Spells of
Mortal
Weaving

Esther M. Friesner

AVON
PUBLISHERS OF BARD, CAMELOT, DISCUS AND FLARE BOOKS

SPELLS OF MORTAL WEAVING is an original publication of
Avon Books. This work has never before appeared in book form.
This work is a novel. Any similarity to actual persons or events is
purely coincidental.

AVON BOOKS
A division of
The Hearst Corporation
1790 Broadway
New York, New York 10019

Copyright © 1986 by Esther M. Friesner
Published by arrangement with the author
Library of Congress Catalog Card Number: 85-91190
ISBN: 0-380-75001-5

First Avon Printing, May 1986

AVON TRADEMARK REG. U. S. PAT. OFF. AND IN
OTHER COUNTRIES, MARCA REGISTRADA, HECHO EN
U. S. A.

Printed in the U. S. A.

K-R 10 9 8 7 6 5 4 3 2 1

For my son, Michael the Bearpaw,
Most Feared Warrior in all the
Twelve Kingdoms

Prologue

"You are a fool, Milkan! Such a gem cannot exist. Even if it did, what would it be doing in a ragtag shop like old Eyndor's? If the stone's as princely as you claim, surely it would be kept under royal guard."

"I tell you, Timor, I have seen it. It lies on a pillow of black satin under the old jeweler's lamp, ready for the taking."

The two men leaned their heads close together in the smoky tavern, speaking in whispers. The first was tall and golden-haired, with a weak chin and watery green eyes. He wore the leather jerkin common to the icy heights of the Kestrel Mountains, seldom seen in the southern lands. The other was swarthy and short, pug-faced. The flowing robes of Vair betrayed his origins. Once their airy gauze had been dyed scarlet and saffron, but years spent in unsavory taverns had dimmed the colors and weighed down the robes with layer upon layer of dirt.

The blond, Timor, poured another cup of wine for his companion and shook his head. "You dream or drink too much," he said. "Eyndor the jeweler has lost his eye and most of his skill. They say that in earlier times he was fit to be jeweler to kings—and more than kings. Age and misfortune have destroyed him. No one trusts him with gems of worth. The jewel you speak of in his shop must be paste."

"I tell you, it's real!" roared Milkan, slamming his goblet down in a rage. A sudden hush in the tavern made him realize where he was. The regular customers of the Hanged Man do not care to be disturbed.

"It is real," Milkan repeated in a whisper. "Who could tell a real gem better than I? In my time I've stolen more gems than lie in the Sombrunian royal treasury itself."

"Too many, perhaps. Your eyes are dazzled," Timor jibed.

1

A dangerous note crept into Milkan's voice and the silver tip of his dagger peeped out at Timor from beneath the table. "It is not friendly to call a man a liar, brother," he said. "Do me the courtesy of seeing the stone. It is in plain sight."

"Very well," said Timor, setting down his cup. "I'll go with you. But I still think it's stupid to risk our necks for cut glass. I could buy a dozen such gems from Fat Katrya in the bazaar."

They left the tavern, slipping between the wisps of fog that glided through the darkened streets. Fog is the friend of thieves, and fog is born in Sombrunia. Droplets of mist glittered in the golden light of street lanterns. The men were no more than shadows.

The shop of Eyndor the Jeweler lay five streets away from the Hanged Man. This had once been a vaguely fashionable section of the city, although it bordered on streets where thieves and ruffians waited, but the well-to-do eventually moved away to fairer parts of the city. Those who did not have the means to depart were left behind; old Eyndor was one such relic.

Above the dim doorway of his little shop hung a wooden placard with a painted crown. In happier days the crown had been gilded and set with false stones. In the spring and summer breezes the sign swung back and forth to the creaky music of its hinges, the jewels catching the sunlight. But eventually the gilding wore away, washed by the rains of many years, and was never replaced. The jewels came unfastened by chance, or else were stolen for a prank by street urchins. The outline of the crown was left, and beneath it the words:

EYNDOR
GEMS FOR THE LORDS OF SOMBRUNIA

"The lords!" snorted Timor. "No lord would come here if he could help it."

"On the contrary," said his comrade, gazing up at the sign with rapacious black eyes. "I hear that the king himself patronizes this place. The gem I saw must be his."

"It's the king's son Alban you mean," Timor corrected. "He's a strange one. They say his life's one long jest, or so it was until his father shipped him off to get some book learning pounded into his skull. He came here on a dare from one of his drinking companions and left a gem of great price with Eyndor. The bet was whether he trusted the old man enough to risk ruining a valuable stone. It was worth a fortune.''

"And?" demanded Milkan, small teeth glittering eagerly.

"A miracle. Eyndor's hand and eye were restored. The gem he carved and set for Lord Alban is a wonder to behold.''

"Then tell me, Brain of a Beetle," said Milkan, lapsing into the Vairish mode, "why it should be impossible that another Sombrunian lord sees fit to trust Eyndor with another precious gem?"

"I concede," said Timor. "Show me this stone and convince me. The time is favorable."

Favorable it was. The hour stood midway between midnight and dawn, when the fog is thickest. Not a living soul was awake in the neighboring houses; not so much as a mongrel dog moved in the street. With hands grown skilful from years of practice, Milkan the thief produced a gleaming picklock from the folds of his robe and coaxed open Eyndor's lock. On silent feet he and Timor entered the shop, closing the door behind them.

Inside, Timor lit a small dark lantern. The light of its flame would be seen only when he raised the small metal gate shielding the lens. Then it cast a powerful beam, directed where its master desired. It was a good lantern in case inquisitive souls should be about, and wonder at too many lights moving through a neighbor's house at that forsaken hour. Like the thieves, the dark lantern was capable of great discretion.

"Well, where is it?" Timor asked, following the dark lantern's questing beam.

"Did you think he'd keep it out here?" snapped Milkan. "Eyndor is old, not stupid. It lies on his workbench. We must go into the back room.''

"Where does the old man sleep?"

"In the loft above the shop. He won't disturb us. Old folks sleep soundly. Come!"

Timor hesitated, remembering his grandmother in the Kestrel Mountains. The footsteps of a sparrow could awaken her. Milkan beckoned him impatiently to bring the lantern.

Eyndor's workbench was a rickety table with a cracked glass lamp hanging above it. The jeweler's tools were arranged in neat rows along one side. There, like a queen on a dust-heap, reposed the most magnificent gem that Timor had ever seen.

It was like no stone he had ever heard of in history or legend. Its beauty held him entranced, unable to do anything but stare as the lantern light called up flames from within the uncut gem's core. He thought it was a ruby, but then a flash of sea blue turned it to sapphire, a glimmer of green haunted it with dreams of emeralds.

"That is no ordinary gem," he whispered to Milkan.

"Did I lie?" the thief replied smugly. "It's fit for gods, that's how big it is."

"Have you noticed nothing but its size? I say there's something peculiar about it. I long to hold it, yet I don't dare touch it. One moment it calls to me, the next it warns me away. There's no good in a speaking stone. Let's leave it."

Milkan groaned. "Are you so afraid of the old man upstairs, or are you merely the greatest coward alive? Dreading the curse of fairies, perhaps?"

"A curse? Yes, sure as I'm born, this stone's cursed. I can feel it. Take it if you like, but I'm going." Timor's voice changed as he spoke, his green eyes staring off into space, growing pale and distant. Milkan recalled a seer he had once met whose eyes also took on that visionary look, and he felt his skin grow cold as Timor went on, saying, "It speaks, this stone. It speaks of a distant place, a place made all of stones like this, a far place of evil. The winds howl wildly there, and the violent sea blasts. Amethyst battlements are guarded by ghosts who howl and howl . . . I can hear them, at the very edge of the world. I hear them . . ."

Milkan struck Timor across the face so hard that the blood ran in a thin stream from his mouth. The green eyes snapped back to life and Timor gasped. "I—I—Let us go, Milkan. Let's be out of here. Please. I've seen that place, the place of this cursed gemstone, and I have no wish to see it again."

"You're mad," Milkan said firmly. "Mad or drunk. Did you hear your ravings a moment ago? Get out, then. I'll take the jewel for myself, and the curse with it." With a taunting laugh, Milkan the Thief reached out one bony brown hand for the shimmering stone.

A cry of pain echoed among the cobwebbed rafters of old Eyndor's jewelry shop. Milkan clutched his hand and stared with terrible fixity at the small, blood-colored insect that perched atop the gem, its tail poised in a high curve above its back, the deadly stinger ready for a second stab.

"A death-kiss," Timor breathed, with fearful respect for the deadliest scorpion spawned in the Desert of Thulain. Milkan was dead before Timor could pronounce the creature's name. The thief crumpled like paper in a bonfire, the light going out of his eyes, his dusky face turned milky pale. Timor was alone in the deserted shop.

The tiny crimson assassin paused a moment, then scuttled down again to crouch hidden at the base of the gem. The spell of death broke. Timor took a deep breath and stooped to raise the lifeless body of his friend before escaping.

"Certainly there is no rush," said a dry voice behind him.

Timor wheeled swiftly, flashing the lantern into every corner of the jeweler's workroom. Motes of dust danced in the yellow beam.

"Come now," said the voice again. "I'm right here. Here, fool, in the doorway."

Timor's lamp swerved and caught the tall, slender figure of a hooded man in the archway between the workroom and the outer chamber. In effect he was barring Timor's escape, a thing no wise person would do to a desperately frightened man. The blade of a flame-knife shone in Timor's hand as he prepared to fight. It took special killing skills to manage the rippled blade, with its two points like a serpent's fangs. In the hands of an expert, a flame-knife's short bit of gilded steel could take out a trio of common swords— and Timor was an expert when it came to killing.

"Put down your weapon," said the black-hooded man. "Your friend was a thief, not you. Are you then a murderer? Have you the inner steel of assassins? You are afraid. Of what? Of me?"

"I fear no man!" Timor said between clenched teeth.

"Ah! Then it must be that you fear the dark. We'll cure that." A hand, elegantly gloved in black leather, made a languid pass in the air. Light blazed in the cracked glass lantern above Eyndor's workbench.

Timor's hands were trembling. "Who are you? By what art . . . ?"

The figure laughed. The black hood fell back. Timor felt himself grow faint as he looked into that thin face. His mind told him that he had never seen the man before. His heart said, "You have seen him all the days of your life." Timor dropped the dagger.

"A wise move," the man said with satisfaction. "You are more prudent than your late friend. A man must protect his treasures, don't you agree? Can you blame me for stationing my little guard here to ward such a jewel?"

Timor fell to his knees, eyes still fixed on the tall dark man. "Indeed, my lord, I could never speak . . . against you," he said hoarsely.

The dark one stepped nonchalantly to the workbench and laid one long finger at the base of the jewel. The death-kiss scampered eagerly onto his fingertip, shining like a single drop of blood.

"Do you hear him?" the man addressed the scorpion. "He accepts my lordship. Not every man is so sage. I have many servants. Too many serve me for their own sakes. They work with one eye on the rewards I promise them. Oh, they come to me willingly enough, but selfishly. Greed blinds them. I prefer this one. He gives me an unselfish heart. Shall I take it?"

The death-kiss balanced on the dark man's finger, curved tail swaying to and fro, a lethal red crescent moon in the shadows. With his other hand the man offered the smoky jewel to Timor.

"Do you like it?" he asked casually. Timor could only nod. "Good. But do you think a lady would like it? They are such unpredictable creatures, the ladies."

"She could not refuse it," replied Timor. Each word came forth with great effort. His head swam as the gem pulsed and leaped before his eyes.

"I hope you're right. The old jeweler promised to carve me a living miracle from this stone, and set it in a silver collar. Gold might dim its brilliance. Would you like to hold it? It won't be the same once Eyndor makes the final cut."

Timor tried to shake his head, tried to reject the stone. He was unable to move. He felt long, cold hands—cold even through the gloves—pressing the gem into the palm of his hand and making him hold it up to the light.

Faces swam in the frozen heart of the stone. Turrets of amethyst raised themselves out of a misty sea and breathed forth hungry phantoms. Now the vision was within those awesome walls, and Timor saw a woman, young and beautiful, flanked by armed men whose faces melted in and out of focus, as if great depths of waters rippled endlessly around them. A grim hall arched into blackness overhead, and at the far end of it stood a black throne where the dark one waited, smiling. They brought the woman to him, those eerie, dream-born warriors, and he held the silver collar out for her to see. She stepped back, only to feel the steely tips of lances forcing her forward to accept it. Head bowed, she fastened it around her neck. The purple stone throbbed scarlet at her throat. Legions cheered with a chilling sound, a hollow voice of autumn winds.

Then the scene dissolved to a single face, the face of a living star, a woman who wept as if the fear of death were on her. But Timor knew that she was already dead. Her image blossomed out of the stone and spread itself across a night of blazing stars; the earth beneath them was barren and blasted, ruled by the dark legions. Tracing the path of her tears, the death-kiss crawled across her moonlit cheek. Timor screamed and dropped the stone.

"Did my little guardian scare you that much?" The tall man smiled. "Or was it . . . her face? In either case, old Eyndor is to blame. Were he not so old, he might know the importance of keeping a closer guard on his shop. Then I would not have to provide one of my own. Perhaps he is *too* old. It might be a kindness to remove the cares of this world from his shoulders. I owe him more than one kindness, and I mean to pay all debts with him once he has cut and set this gem to my liking. You will find that I am kind, but just. Now, as for this one"—he gazed at the scorpion—"we shall punish him."

The world became a sea of red and blue and purple hues seen through a sparkling glass. Timor's sight came in a hundred facets, the single image of the dark man multiplied and mirrored in every one. He heard the dark man speak, then saw him glance down at the crimson blot on his fingertip. He breathed upon it once. The scorpion curled in on itself and tumbled to the floor with the dry sound of an empty seed-pod.

When old Eyndor came down from his lodgings in the morning he found much to wonder at. On the table lay the gem, just as he had left it the night before, and on the floor beside it sprawled the body of a dead man.

In a corner of the shop—a corner that brimmed with shadows even in the brightest day—there crouched a lunatic. He held a small round red thing in one hand, and shook it near his ear from time to time. The hollow rustling it made appeared to delight him.

He must be an ancient madman, thought Eyndor as he gazed at the pitiful sight. *His hair is twice as white as mine.*

The old jeweler sighed. There would be no getting to work until this mess was cleared away. His bones still ached from a poor night's rest, although his slumber had been deep. He flexed his hands and noted happily that the miseries in all his other bones had blessedly left his hands alone. It was as if his youth remained in his fingers. Ah, a youth such as few men enjoyed!

But what good did the memories do him now? He couldn't recount them without seeing his hearers exchange clandestine smiles and tap their temples knowingly when they thought he wasn't looking. For them he was only another old gaffer, whose mind had misted over until he didn't know history from dream. Old Eyndor rambling on about the ancient days, the days when the gods walked the earth with men, the days too ancient for any man now alive to have experienced. Poor, mad old Eyndor.

He grumbled and reached for the ragged cape hanging on its peg beside the front door. Mornings in Sombrunia still held some of the night's fog and chill. He pulled on a pair of thick wool and leather gloves as well. No need to hurry—the corpse wasn't going anywhere, and the madman would be easy enough to trace should he decide to run away. Eyndor wasn't going to risk the health of his hands for anyone, sane or stricken. He locked up securely and set off in search of help.

Outside the shop his breath made little runs of mist. The fog from the Opalza Sea was still thick, but the rising sun was beginning to burn it away. It tattered as he passed, appeared to form a portal through which stepped two men. The harried jeweler bustled by, ignoring them. Truly, to a casual observer there was nothing extraordinary about them, nothing to merit more than a passing glance in the street.

"Where do you think Eyndor's off to so early, Ayree?" the black-haired, black-bearded one of the pair asked. He wore the rusty robes of a scholar, and his eyes glittered behind bright spectacles.

His companion was taller and looked younger, but that illusion lasted only until a person saw his eyes. They were the color of a glacier's soul, just as hard and old as the immortal ice of the farthest northern lands. Now they were shadowed by the drape of his hooded tunic. A wisp of white hair brushed his cheek as he answered.

"Who knows? It's just as well that he's gone. You know how proud he is, how fiercely he guards his handiwork. He'd never let us take a jewel once someone else entrusted it to him."

The black-bearded man laughed. "You make us sound like common thieves, Ayree."

Ayree's eyes flashed in shadow. "Isn't that what we are, Paragore-Tren? Isn't that what we've been reduced to? I can't number the spells I've sent out from Castle Snowglimmer, seeking the stone, trying to destroy it, trying to destroy *him* . . ."

"I know." Ayree's friend lowered his voice. "I have been doing the same. The very trees of the Naîmlo Wood shook with the strength of my spells, but it did no good. We must resign ourselves;

this is no matter for wizards or witch-kings alone. The prophecy will not be denied. What mortals have marred, mortals must undo."

Ayree's jaw tightened. "I will not submit to prophecies. What are they but empty words?"

"Not so empty, or they wouldn't have angered you." The wizard's eyes grew soft with sympathy. "You scorn the prophecies, but you also fear what they hold in store for your family, your sisters. And you abide by them, isn't it so? That's what has made you lonelier than any other being, human or divine, who walks the Twelve Kingdoms: the words you call 'empty'."

"I am used to it." Ayree shrugged. "We're wasting time. There's old Eyndor's shop. We'll have the gem before he returns."

Wizard and witch-king entered the shop openly, with none of the nonsense of picklocks and dark lanterns used by the unhappy mortals Milkan and Timor. Later, a witness would say that a patch fog had drifted up against the wooden door and seeped into the grain.

Fog did funny things in Sombrunia.

They found the gem where Eyndor had left it, and the body of Milkan. A second corpse lay across the first. The white-haired witch-king hooked his hand under Timor's shoulder and rolled him back. A jagged slash had opened the great vein in his throat. The flame-knife fell from its master's fingers, its wavy golden blade stained red.

"Morgeld reaps his harvest already," Ayree said grimly. A touch of his hand closed the gaping wound. The worst of the blood vanished. He let Timor's corpse slump back to the floor.

"When Eyndor brings the men of law, there will be a mystery. A dead man without a mark on his body," Paragore-Tren said.

"They can have their mysteries. Take the jewel and we'll give them two for the price of one."

The wizard chuckled at Ayree's peevish tone and reached for the gem. Red lightning crackled in a sphere around it, searing the wizard's fingers. Paragore-Tren howled and jerked his hand away.

"You damned icemonger, use *me* as your catspaw?" The wizard shook his injured hand and glared at Ayree. "Snag it yourself! Go on—take it!"

Ayree pulled back his hood, releasing a mane of silvery hair. Many called such hair the mark of sorcery, but the powers in Ayree's blood went back beyond the times when men first learned to call the hidden powers their own. He had been born to magic, and his twelve sisters with him, as some men are born to thrones. Was this birthright curse or blessing? Not even the young warlock knew the answer to that riddle.

"Give me your hand." Ayree took the wizard's fingers and murmured a few words over them. The look of pain washed from Paragore-Tren's face, but the resentment did not. "The stone is carved from Helagarde itself, and all of Morgeld's reawakened magic is in it. This is the bondstone that the prophecy foretold, the gem that must be cut by Eyndor's hand alone."

The wizard frowned. "You're sure? Maybe my powers aren't enough to break through whatever shielding protects it. I'm . . . only an upstart mortal, you know." The frown twitched slightly, wanting to turn into a mischievous smile. It would take much to submerge Paragore-Tren's sense of humor for long.

"Upstart mortal." Ayree repeated the wizard's words and could not help smiling himself. "That's a fine jest. And who was it set the bonds on Morgeld himself but another upstart mortal? A lovelier one than you, to be sure."

He slowly extended his hand, palm foremost, toward the gem. The red aura grew and shivered into sparks as the witch-king's hand came closer. He drew it back before actual contact.

"Here at least the prophecies seem to be more than wind," Ayree said. "No child of sorcery may interfere until the bondstone has found its place."

"No stepchild either?" The wizard's black brows rose in inquiry. "No, I guess not. So! It seems that old Eyndor keeps his stone and satisfies his client. That's good. I'd have hated to see the old man run afoul of *that* one. A gem carved by Eyndor's hand alone, eh?" He knelt to study the deadly amethyst at eye level.

Ayree nodded. "Even I cannot number all the mortal souls who served the gods in the good days when gods and men walked these realms together. Eyndor was only one. For their services they were allowed to choose their own rewards, but with this condition: that if a time of darkness should come, they must agree to play a part in fulfilling the prophecies that would end it."

Paragore-Tren straightened up. "I'd say Eyndor's done his part. Now it's time for me to do mine."

"Where do you go, my friend?"

"To the north, to find Lord Halbor's son. Lord Halbor of Sombrunia is old and ill; he may be dying. I may not know as much of the prophecies as you do, Ayree, but I know that Morgeld's doom must spring from Halbor's line. Once the lord of Sombrunia had four sons. Now he has only one, a good lad, Alban. He is a student at Panomo-Midmists. I go to fetch him home.''

"And to protect him?"

''If I can, Ayree, if I can. The question is, will the prophecy allow it?''

There was no hint of hope in the witch-king's pale eyes. "I can't say. You must try. And I . . . there is a second branch of blood that must unite with Halbor's line to destroy the lord of Helagarde. They are northern folk. I will watch over them as far as I can.''

Paragore-Tren sighed, ''That may be all either one of us will be able to do, in the end: watch.''

A small smile brightened Ayree's face. ''In the end, my friend, who knows if the gods themselves can do anything more?''

Chapter I

LORD PRINCE ALBAN

The Council of Sombrunia thronged the narrow hall leading to the Veiled Chamber. Whispers scurried back and forth like mice. Sometimes a man would raise his head as if to sniff the air, or perk his ears toward the black door at the end of the passageway.

Sunlight washed the hall. The sweet smells of high summer called to the twelve men who waited. It was useless. Their hearts held winter just as surely as their hands held their twelve ceremonial spears. They were the supreme governors of Sombrunia, second in rank only to Lord Halbor—sometimes called King—and men of proven worth and varied duties. One such duty was to escort their sovereign through the uneasy hours before death. Now that duty had come due.

Lord Regis was the oldest there. White-haired, eyes rheumed with age, his palsied hands could barely close around his spear, a marvelous weapon hafted with lapis lazuli and tipped with silver.

"Lord Halbor is younger than I by many years," said the ancient one. Although Lord Regis had been the last to arrive and assume his post, age had not dulled his desire to know everything going on around him, especially when it involved the imminent death of his king. "Was it some accident in hunting or at sport? Was it the plague?"

Red-haired Lord William replied in a voice loud enough to pierce old Lord Regis's encroaching deafness. "None of these, I fear. We were all as surprised as you at the summons. One morning, not a week ago, Lord Halbor rose from the council table and sighed, his right hand on his ribs. We thought he just had a slight stiffness, from too much close work. But the lords of Sombrunia always know when they are going to die; it is a gift from the Lady. He put on the white robe and ordered the servants to clear the Veiled Chamber. There he retired before sunset. There he still sits, in the golden chair facing the open window, waiting for the end to come. You know how we were all summoned to attend him."

"True, true," sighed old Lord Regis, shaking his snowy head. "The gold chair at the window, you say? He thinks of his son."

"Better Halbor should think of his people," snarled Lord Bran, joining their conversation uninvited. Tall and thickset, skin burned swarthy from many missions ridden against desert raiders, his pugnacious temper made him a popular commander in the Sombrunian army. Off the battlefield he was not so popular. He had never quite mastered the art of knowing when to call off the attack. "What's going to become of this land? Prince Alban's not the man his father was."

Lord William answered Lord Bran's words calmly, but with a certain threat implied. Like most of the other Sombrunian lords, the redhead did not care for Bran's overly forthright nature. "You are too quick, my lord. Do not say *was* of a man who still *is*. Our lord is not dead yet, and we can always hope for his recovery. We are here to comfort Lord Halbor's final moments, not to listen to ill-thought talk. And we are all armed." Here he shifted his spear from hand to hand. The haft was amber, the tip silver. All the council spears were tipped with moonshine metal, each hafted with a different kind of fair and costly stone.

"And what if we are?" demanded Bran, always the warchief, unused to being the object of threats.

"Well, Lord Bran, we'll use our weapons since we've got them, and above all we'll use them on traitors. Traitors are unusually quick to kill a king. Even with words."

"I only made a slip of the tongue," sulked Bran. "I'll defend our young prince's right to his father's throne as well as any of you. When does Prince Alban return?"

Pacified, William shrugged. "Yesterday a messenger was dispatched. I couldn't say how long the journey will take."

His malachite spear the same bright green as his eyes, the courtly fop Lord Darr sidled up, eager to amaze his peers. A born gossip, he fluttered his fingers for attention and confided, "It won't take *that* messenger long at all. No, no, not long, if you knew who the messenger is. *I* know, and it was supposed to be a *deep* secret, but now that he's on his way, I guess there's no harm in telling." He dropped his voice for effect and whispered, "Paragore-Tren, mage of mages, is entrusted with this mission." The reaction was not all Lord Darr could have desired.

"What'd he say?" shouted old Lord Regis, cupping his good ear.

Lord William obligingly repeated the news, but without appearing too impressed by it. Very little ever got the red-haired lord in a dither. "Darr says Paragore-Tren's gone to bring Alban back," he bellowed into the old man's ear. In a normal voice he added, "If a wizard's the messenger, he rides the winds. Our prince will be with us soon."

Cantankerous as always, Bran pulled a grim face. "I've lived long enough to know that the world's uncertain. There are many who would not like to see Lord Alban on the throne of Sombrunia. And some legends say . . . ."

"Legends!" laughed William, abruptly looking very young. "Do you believe such things? Tales of prophecies and bindings, spells and counterspells. Well, if you believe in them, be comforted. The one you fear has long been bound in fetters made strong by silver magic. He cannot escape to trouble the world again."

Bran shook his head. The Sombrunian commander had seen too many battles to share Lord William's faith. "What's destroyed can't return," he said, "but what's only bound *can* be set free. There are too many prophecies, and we only know half of them. We must wait and be wary."

Lord William shook his bright red hair and gave Lord Bran a skeptical smile. Shouldering his spear, he joined another knot of council members who were discussing matters more serious than prophecies and legends.

Within the Veiled Chamber, Lord Halbor sat propped in the golden chair and let sunlight warm his careworn face. Lord Regis was older, but Lord Halbor's hair was whiter, his beard like a silver river. The golden diadem of Sombrunia winked and shimmered on his head.

From far away he heard the hushing sound of the Opalza Sea breaking on the rocks below Castle Pibroch. The salty smell took him sweetly back to the days when he had gone voyaging along the borders of the known lands. Half dreaming, he touched the medallion he wore beneath the white robe of waiting. The chain was thin, and snapped at a twitch of his hand.

"I am still strong," he murmured. He raised the charm to his eyes and gazed at the glad young face engraved there. "Alban," he sighed. "I had hoped to see you again. At your age I sailed the world to learn of other places and other peoples. Today you learn the same hunched over a pile of tattered scrolls. How can paper teach you all that I have learned? And yet, you'll have my last words to you on paper, not from my lips."

Lord Halbor's hand dropped to his lap, and he closed his eyes. "I am so tired. I want to rest," he breathed. "All that keeps me alive now is hope. Paragore-Tren is lord of many magics. He might transport you here by enchantment, and then I'll see you again after all. I must wait . . . a little while longer." The warmth of the sun and the cool sea breezes comforted the pain in his side. He let himself drift toward sleep.

A shadow fell over his face, waking him. Old battle instincts made him jerk up his head and reach for the sword he no longer wore. Alban's likeness fell jingling to the floor.

"Greetings, Lord Halbor," said the dark man who stood between him and the sunlight. "I had not hoped to see you so soon."

Lord Halbor's face tightened as he took in each feature of that dreaded face, each movement of the juiceless body. Pale skin pressed tightly over high cheekbones, skin that concealed little flesh between it and the skull. Dark eyes burned deep into Lord Halbor's own: unchanging eyes, long and ageless, speaking of timeless voids that lie in regions where the stars themselves dare not go. The visitor smiled between thin, humorless lips, and bowed before the aged king.

"Impossible," said Halbor. "By what evil trick do you send your image here to taunt me?"

"I am no image," said the dark man.

"You must be an image! You lie bound in the depths of cursed Helagarde."

"Did you believe any bonds could hold me forever? My faithful servants labored long to free me, and now I am free. She who spun the thread that fettered me has long been dead, her bones dust in the desert."

"Janeela," whispered Lord Halbor, smiling at the melody of that name. "Janeela, the Silver One. With love she lured, with silent purpose wove, with patience walked the walls of Helagarde until the night that starlight touched her weaving. Magic made it strong. By night she came on silent feet to bind the evil one by hand and foot and save the slumbering world. Then Janeela climbed the pinnacle of Helagarde and the north winds bore her away." The king's voice rose as he chanted the tale of Janeela.

The dark man's smile vanished. "You praise her, when she was a traitor of the worst kind. Have men begun to adore traitors?"

"To betray you is not treachery," returned the king. "You were bound once and you shall be bound again. The prophecies say—"

The dark man raised one hand. "I know the prophecies. I've heard that you take an unhealthy pride in them. It's said that one of your direct line will defeat me, and another will be my doom. I am surprised at you, Lord Halbor. With so much depending on your descendants, why did you have only the one?"

"I had four sons once, demon!" shouted the king. "Three died. How long have you been free? Was it your hand that drowned one, poisoned one, and made the youngest lose his footing on the cliffs above the sea?"

"Yes," confirmed the visitor. "I was freed on the day of an auspicious birth. You know only half the prophecy. Your son might defeat me, but I can return. My doom, my final death, lies with the line of a certain lady of the northern lands. When she was born I broke my bonds and left fair Helagarde. I go to find her, now that she is a woman. She shall be my bride, and once she is mine, she'll be cut off forever from bearing the child who might destroy me."

Lord Halbor forced himself to stand. "I know the prophecy!" he thundered. "The lowest beggar in my land sings the song of 'Morgeld's Doom.' Do you think I did not intend to marry my son to that lady? They'll be betrothed next year, to fulfill—"

Morgeld opened the palm of his hand as daintily as the parting petals of a water lily. A silver collar set with a bedazzling purple stone twinkled there. He touched the stone to Lord Halbor's chest. The old king gasped as the heart of Helagarde touched his own, and fell back into the golden chair. His sightless eyes stared out the open window, death's glaze sealing the final look of fear upon them.

In the hall outside the Veiled Chamber a fearsome commotion began and grew. The twelve lords gazed at the ceremonial spears and shouted their amazement. The silver blades were dead, turned to lifeless black stone. Men spoke of portents and prophecies as they ran back and forth in the narrow passageway. Within the Veiled Chamber, Morgeld allowed himself to smile.

Chapter II

PANOMO-MIDMISTS

The minstrel who entered the Book and Scroll tavern was a small man with a small voice. Pride made him fancy himself a musician. He had not been on the road very long, and the few times he stopped to ply his trade at village fairs or country inns, the people were too deep in their wine to care if he sang off-key. They pounded him on the back, called him a good fellow, and gave him a little food and money for the road.

Encouraged, the minstrel resolved to take his talents before an educated audience. They would appreciate him; he was tired of receiving mere cash and bits of bread for his music. So he went to the great university city of Panomo-Midmists, eager for the headier tribute of the wise man's applause.

The Book and Scroll tavern, like all taverns in Panomo-Midmists, centered on the students. The town itself was an outgrowth of the university. The students ruled the town and the faculty tried to rule the students. In the classrooms they could control them, but after class all restraint was gone.

The minstrel took a seat at the fireplace and tuned his lute. He tied a bunch of jinglebells to his right ankle, for it was his habit to stamp his foot in time with the song, whether it was a gay harvest tune or a mournful dirge for a dead hero. His preparations made, he announced that he would sing the famous "Triumph of Elaar."

He was at the second verse when a score of students seized him by the seat of the pants and the scruff of the neck. A smiling barmaid held the door open and the minstrel went sailing gracefully through the evening air like a puff of dandelion down. He landed with a splash in a rain-drenched gutter.

From the tavern door a tall, blond young man addressed him cheerfully. "The 'Triumph of Elaar' is a masterpiece of the old songsmiths, Minstrel. When properly sung, you can hear the waves and learn the language of rainbow fishes. But you've churned the sea bottom to mud. Here." He tossed the soggy singer a purse with a few pieces of silver. "Use that for traveling money. And praise the gods you came to this tavern. The music students frequent the Singing Bird, and they'd have killed you."

The minstrel picked himself out of the gutter and tried to wipe his lute with the corner of his sopping cape. The jinglebells around his ankle were clogged with mud.

"You are no critic," he informed the young man. "I'd like to hear you do better as a minstrel. You haven't the strength needed for the profession."

"Oh, I can run away as fast as you can," chuckled the young man. "But why should I want to be a minstrel? A sorry, wandering life, with no idea of where the next day will bring you."

"It has its advantages," replied the minstrel. "There are always the ladies."

"What! Ladies follow after a ragtag fellow like you?"

"Not yet," the minstrel admitted. "But to all minstrels there eventually come two magics: the blessing of the ladies, and the curse of love."

"Who would want a curse to come to him?"

"You misunderstand. The minstrel does not feel the curse. He casts it on his enemy. It condemns the wretch to fall in love and follow the lady of his heart through long despair and countless perils."

"I think there are ladies enough in the world," said the youth. "If I can't have one, her sister will do as well. A useless curse!"

The minstrel cocked one eyebrow. "That may be. But if I knew who provoked those louts in there into tossing me out like a sack of rubbish, I'd try the curse on him and we could both see if it worked."

The young man laughed and patted the minstrel on the back. "I stand ready to receive it. Do your best. It was my idea to toss you out. That's why I came to see you how you are, feeling responsible."

"Oh?" remarked the minstrel. His voice was dangerously soft. "What's your name, lad?"

"I'm Alban; Alban of Sombrunia. And you?"

"My name doesn't matter. A man must know the name of one he curses. The minstrel's curse I lay on you: Alban of Sombrunia, may your dreams be haunted with beauty and your heart with longing. May you find love and lose love and not rest until you find it again." The minstrel turned and hurried away into the purple shadows of evening. Alban wore a puzzled smile as he watched him go.

The tavern door opened and a small man joined Alban in the street. "What's keeping you?" he asked. He barely came up to Alban's shoulder. Thick dark hair lay above pale green eyes the tender shade of young river reeds.

"Ah, Lymri, I've had an interesting time out here. The tone-deaf minstrel laid a curse on me, if you please."

"A curse!"

"No need to worry. It was something to do with love, and you know my thoughts on that subject. I'm not one of those poetical young men doomed to be a sacrifice to Krisli."

"Have a care, Alban," Lymri said in a quiet voice. "Wise men don't mock Krisli. He rules the human heart, and the heart rules the man."

"My *brain* rules me," answered Alban. "Come, we've wasted enough time with wine and minstrels and mumbo-jumbo. I hear the call of scrolls to read and books to memorize. It's a weary life we live here, tossed back and forth between our studies and our small pleasures. A very weary life indeed."

The students linked arms and strolled back toward the university. In the twilit streets the tantalizing fragrances of hidden gardens caressed their nostrils. From a lighted window came the voice of a girl singing an old love song. Their way led them out of the tavern streets and into more elegant byways. Arcades of flowering trees lined a broad avenue where rich merchants and lesser nobles dwelt. Hanging lanterns amid the leaves bobbed and swung in the gentle summer breeze like tethered ships on invisible waters.

"This is a night for love," murmured Lymri.

"Enough of love!" said Alban. "It's a fine summer night like any other. Leave it—"

A muffled figure rounded the corner and ran headfirst into Alban, knocking him to the ground. Swiftly he recovered and threw

his assailant over, pinning the caped one while he drew the short
dagger from his belt.

"Who dares to attack us here?" Lymri wondered aloud. "The
hour is too early, the street too bright."

"We'll soon find out," muttered Alban, seizing his prisoner's
wrists. He marveled at them, so slender for a street marauder. He
pulled aside the hood, the color of autumn leaves.

"By all the gods," breathed Lymri. His voice was a wraith of
smoke.

The woman looked up at Alban with eyes like green stars, flashing fright and defiance. A cloud of honey-colored hair tumbled
loose, framing her face in dark gold.

"Let me go!" she commanded. "Let me go, or I am a dead
woman!"

Alban did not move. He dropped her hands and did not resist
when she pushed him aside and leaped to her feet. Like a harried
deer she turned her head this way and that, confused.

"Curse this town! What direction did I come from?" she demanded of Lymri.

"From there." He pointed. Approaching footsteps echoed from
the shadowy street. Even as the woman drew her hood on again and
took to her heels, her pursuers rounded the wall and were on her.

Four stout men-at-arms clad in the flexible mail of the northern
warrior-lords grabbed her. Following them came a fat, mustached
fellow who reminded Lymri of a walrus. He puffed and wheezed
as he caught up to them.

The soldiers seized the woman so gently that Lymri stood bewildered. "Strange treatment if she's a lady's maid who's robbed
her mistress," he thought. "She must be the lady herself, but why
she flees or what she fears is a mystery."

"Ungrateful child!" the fat man panted. "Is this my reward? Is
this the obedience you owe your father?"

The woman set her mouth and would not answer. They glared at
each other like a pair of feuding basilisks.

"Obedience?" came a voice from nowhere. "She doesn't owe
you obedience after the fate you've got in store for her, Father!
You're selling her like a sheep at a fair. And for what?"

"Silence, girl!" thundered the lord. "I see your hand in her escape. When I get the two of you home, you'll learn some discipline.
As for you, Ursula . . ." He turned his attention back to the golden-
haired woman. "As for you, we'll change your maids for older

women to chaperone you until we're safely home again. Mizriel, I want—Mizriel, where are you?''

The fat lord darted glances into the gathering night. Laughter glittered in the air around him.

''If I show myself, you'll give me a thrashing,'' teased the voice. ''No thank you, Father. I'll stay invisible.''

''Mizriel, I have enough trouble with your sister. Come here now, or when you finally *do* choose to appear it will be hard for you.''

''Oh, all right.'' The voice was crestfallen. The small shadow of a maiden wavered beside the golden-haired woman and grew solid. Hair white as frost fell in lacy ripples down her back. Her face was thin and pointed as a fox's, and her eyes were an unsettling russet hue.

Silver head leaned close to gold as Mizriel said, ''Come, Ursula. Next time we'll save you.''

''There will not be a next time,'' said Ursula, head bowed. ''My fate is set.'' The sisters clasped hands and departed the way they had come, followed by their father and his men.

''Well!'' said Lymri, much insulted. ''How do you like that? Not a word to acknowledge our presence. We could have been a pair of extra trees on a promenade. That fat pudding must be one of the high mucky-mucks, or a northern lordling. They give themselves airs enough to be kings.''

''That is she,'' said Alban.

''What?''

''That is she, Lymri. I'm dead if I don't see her again. She's meant for a throne. If she doesn't have one of her own, she'll have mine. Who is she, Lymri? Where did she go?''

Lymri grabbed Alban by the shoulders and studied his face. A mild, sheepish smile played across his lips. His eyes wandered, giving him the look of a half-wit or a daydreamer. Lymri shook him violently until some scrap of understanding came back into Alban's eyes.

''What . . . happened?'' he asked, reviving.

''You saw a lady—I think her name is Ursula—and the minstrel's curse came home. Unless it was a weak curse. You seem normal now.''

Alban shook his head wistfully. ''If my life is short, the curse will be short. I love her, Lymri. I think I was meant to love her even without the minstrel's curse. Let's follow her.''

"Whoa, Alban! Just a minute!" shouted Lymri, trotting to keep up with the Sombrunian's long strides. "Where do you think you're going? What makes you think that fierce father of hers will be so glad to see you?"

"I am a prince of Sombrunia," Alban replied with happy pride. "Someday the throne shall be mine. Who'd deny his daughter a kingdom?"

"So you're a prince? I know it and you know it, but look at you, dressed like every other student here. What proof do you have of your rank?"

"In my rooms I have a bauble or two that would take that rustic lordling's breath away," said Alban.

"Good. Then fetch your proof before you go courting. The hour's late; I suggest we retire for the night and present ourselves formally in the morning, in royal robes and bearing gifts."

"I won't sleep without a second sight of her," said Alban.

"Try," answered Lymri. "Remember, friend, you have no guarantee that the lady wants a second sight of you. And wash your face. It always makes a better impression on a woman if you wash your face."

Alban shrugged and let Lymri take him back to their rooms. Well pleased with himself, the little man threw himself down on his bed and fell asleep grinning. Sleep was a great cure-all. Alban would have forgotten all about the woman by morning.

Lymri was still deep in his dreams when an imperious hand shook him awake. He grumbled and tried to burrow into the pillow.

"Lymri, get up. I want to say goodbye."

"Goodbye and drown! Let me sleep some more, Alban. It won't be the first time I miss a lecture."

"It's not time for classes. It's not even time for breakfast."

Lymri sat upright in bed, clearly enraged. After food, music, and sundry other pleasures, he was fond of his sleep. "Then why disturb me? What kind of friend—"

"I thought you'd want to say farewell. We've had some good times together, Lymri," Alban said with a wistful hint of sorrow.

"What? Farewell? Where are you going? If you're off to find that girl at this hour, her father will slit your throat. *I* almost did."

"She's not here anymore. They left their lodgings. They're heading for home. I must follow."

"And where's home?"

"Her father, Lord Blas, holds Dureforte Keep. A little judicious gold given to the ostler and the maids at the inn gave me her whole family history.''

"Dureforte Keep," mused Lymri, calling up images from maps. "That's a far distance. How will you go there? Have you enough for a horse, supplies, and lodgings on the road?''

"I have all I need." Alban smiled. It was then that Lymri's sleep-fogged eyes first saw what his friend was wearing.

From the tips of his stout leather marching boots to the top of his thick woolen hood, Alban was the picture of a highway wanderer. A sack of provisions was slung over one shoulder, a deep-bellied lute over the other. Heavy brown hose sheathed his long legs, and a rust-colored tunic showed beneath his cape.

"You're . . . *walking?''* ventured Lymri.

"I must. I haven't enough gold left to ride and I haven't the time to wait for the next allotment from home. If that so-called minstrel last night can make a living out of songs, so can I.''

"Krisli's Fool," Lymri said under his breath. The sickness afflicting Alban was well known. To the prince he said, "You don't know a thing about life on the road. It's dangerous.''

"I'll learn. I'm a student, after all.''

"Well then, so am I!" cried Lymri. He jumped out of bed and dressed himself hurriedly.

"Lymri, what are you doing?''

"Getting ready to go with you," panted the little man. "And don't try to stop me.''

"Never while I live," said Alban. He embraced his friend and helped him pack.

The morning bells of the university called sleepy students from their beds to musty lecture halls where old men droned on and on about the priceless wisdom hidden in old scrolls. In the pell-mell rush to class, scarcely anyone noticed two merry wandering minstrels as they sauntered out the great black gates and turned their faces to the sun.

One of the hurrying students paused to watch them go. He was a dreamer who spent his time drawing caricatures of the lecturer for his own amusement. He had a good mind for faces, and those two tatterdemalions looked mighty familiar. He was still cudgeling his brain for their names when a rider came galloping through the gates.

The stranger wore black and silver and sat astride a rattle-ribbed mare. The student looked up at the man's thickly bearded face, and his small eyes peering sharply from behind wire-rimmed spectacles.

"Where's the gatekeeper's office?" the rider asked.

"By the gate," replied the student, meaning no malice. "Why? Looking for someone?"

"A Sombrunian. Tall, fair-haired, named Alban. Do you know him?"

The student pondered the name. Very familiar. Suddenly he beamed up at the rider and said, "So *that's* who it was. And Lymri with him! I wonder what they think they're doing? You know, sir, funny you should be looking for Alban when just a few moments ago he went right out the gate there." A brazen bell pealed once in the tower and the student blushed. "Sorry. I mean it must have been an hour ago he went. I've been standing here trying to recall his name, and I've woolgathered right through the first hour's lecture."

"Then you'd better be on your way before the second hour eludes you," the rider said crisply. The student shuffled away. Alone in the courtyard, the black-bearded one plucked a sphere of crystal from the air and searched it. His mare stood perfectly still, only her ears twitching at the flies. At last he looked up and muttered, "Well, if I can't find him, neither can Morgeld. Perhaps it's for the best. We must wait and learn."

Putting spurs to the mare, he raced out through the iron gates and away from the city. In a secluded grove of willows he dismounted and stroked the mare's muzzle. "Your job is done. I free you," he said.

An almost imperceptible quivering ran along each line of the mare's body. She seemed to melt into air, then to shift back abruptly to solid form. An eagle's beak clashed beneath the gold eyes of a tiger. Shining claws sprang from hooves that turned to massive tawny paws, while rainbow wings sprouted in fiery glory from the creature's shoulders. With a proud cry the gryphon mounted the wind and flew into the west.

The wizard watched her flight. He had never quite grown tired of wonders, even when they were of his own creation. When she was gone, he looked again into his crystal and called, "Ayree . . . Ayree, my friend . . ."

The witch-king's drawn face answered, his frosty hair filling the crystal with a comet's light. *What would you have, my brother? Have you found the prince?*

Paragore-Tren looked glum. "Not only haven't I found him, I can't even see where he's gone. It's as if I were an apprentice again and the only vision I could get in this crystal is my own reflection."

You can't scry him? Ayree's brows came together. *That's bad.*

"Or good, depending on how you view it," said the wizard. "We're not the only ones looking for Prince Alban, you know."

Ayree continued to frown. *I would say the gods are in it, but it has been so long since they . . . No, better not to depend on them in this. I will do what I can from here.*

"You are in Castle Snowglimmer?"

I am. But I intend to travel down to Cymweh soon. I must speak to others of our kind. Morgeld is growing too arrogant too quickly, and not all the magic-makers of the Twelve Kingdoms believe how serious matters have become. The witch-king's scowl darkened. *He has already sent his creatures against my sisters.*

Paragore-Tren looked truly horrified. "Sweet Lady protect them! Were any of them harmed?"

The youngest was taken from her play, lured off, but she was rescued before anything could happen to her. Rescued . . . by a mortal man. Ayree's face vanished from the crystal, displaced by the image of a dark young man who wore first the furs of a northern traveler, then the lighter robes of Vair. A small dog frisked by his side.

Know this man, my friend, said the witch-king. *His name is Mustapha, a traveling player. It may be that he will have a greater part to play for us than a mere animal trainer. At any rate, he was the one who saved Basoni.*

"I will remember him."

And I will go south, to Cymweh. Farewell.

"Farewell."

Chapter III

URSULA THE ACCURSED

The tower room faced the forest and the forest went on forever. Since her childhood, the forest had defined eternity for Ursula. No man knew what lay beyond the forest. It was written that the gods lived there, for the gods are fond of trees and the quiet green places of the world. But the forest was also a place of hidden fears—the lair of strange beasts, wild men, and monstrosities that could not be called men or beasts.

The castle of Dureforte Keep was worthy of a king. Its rooms were light and spacious. The lawns and gardens were spread at the foot of the castle walls like pearls at the hem of a gown. Peacocks strutted and spread their tails under arbors of climbing roses, while fountains played liquid music. And in spite of the pleasures of the palace and the perils of the endless forest, the lady Ursula wished herself a hundred leagues to the east, deep in the wicked woods.

She sat by her loom in the tower room and sent the shuttle back and forth to weave her wedding present to her future husband. Her father had chosen the scene, a popular one for wedding tapestries: the Marriage of Love and Music. But Ursula chose the funereal colors—shades of gray and purple and ochre, dull reds like murky rubies, dim and gloomy blues.

The door opened and Mizriel came tripping into the room.

"Ugh," she said, looking at the tapestry. "Depressing stuff. Can't you do any better?"

"For what?" Ursula said frostily. "I'm not about to celebrate this marriage, although you seem resolved to enjoy it. Thank you, Mizriel. I know I owe it all to you."

26

Mizriel gave a comic groan. "Not *that* again, Ursula. It's ancient history. The one time I cast a spell on you, the only time, and you're forever blaming all your misfortunes on me!"

"A spell that you can't lift to this day! A spell that's ruined my life!" countered Ursula. "I'm over eighteen and unmarried because of your spell. No man wants me. Now here comes a suitor I don't want, and Father orders me to wed him because he sees no other chance of getting rid of me!"

Mizriel stared at her toes. "Then blame Father, not me. Why do you have to get married? I don't want to. After Father's gone, we could hold Dureforte Keep ourselves. There have been chatelaines before us. There are even women warriors, like the shield-maidens of Braegerd Isle and the fighting women of barbarian Vahrd."

"You speak of the southern lands. In the north a woman rules a castle only until the man can return."

"Then it's time we changed things in the north," said Mizriel.

Ursula set down the shuttle. "Mizriel, who lives to the north of Dureforte Keep?"

"Lord Thaumas," replied the white-haired girl, wondering what her sister meant by such a pointless question. "Poor old Thaumas! His daughters are the ugliest things since thirst and hunger. One looks like a goat and one looks like a cow."

"True. But a married goat. A married cow. Their husbands are knights with no property, but with a hundred men-at-arms between them. They've all settled in with their father-in-law, and they have healthy appetites. Lord Thaumas rules a rich domain, but not as rich as ours. He's been dropping hints about what fine warriors his sons-in-law are. If we're to prevent them from picking a quarrel for our lands, Father needs a powerful son-in-law himself."

"Just let Thaumas try attacking us!" cried Mizriel. "I'll cast a sickness on his troops and a blight on his ugly daughters."

"You couldn't cast a fly to a starving trout," said Ursula. "You are mistress of seldom magics."

Mizriel ignored the jibe. "It's not my fault that my tutor died. Poor old Perquis! She was a wise woman."

"Not wise enough. Not even she could lift the spell you put on me. Sometimes I wish Father had found another tutor for you: a competent one."

"Perquis was as skilled a magic-worker as any in this domain," Mizriel said hotly, coming to the defense of her former teacher. "If

Father never found anyone to replace her, I think it was because he was always a little afraid of my talents.''

Ursula laughed without joy. ''And with good reason. If your talents are so great and your teacher was so wonderful, why could neither one of you undo what you did to me? If you had, perhaps I'd have married by now, and married a man I could love.''

''Why not love the one you've got?'' asked Mizriel. ''He seems eager to please you.''

''There's little love in his eagerness,'' replied Ursula, shuddering as she thought of her betrothed. ''He is too pale for my taste, and old beneath his smooth skin. His bones are too long, as if he'd been stretched the way no man should be stretched. Do you recall how the dogs slunk away growling at first sight of him?''

A discreet cough made Ursula turn to see the major-domo standing behind her. ''My ladies, you are summoned to the banquet hall.''

''Another meal with him,'' said Ursula. ''Soon, all my meals and all my life with him. I'd rather die.''

''Then refuse to marry him,'' Mizriel said hotly. ''Father can't force you. If you're firm, that creature will pack up and go back to where he came from. No man wants an unwilling wife.''

''This is no ordinary man,'' Ursula said with conviction. ''We know almost nothing about him. He showed up one morning at the castle gate, leading a reassuring troop of armed men, and asked Father for my hand.''

''He has to have a name!''

''He calls himself Lord Glamorgan of Glytch. Well, I'll do as you advise, little sister. I'll refuse him. Let us go down to the hall.''

The banquet hall was loud with revelry. Lord Blas sat on the dais and contentedly surveyed the tables. His guests and dependents were making merry at his expense, but with the marriage of his elder daughter so neatly taken care of, he could see them indulging the most voracious or frivolous appetites and never feel a qualm. Indeed, he had planned the feast to suit everyone, from the most finicky gourmet to the most omnivorous trencherman.

Slabs of homely roasted beef lay side by side on the board with delicate singing birds from the Kestrel Mountains, their tiny bodies laced with the same honeyed sauces that had been used to lure them to the fowlers' nets. Clear, perfumed broths spun from the seaweed called Elaar's lovelocks were served up in petal-thin porcelain bowls. Indifferent servants piled these treasures on the same trays they used to clear off the huge oakwood bowls for savory boar stew. Down at the far end of the room, Lord Blas's wine steward was having a conniption fit trying to direct his underlings to deliver the proper vintages to the guests. It was no easy job when the sweet yellow dessert wine went wandering up to the man gnawing a leg of venison, while the heartiest red wound up in the goblet of an airy young lordling who simply could *not* abide anything but candied water-root imported from Cymweh.

Well, wine stewards were expected to have conniption fits. It was part of their job. As for Lord Blas, he could rest easy. His future son-in-law sat on his right. He was not too fond of the quiet man, but he was more than happy with the knights Lord Glamorgan controlled.

Lord Glamorgan sat silent, ignoring a plate piled high with the best bits of the feast, sipping a thick red wine from his goblet. His velvet robes were the color of the wine, a red so dark as to be almost black.

Ursula and Mizriel entered the hall and all the nobles rose to welcome them. Ursula looked grim but determined as she approached her father. Mizriel wore a secret smile.

"Ah, my lady Ursula," said Lord Glamorgan, letting the lady's name slip lovingly between his teeth. "Come and sit beside me. I have a gift for you."

"My lord," said Ursula, curtseying and ignoring his invitation, "keep your gift. I have something important to say."

"Ursula," blustered Lord Blas, "if this is more of your waywardness, this isn't the time or place for it!"

"No, Father, this *is* the place. I am sorry, Lord Glamorgan, that I waited so long to say this. I apologize, Father, for the expense of my bridal clothes. I won't marry this man. If it means I never marry at all, so be it, but I won't be his bride."

There was a stunned silence followed by the confused babble of many voices together. From the tables where Lord Glamorgan's men sat there came the scraping of swords being drawn. Blas was on his feet, raging like a surly lion. Glamorgan also arose, but slowly.

"Lady Ursula." Glamorgan's voice was dry as fallen leaves. "Lady Ursula, the northern customs are plain. Your father gave me your hand and you said nothing. You have lost the right to reject me. We will marry, and if the gods are kind, perhaps you will come to love me. If not . . ." He shrugged.

"I will not! I claim my right, my right to a combat. One good sword raised in my name will save me from marrying you." She cast eager eyes the length of the hall. No one moved. The stillness mocked her.

"My lords," Ursula said calmly, addressing her father's guests, "you have known me since birth. You know why no man has asked to marry me. You know my curse. But I tell you now that I have come to realize that I would rather live cursed and alone than wed to this man. Will none of you defend me? Or must I take up the sword myself?"

"This is an outrage," hissed Glamorgan. "I don't appreciate humiliation, lady. When you are my wife, I will remember this."

"She will not be your wife!" a clear young voice proclaimed. It was the son of one of Blas's nobles, newly knighted. "If the lady won't have you, I'll defend her right of refusal."

Lord Glamorgan regarded him dispassionately, replying in a voice of iron on stone. "You are a fool. No one refuses me."

"*She* does, and my sword protects her!" replied the young knight. "Fight for her or abandon your claims."

Lord Glamorgan stepped primly down and faced the lad. He wore no sword. "Why do you anger me?" he asked the knight.

"I challenge you to single combat," replied Ursula's champion. "All your power"—he indicated the men-at-arms—"will not help you there."

"You think you know me. You are wrong. Farewell, Sir Fool," Glamorgan whispered. He touched the young man on the wrist.

The knight gasped and died under his father's horrified gaze. When the young man's sword clattered to the flagstones, Lord Glamorgan picked it up and crushed it to blue-gray powder between his hands.

"I tire of this masquerade," he said wearily. "I am Morgeld."

He expected shock, but not panic. In the northernmost realms where life was harsh, the harshest legends held most power, but the people faced them. Lord Halbor had called Morgeld a demon before he died. In the sweet, soft, southern lands they fancied him a god. The truth lay somewhere in between—in the fruition of an unsung, unwilling coupling forced upon Inota, Lord of Battles, by a night-spirit. The shameful thing had come to pass in a nameless cave, where that elemental creature of darkness kept Lord Inota himself captive until he gave her a child. Such a child! No sooner born than the capricious mother gave him into his father's care, a reminder of the galling time when even a god had to submit to the powers of night.

Hot-tempered Lord Inota did not care for such a reminder.

In the banquet hall commotion rose, fell, and redoubled. Morgeld himself wondered that his revelation could cause so much excitement. Then he saw the second reason for the panicked rumblings of the guests. Beside the body of the fallen knight there squatted the hulking form of a great brown bear. It pointed its muzzle skyward and bleated its woe, then shambled clumsily from the hall while frightened pages scrambled out of its way. Mizriel of the White Hair ran after it.

"So that is the curse," said Morgeld, resuming his seat and helping himself to wine. "Can she rule her transformation?"

"No," rasped Lord Blas, staring at the body of the boy whom he had knighted scarcely six weeks before. "It comes when it will. Her sister Mizriel put it on her when they were both children."

"In a fit of temper, I suppose. One daughter a bear and one a sorceress," mused Morgeld. "A good family. When she has a woman's neck again, I will give her my gift."

From a black leather pouch he poured a silver necklace set with purple stones. The links were thick, yet flexible, like those used to collar the most pampered slaves of the southern lands, and the central stone blazed with its own life. It was a thing of great splendor, but it was still a collar for a slave.

"Pretty, isn't it?" Morgeld smiled. "Perfect for her. And it will make her mine—safely mine."

Mizriel didn't have any trouble following the she-bear through the castle; Ursula left a trail of quaking maids and crying pages. But Mizriel lost the track in the lower reaches of the castle. Either her sister was hiding or had found a way outside.

"Or returned to human shape," said Mizriel to herself. "I'll find her later. So that is Morgeld! The rumors from the west are right, then. He *is* free. We'll face hard years. And my poor sister, to be his consort! There's no way out of it. Father won't dare object now. Poor Ursula." And Mizriel trailed back into the banquet hall.

Outside, the moon had risen, shedding a lustrous light over the pines of the sleeping forest. A shaggy shadow lumbered over the starwet grass. The bear paused and glanced once over its shoulder at the twinkling castle towers, then went resolutely on.

At the edge of the woods, the bear hesitated, sniffing the damp, chill air that blew from the trees. Not even the fresh, friendly odor of fallen pine needles could disguise it. The bear shivered, fur bristling. It was not so easy to enter this forest. It sent a message of warning to all the senses at once, a warning that spoke to the soul in its own language of hidden terrors. The traveler on the edge of this wood did not need to be wise to keep out, but had to be in the last stage of desperation to go in.

She stood there, torn between fear and flight. One pace either way would decide her. Morgeld's face danced in the gray and silver shadows of the trees. Could she be certain that he would not follow her, even if she dared the forest? Men were afraid of it, but Morgeld was something more than a man.

As Ursula lingered, wondering and afraid, a sound of soft music drifted toward her. It was man-made song, the gentle complaint of a burnished lute, the silver traceries of a minstrel's piping.

A curl of smoke twined upward on the breeze to meet the moon. Twigs crackling on a fire lured the bear away from the lowering pines. She followed the tune. In a shallow dell she saw a small camp. Two men sat by the flickering light of the fire and deceived their lonesomeness with song. The bear forgot she was a bear and came into the circle of firelight to join them.

The flute player's fingers froze on a single note. He threw down his instrument and tumbled backward, trying to escape the beast. His friend was calmer, his fingers never leaving the lute strings. He went on with his melody as if he played for bears daily.

"Alban, are you crazy? A wild bear! You'll be dead where you sit!"

"Hush, Lymri," said Alban, still coaxing pensive music from the lute. "Do you see it attacking me? I think it likes my song. There's understanding in those eyes. If the bear won't bother me, why should I bother the bear?"

"You're too kind to be healthy," said Lymri, keeping Alban between him and the animal. "Now that we're almost at our goal, you'll get yourself killed by serenading bears!"

"They say that Insar, the son of Asira, played to the animals on his lute and they followed him like children. He called them his children. Always remember the gods, Lymri. See, the beast sits down as gracefully as a lady."

"Getting ready to spring!"

"Nonsense. This must be a tame bear from Dureforte Keep. She's very beautiful."

Lyrmi snorted. "How can you call this brute beautiful? You must be mad."

"I am, I am," sighed Alban. He gazed at the bear gently across the crackling flames. "I'm in love, and so I walk among miracles."

"Miracles, is it? I say you walk—Oh!" Lyrmi caught his breath and sank trembling to his knees. It seemed the wavering light of the fire was playing odd pranks. The outline of the bear appeared to blur, then to grow tall and slender, to cast off paws, snout, and fur. The Lady Ursula stood by the campfire, smiling mildly down at them.

"A sorceress!" hissed Lymri. "A witch! Oh, this is worse than when we only faced a bear!"

Alban ignored Lymri. He knelt before the lady, head bowed low, not daring to look into her eyes. "The gods do not forget me," he murmured. "I am here to serve you, my lady."

"I know you," Ursula said carefully. "You were the man who blocked my escape at Panomo-Midmists. Get up, please, I don't want your services."

"Escape? What were you fleeing? If you could have named your troubles, I would have slain them, even were they the spirits of darkness themselves."

Ursula studied her own clasped hands. "Never mind. There is no escape for me. If you truly want to serve me, sing for me. Sing the ballad of Ursula the Accursed."

Automatically Alban's fingers strayed to the strings of his lute, drawing forth the familiar chords. Lymri, entranced by the lady, the look in Alban's eyes, and the night-magic, began to sing the old, old words in his tender, liquid voice.

> "Ursula weaves by the chamber door
> A tapestry of grand design.
> Her needle works a tale of war;
> The work is swift, the work is fine.
> Below her window, on the plain,
> The sounds of arms and armor meet,
> A battle cries the cries of pain,
> A living pattern at her feet.
> A faithless knight is cause for war,
> A lady is a fragile thing.
> Her honor is worth dying for,
> Or so the sheltered poets sing.

A lady's love is swiftly won,
A lady's honor quickly gone.
A lady's father and his son
Are laid in tombs of chalcedon.
The torches gutter dark and low,
The clash of armor fades away,
The ghosts glide softly to and fro,
The war will last another day.
A child is weeping in the night,
A child is born to swiftly die.
The lady's torches all burn bright
And yet she fears, she knows not why.
Ursula weaves by the chamber door
A royal shroud of grand design.
Her needle works a tale of war;
The work is swift, the work is fine."

Lymri's song faded, rising with the smoke of the campfire. Ursula drifted past the two musicians, her face set toward the forest.

"No!" cried Alban, vaulting the fire to stand by her side. "You shall not go into that evil wood. What do you fear? What do you flee? I swear by my sword, I'll protect you from it to my death."

"You are bold for a wanderer," said Ursula. "I see no sword for you to swear by. Yet a wanderer . . . a wanderer might be just the man I need. Do you know the Twelve Kingdoms?"

"Northern and southern lands, and the islands in between," Alban said proudly. "I am Alban of Sombrunia."

"A southerner! That explains your kindness. I hear that your folk are gentler to the ladies than the rude men of the north. Very well then, Alban of Sombrunia. Serve me. Take me away—far, where my name will be nothing, and where Dureforte Keep is a memory."

Alban tried to keep back the dance of joy he felt stirring in his feet. "Gladly," he managed to reply. "I'll take you to the farthest pole, to Sombrunia, to the stronghold of Castle Pibroch itself."

"You are good, Alban," said Ursula. "I wish the northern lands gave birth to men like you. You saw me with my curse upon me, the bear shape, and you didn't run away or try to slay me. Brave beyond your kindness, and kind beyond your birth."

"Hey!" protested Lymri. "Don't speak too quickly of Alban's birth, m'lady! You'd better know he's—"

"—very pleased to serve you." Alban covered Lymri's words. "We leave at once. First, south to the great port of Cymweh, there to take ship for Sombrunia. Are you ready?"

Ursula laughed for the first time in months. The hem of her palace dress was torn and stained. It would be in worse state before they reached the sea. "I am ready," she said. "I have no choice. My jewels will see us through. I can never go back to Dureforte Keep again." Her voice changed slightly as she allowed herself one last look at the far-off towers. "And yet, there is something . . ." Her voice trailed off wistfully.

"Name it!" cried Alban.

"My sister. I would like to say goodbye to my sister, Mizriel. But how can I? I can't go back."

Lymri made an elaborate bow. "Leave that to me, my lady. Saying goodbye began this journey for me. You and Alban go on your way. I'll meet you on the road, after I deliver the lady's message to her sister."

"You can't mistake her," said Ursula. "They call her Mizriel of the White Hair."

"We must go swiftly," cautioned Alban. "If we don't meet on the road, seek us in Cymweh."

Alban's words followed Lymri like friendly birds as the little man trotted away through the dark.

The moon-white towers of Dureforte Keep waited.

Chapter IV

MIZRIEL OF THE WHITE HAIR

Lymri spent what he then thought was the worst night of his life. By the time he reached the castle, the gates had been locked and secured till morning. No guard in his right mind would open them to admit a scraggly minstrel. He circled the castle, looking for a way in; found a low wall and scaled it, only to find that it was merely the fence around a dainty private garden. The door from garden to castle was thick and well-bolted. The man who had raised Dureforte Keep was no fool.

It was too late to abandon his errand and rejoin Alban. Besides, he disliked thinking of what the lady would say if he came back without fulfilling his promise. Those eyes of hers, he mused, were the sort to see through lies. He curled up to sleep under a rose tree whose pale flowers graced the night with a dozen fragrant stars.

The morning dew awoke him to aches and soggy clothing. He groaned and stretched, feeling altogether miserable, and thought with longing of his poor but cozy room at the university.

"Alban is Krisli's Fool and I'm a bigger one because I'm Alban's Fool," he growled. "Does friendship breed stupidity? A magnificent stroke of luck last night: the lady he was seeking blunders right on top of us, and he won't even let me tell her who he really is! One whisper that her lover's a royal prince and she'd be his for the asking. But no. Our Alban must keep up his minstrel masquerade. The man is fairly mad."

Lymri would have said more, but the sun rose over the garden wall and reminded him of his task. "The sooner I see the end of this stupid venture, the better. I'll find the front gate and ask admittance." He was on the point of clambering back over the wall when the rasp of a bolt being drawn stopped him.

There was no time to get away. Lymri conquered walls by diligence, not skill. Whoever came would find him trespassing in the garden before he was even halfway over the wall. So Lymri obeyed his instincts, all of which bid him hide, and plunged into a thicket of barberry without regard for the thorns, an action he later regretted.

Mizriel of the White Hair came into her private herbary. From his ambuscade Lymri suppressed a glad cry. Then he saw that she was not alone. With her was a tall, thin man whose smile curved hard, like a hungry sword.

"You can follow me up and down stairs, in and out of closets, back and forth until we both drop," said the girl, in the last throes of exasperation. "You give me no peace, but my answer is the same. I tell you I don't know where my sister is. If I were her, I'd be at the bottom of the moat, except Dureforte Keep hasn't got a moat."

"So you think your sister is wise to shun me, little Mizriel?" asked the man.

"Even before we knew you to be Lord Morgeld, I said she shouldn't marry you," snapped Mizriel.

"So fierce? You might be right, my lady. If your sister hates me that much, I ought to look elsewhere for a bride. But I do desire alliance with your noble house so very much." He smiled coldly. "What am I to do . . . but marry you instead?"

"I'll see you at the bottom of the sea first!" retorted Mizriel. She tried to push past him, but he gracefully stepped between her and the door.

"You speak in haste. Would your father deny me your hand? He wouldn't dare. He would do everything in his power to marry us, rather than displease me. And what could you do to stop it?"

"You forget, Lord Morgeld." Mizriel raised her chin, looking absurdly small and foolhardly against the great black curtain of his armored chest. Fragile whiteness trembled against the depthless dark. "You are not the only one who rules by magic!"

"You are young," said Morgeld, "and your incompetent witcheries are a grain of sand that the waves wash away and never notice. It would be good to have you for my bride. I could train you. I could breed you to magic arts you never dreamed of. I could make you a sorceress-queen, and together we might ride down the winds of the world.''

Morgeld's black eyes glittered with a sudden spark. He took a step toward Mizriel, who backed away. He wore his mother's mantle, the powers that differentiated the elemental beings from the gods. The gods could both create and destroy—even Inota, the violent Lord of Battles. Had not his willing mating with a fire-spirit given birth to Krisli, who ruled the human heart? But elementals could only destroy. The breath of Morgeld's night-spirit mother clung to him. The flowers he touched in passing seemed to put on a dusting of ashes. Mizriel screamed.

''The lady does not want you!'' cried Lymri, jumping out of the shrubbery. His clothes snagged on prickles and he gritted his teeth when his flesh did the same. He had no sword, so he flourished his silver flute and tried to look taller. Even as he leaped forward, he condemned himself for ever calling Alban a fool. Mizriel looked twice as surprised as Morgeld to see her unexpected champion.

''Well,'' said Morgeld, retreating a pace or two. ''My lady grows strange things in her garden. Who might you be, manling?''

''My name is Lymri, and who I am doesn't matter. I am not going to let you bother this lady, that's all.''

''Whoever you are, wherever you come from, go away,'' urged Mizriel. She ran to Lymri's side and gave him a push toward the wall. ''Save yourself. You don't even have a weapon.''

''My legs are too short for running away,'' returned Lymri. ''His legs are longer. Let him run.''

''I think,'' said Morgeld, holding his bony hands together as if in prayer, ''that there is more to this mannikin than meets the eye. Are you a hero? A dragon in disguise? A mighty sorcerer? Tell me, Lymri the Brave, what lady do you serve? Surely not this girl's sister, the fair Ursula?''

''Never heard of her,'' Lymri said suspiciously. He attempted to keep his eyes from meeting Morgeld's.

''Oh, but you have! You have seen her and spoken to her. For her sake you've come here seeking Mizriel. Don't deny it, little man. Ursula is touched by her sister's childish magic. Once an enchantment is cast, it leaves a mark that any mage can read. And I, who am more powerful than any sorcerer living or dead, can sense the presence of magic as surely as a man can follow the perfume of a rose into the heart of a garden.''

"If you're such a good hunting dog, find her yourself!" said Lymri.

Mizriel's hands flew up like startled doves to cast protection over him, a sending from the heart. Morgeld's cold eyes sent a killing at Lymri, only to meet the barricade of Mizriel's counterspell. The dark one looked perplexed. Lymri stood alive, taunting.

"What meddling magic is this?" Morgeld asked himself. His hands tingled; he brought them within an inch of the small man's body and could go no further.

Mizriel laughed.

"A surprise, it seems," said Morgeld. "Do you enjoy surprises, my lady? Then take this one, and with my compliments!"

Morgeld's rage blazed up like burning crystal. Lymri thought he could see a coldly sparkling ring of light, like the trapped fires of great gemstones, enveloping the dark one. It flamed without warmth, and its very strangeness made the little singer shiver with fear. Suddenly he was overwhelmed by how deadly chill Morgeld's wrath could be.

Mizriel clutched her throat in horror; her hands met a loop of lead.

"Charitable to protect others and forget yourself," said Morgeld. "You now wear my thrall collar, lady. It is not so fine as you might desire. Smooth lead, so thick and dull and heavy, without a stone to set it off or a clasp to set you free. A silver necklace would look sweeter, yet for now this leaden one will do. I cannot harm your new friend, nor can he harm me. You must be our battlefield.

"I don't want much," Morgeld continued. "I only want to have my bride again. This man knows where she is. If he refuses to tell me, he may depart unharmed. But hear me, little man! Each day that passes without Ursula by my side, that collar on the lady will grow tighter. Each day the leaden noose will shrink. If I don't find Ursula, the day will come when it tightens for the final time."

Mizriel sobbed aloud. Blind with anger, Lymri flung himself at Morgeld. But the student hurtled through naked air; his hands closed on emptiness. Many yards away the dark one lounged with a grin beneath the rose tree.

"What shall it be, Lymri?" he asked. "Cooperation, or death for the lady? She is nothing to you, yet chivalry can—"

"I'll talk," Lymri said slowly. "I'll tell you all I know, but you must promise to release her."

"By the spirits of night, I promise."

"Ursula is escaping. I don't know where she is or on what road."

"That's less than nothing. I won't free Mizriel for that," said Morgeld impatiently.

"But I do know her goal. She makes for the great port of Cymweh, and from there for the southern lands. That's all of it. Now release the lady Mizriel."

Morgeld appeared not to hear Lymri's last words. "The southern lands," he mused. "That's not good—*he* dwells there, and she must not meet him. She must not leave Cymweh." Muttering to himself, Morgeld strolled into the castle. Lymri ran after him, seizing him by the cape.

"Free her!" he shouted. "Now!"

"Free her?" repeated Morgeld, dreamy-eyed. "Oh, the collar will come off when I find Ursula. Not before. Did I promise *when* it would come off? You will accompany us to Cymweh, little man. I think you'll have your uses. You'll learn the songs of Helagarde to play upon your flute. No mortal musician has ever played that lissome music. You will thank me." He passed into the castle like a specter.

The next morning a troop of black horses stood outside the gray gates of Dureforte Keep. A white mare and a small piebald gelding whickered nervously behind them, pulling at their tethers. Beside each raven steed stood a hooded man in smoky armor. At last the castle gates released a glorious blue-black stallion, eyes like living emeralds, with Morgeld astride. Two small, pale figures followed him on foot and mounted the white mare and the piebald.

Fat Lord Blas watched his child being led away. He stood at an upper window and watched, his heart swollen with sorrow and helplessness. The sinister horsemen mounted and formed two columns behind their lord. A group of four stationed themselves behind Lymri and Mizriel before the double line rode away south to Cymweh.

"My lord," said the gentle voice of Mizriel's old nurse, Hadolor. "My lord, what man can do anything now that Morgeld is free again? Submit and pray."

The sound of iron hooves grew fainter in the distance. Blas turned furiously on the old woman. "Submit! Pray! He's driven Ursula from me, and now he takes Mizriel. I curse the day I failed to see through his guise of Lord Glamorgan. I'll give him a spear through the heart for each of my sweet girls, and no one will stop me! By all the gods, has he made me forget myself?"

"My lord, no one can fight him and win," counseled Hadolor.

"Go back to your spinning, woman. Leave fighting to me. He casts a spell of fear that steals a man's marrow, but he can be defeated. I've lived a life of ease here, forgetting I'm a warrior. I'll forget it no more! By Janeela's silver hand, I'll snap his spells with his bones. My men! My men to me! Make ready for battle. We follow them!"

Chapter V

LYMRI RIVERBORN

The sound of running water sent a delicious thrill through Lymri, raising his spirits. It didn't matter that Mizriel hadn't said a word to him since they'd defied Morgeld together in her garden. It didn't matter that he now rode among a troop of mute, menacing horsemen led by Morgeld in the flesh. He heard the water, and misery and gloom were banished.

"I was born beside a river," Lymri remarked out loud. He looked at Mizriel hopefully, awaiting a reply. He got none. "I was. It's true. I can't think of a better place to be born. That's where my foster mother found me, in the reeds beside the River Salmlis."

"Your foster mother?" Mizriel asked dully. The lead collar had sapped her. Lymri's light talk revived her a bit. "What happened to your real mother?"

"I don't know," he shrugged. "My foster mother said some evil must have befallen her. The Salmlis runs between Clarem and the unknown lands. Some creature from the western bank may have stolen her away after she bore me. Life is uncertain when one lives too close to magic."

Water pouring over golden sand, louder now. Lymri pricked up his ears and smiled, wishing for a sight of the river. Mizriel studied Lymri's avid face with interest.

"That's the River Carras you hear," she told him. "It feeds into the Opalza Sea at Cymweh's delta. It isn't much of a river, you know."

"Ah, any river's a fine thing to see!" said Lymri. "Each one's ruled by a different spirit, and each has a different song to sing.

42

Some house more than one sprite, and some are the glittering water-palaces of whole families of riverfolk.''

"You speak as if you know the rivers; all the rivers in the world.''

"I wish I did. I've studied maps of them and read what I could. You take your River Salmlis, for example. He's born in the heart of the Kestrel Mountains, and he's like the souls who live there. He's an icy river, blue-white with melting snow, businesslike and hard-working with no time for nonsense. But then he leaves the mountains and enjoys himself a bit, splashing over great black boulders and singing through the rapids until he's had enough of that and slows to a majestic flow when he enters the unknown lands. 'I am a river of grave secrets,' he says then. 'I must bear them solemnly to the sea.' ''

As Lymri spoke, he saw a silver sparkle through the trees, and then the River Carras spread its pale blue waters out for admiration. Bright yellow flowers decked the banks and leaping fish broke the surface of the water. Diamond sprays danced in the sunlight. Diving swordbills, those darting green-plumed fliers of the riverside, speared trout as neatly as seasoned fishermen could desire. Clouds of heartsbreath rose from the reeds—flying marvels, part insect and part blossom, whose rosy wings perfumed the air, but whose fragile bodies melted into a sour-smelling puddle in the hands of children cruel enough to catch them.

White flocks of geese mingled with brown and tan ducks paddling close to the bank. If they belonged to any man, they went unherded. Old tales claimed that the waterfolk who haunted Carras' stream were more beautiful than any others of their breed. To send a child to tend the geese was to lose him to those exquisite beings forever.

Down the middle of the stream sailed the heavy wide-bottomed barges of the river. Broad as the Carras was, it was shallow. Only a barge could safely ply the length of its waters.

Morgeld reined in his horse and dismounted. His men did the same, the rearguard making sure that Lymri and Mizriel obeyed. Small pumice-colored tents sprang up like toadstools under the willow trees, and the troops disappeared inside them. Lymri and Mizriel were shoved into a single tent with two armed guards posted outside.

Although the daylight outside was clear and growing brighter, inside the heavy tent all was night. The gray walls were thick and opaque as woven stone. In the darkness, Lymri fidgeted with longing for the river. Mizriel spread her blanket on the earth and lay down to sleep while Lymri paced the ground like a caged cat.

"Get some rest," she murmured. "Morgeld prefers the night for his travels. We'll most likely camp here until sunset, then move on."

"I can't help it," Lymri said curtly. "There is the call. By moonlight it won't be the same."

"What won't?"

"The river. By day the gentlefolk of the waterways play there, but by night some other breed of spirit dabbles in the moonlight. I don't like a starlit river, Mizriel. It's not water anymore."

"What is it, then?" demanded the girl.

Lymri's eyes stared into the artificial night of Morgeld's tent as if trying to burn the shadows away. "I don't know. Sometimes I think it's a road I see, when the moon streaks silver across the river. A perilous road, with someone waiting for me at the end."

"Well," yawned Mizriel, "you speak more riddles than natural for a mortal man. I like the river well enough, day or night. And so did Ursula. I'll wager she told a good lie to a bargeman and wangled a ride down to Cymweh while we're slogging along by land. We might catch her if we took ship, but Morgeld hates living water more than he hates sunlight. He'll only cross it when he must. I'm glad. Let my sister escape at least, even if I"—she slid two fingers between her neck and the collar—"cannot."

"Oh my lady!" Lymri's voice was heavy with pity. "Has it gotten smaller?"

"Just as he promised it would," said Mizriel, smiling ruefully. "Sleep, Lymri. Your waking can't help me."

Lymri lay down wrapped in his cloak. The earth was a hard but familiar bed. In the murky shadows of the tent Mizriel's white hair and pale face shone like the silvered foam of the sea. He watched her until he fell asleep.

A black-garbed guard woke Lymri with the tip of his boot. Lymri in turn woke Mizriel, before that same ill-favored fellow could touch her. Together they stumbled from the tent to greet the midnight sky. Morgeld and his men were already mounted, in serried rows of black against the night like a range of goblin-haunted mountains.

Lymri helped Mizriel to the saddle, then mounted the piebald. A low hum passed through the black horde and they began to move south.

"Mizriel?" Lymri called softly. The ghostly presence of the

white girl on the white mare moved beside him, a phantom. "Mizriel, are you all right?"

"I'm sad, good Lymri. This feels like my funeral cortege I ride in, with black demons around me ready to snatch my soul. Lymri, you carry a flute. Can you play it?"

"Yes, my lady."

"Music would be good to hear."

He felt for the cool slimness of his flute. He wore it at his waist as a warrior wears his sword. Setting it to his lips, he played a merry jig that set the silent waters to dancing.

Mizriel clapped her hands in time and laughed. Lymri changed the tune to a gay village dance, but before he was into the chorus a large hand snatched the flute from his lips and snapped it like a birch twig. Yellow eyes glowed at Lymri from beneath the brim of a gray steel helmet. Morgeld's man intoned, "You will play no more."

The hooves of the black horses trampled the silver flute into the earth.

"So, I shall play no more?" Lymri seethed. "Very well! But my lady asks for entertainment. I am bound to please the ladies. I'll sing."

"Please, don't," begged Mizriel.

"My voice isn't that bad!"

"Lymri, you mustn't. They'd snap you as easily as they snapped your flute."

"It wasn't the music that made Morgeld tetchy, but the happy tunes I played. Listen. I'll sing a solemn song and you'll see that he permits it. Any music's better than none."

"You're right," whispered Mizriel. "Sing on."

The little minstrel sat back in the saddle and raised his face to the moon.

"Sail swiftly, moon, across the sky.
The jeweled stars begin to die
And day will overtake thee soon.
Sail swiftly, moon!
Glide, golden one, from out my dreams.
Fall gently on the waking streams,
For dawn comes on and night is done.
Glide, golden one.
Fade, goddess white, before the day

Shall cruelly thy fairness slay
And steal from dreamers' eyes their sight.
Fade, goddess white.
Return, my heart, to morning cares.
The sun with heartless brightness glares
To show to souls their poorest part.
Return, my heart."

Night slipped into day, day into night, in an indistinguishable
monotony. Sometimes the horses would throw themselves into a
wild gallop, red sparks flying up from their hooves. Sometimes they
moved like dancers in a grim sarabande, the road flowing slowly
beneath their iron-bound feet.

Then one awful evening a great darkness descended on them.
Lymri heard a noise like the rushing of large leathery wings, and
held tight to his saddle. A bitter wind lashed him, and he thought
he felt long, thin fingers trace clammy paths across his face while
the muffled laughter of mindless things rang horribly in his ears.
Finally the darkness lifted and he drew deep breaths of earthly air
again, noticing that the dawn was beginning to show a thread of
scarlet in the east.

"Lymri, are you there?"

"Yes, my lady," he called back. His breath came out in a rush.
"By Ambra! What manner of ride was that?"

"A ride of wickedness, Lymri," answered Mizriel. "Last night
we lay far from Cymweh. Then Morgeld tired of slow pursuit. He
chose a road beyond mortal eyes, and we rode it. Look southward.
Smell: the sea sends its first tang of salt. By full daylight we shall
see Cymweh and be there by evening."

"Good," joked Lymri. "It was a less tiresome way to travel,
Morgeld's road. I'm grateful to him for sparing me some saddle
sores."

"You're lucky you're alive to feel them, minstrel," said Mizriel. "Where we rode, dark beings fluttered around us, seeking their
food. It seems my spell of guarding still protects you. Frankly I
didn't expect to see you again."

Lymri remembered the cold, searching fingers on his face and
shuddered.

As Mizriel predicted, evening brought them to Cymweh. The
streets were paved with smooth white stones veined with lavender.
The houses and the titan warehouses too were built of stone, shel-

tering trade goods from many lands. The scents of a medley of spices and other tantalizing perfumes from the warehouses—cloves, nutmeg, cinnamon, star anise, oranges, and dried citrons—met the traveler's nose mixed with the more pungent smells of brine, seaweeds like green lace, and clumps of mussels which shone like black opals on the wharf pilings.

The lanterns were the golden eyes of sleepy dragons, casting a warm, hazy light over the passers-by. But not even their enchanted glow could soften the sharp outline of Morgeld's men as they rode their horses down to the edge of the Opalza Sea.

An old sailor sat on a rickety brown pier, watching the stately departure of a delicate merchant ship with azure sails. Morgeld gave no sign, but one of his men dismounted and presented himself at Lymri's side.

"Ask that sailor about the Lady Ursula," said Morgeld's creature. "Make haste."

Lymri glanced briefly at Mizriel. The girl looked ill, her fair face sallow. The leaden collar had grown too tight for comfort. Privately he gave thanks for the ghastly shortcut Morgeld had taken. Without it, she might have died long before reaching Cymweh.

"Sir," said Lymri, laying one hand on the old seaman's stooped shoulders. "Sir, I'm seeking a lady."

"Aren't we all?" chuckled the sailor.

"A lady," Lymri persisted, "recently come down to Cymweh. You look like a man who notices such things."

The old sailor stroked his grizzled chin and shook his head until Lymri came up with a packet of russet tobacco and a silver coin from his traveling pouch. The seaman pocketed all and regained his memory.

"A lady lately come here? Must be remarkable special for you to think I'd know her. A real lady, you must mean. What's she like?"

"Tall and straight as a young rowan tree, with honey hair," said Lymri. He dropped his voice and added, "A lady not alone."

"Ah!" The graybeard nodded. "I've seen that one, then. You may see her too, if you've got good eyes."

"Where is she?"

"There," said the old man, pointing across the wavelets. "There she sails, your lady aboard, bound for Sombrunia. Fair weather attend her and all who sail on *Elaar's Eye.*"

The sails of the little merchant ship were a smudge of blue on the horizon. Reluctantly Lymri returned to make his report.

"She's gone?" asked Morgeld in a voice as soft and thick as winter mud. He rode his black steed to the edge of the pier and gazed after the vessel as night took the sky. "Impossible. How could anyone outride . . . ?"

Morgeld fell silent, sifting his own cold thoughts. Lymri watched, fascinated. It was like seeing a snake threading out its hunting path through tall grass, choosing one turn over another for reasons only it could know, coming at last to the place where its prey crouched in useless terror.

"Ah," Morgeld said at last, nodding with disquieting satisfaction. "I *thought* I felt something barring our passage. Oh, a very gentle force, so shy, tugging us back, hindering ever so slightly. . . . At first I believed it was just the influence of the river, the living waters that do not willingly let my troops pass. But this was stronger. Strong enough to buy the lady Ursula some time."

His laugh was short and hard as a dagger's blade. He did not seem to be speaking directly to anyone present. "I wonder how much time we have lost? And by whose hand? Do I sense you near, Ayree? Don't you dare to come any closer? Do I frighten you so much? Hinder me all you like; you only postpone the inevitable. We shall take the ship in pursuit—"

A clatter of hooves on Cymweh's violet-veined cobblestones drowned his words. A mass of horsemen, riding hard, poured into the plaza. On one side was the sea, on two sides the blank facades of warehouses, and closing the square was a narrow street and a humble tavern whose jolly red lantern lit the sign of the Merrie Manticore.

Fat Lord Blas came at the head of the riders. His men filled the square with steaming horses and the shine of steel. Swords hissed from scabbards, lances clashed together, and there was the dry whisper of feathered shafts drawn from their quivers, nocked to the bow. There was no retreat for Morgeld and his legion.

"So." It was a whisper from Morgeld's lips. "The magic that hinders one, speeds another. And did this thick northern lordling even realize it when enchantment devoured the road between his castle keep and Cymweh?" The notion of Lord Blas unknowingly galloping over a sorcery-shortened road amused Helagarde's lord. Grim northern faces ringed Lord Blas as he dismounted and brandished the heavy two-handed sword of his fathers. They called it

Bloodthirst, but it was older than that, and rumored to be one of the three swords forged from the pieces of Oran's shattered blade. Calmly Morgeld reined his horse around and went to meet Lord Blas, the huge black hooves mincing forward like a dancer.

"Morgeld," thundered Blas, "by deceit you entered my home. By trickery you got my consent to have my daughter Ursula for your bride. I blame myself for that, but now I tell you that you shall not have her sister! I am no raw boy. My men follow me to the death against you. You've been free too long already, and I swear by all gods that I'll bind you down with death itself. Will you face me at the head of my men, or will we settle this in single combat? Choose, Morgeld. I want you dead."

Morgeld twitched his horse's reins slightly and leaned forward over the saddlebow. "I choose," he replied. "Let it be between us alone. The air about you reeks of spells and counterspells. Do you dream they'll be good enough to stop me? But let it be settled with swords, and nothing but swords. To the death."

Morgeld dismounted and thrust his right fist skyward to wrench a sword out of air. Amethysts winked on the blade. Lightning split the clouds above the plaza. Lord Blas's men and Morgeld's legion melted away like forgotten winters.

"Don't fear for your men, Lord Blas," said Morgeld, taking a fighting stance. "They are safely back at Dureforte Keep. If this is to be a private battle, we shall not be disturbed."

"Devil!" shouted Blas, swinging his sword overhead with both hands. "Janeela bound you once, but your final bonds will be forged by a man!" With his old battle cry on his lips, Lord Blas attacked.

Steel on steel rang harsh and hard in the twilight. Lord Blas and Morgeld met each other's strokes with counterstrokes and parries. Morgeld slipped across the cobbles like the shadow of a bat, the amethysts gleaming on his gray sword. He led Lord Blas through the figures of a secret dance.

The first ferocity of Blas's attack waned and dwindled. Morgeld kept always an inch beyond the range of the broadsword. Years of peace had added too much to Lord Blas's girth, too little to his battle skill. He imagined himself a young fighter again, defending the lands of his king and receiving Dureforte Keep as his prize. Again Blas saw the bright green eyes of Mellicent looking down on him with favor from her distant tower. She leaned forward, dropping her glove as love-token. As he recalled kneeling to pick it up, Morgeld's sword caught his at an awkward angle and sent it flying from his hands.

"So, Lord Blas, it ends," said Morgeld. He played the point of his dismal blade above Blas's heart.

"He's unarmed!" protested Lymri. "You can't—"

Mizriel wailed and threw herself past Morgeld to cling to her father. "Spare him, Lord Morgeld. Spare him and I'll use my own spells to find my sister. I'll do anything you say. Please, please spare his life and take mine!"

Lord Blas embraced his daughter. "My Mizriel," he said in a voice so tender it surprised memories of old loves in his heart. "My little daughter, offer him nothing. His doom is written in the stars. It seems the honor of it is for a younger man. Shed no tears; I am glad to die in battle." He kissed the sobbing Mizriel and gently pushed her away.

"Prettily said, Lord Blas," said Morgeld. "But very foolishly done. You shall be my jester in the purple walls of Helagarde." His blade licked out and ended Blas's life.

"Now," said Morgeld.

"Now fight! Fight someone who's neither old nor unfit for battle!" shouted Lymri, brandishing Lord Blas's broadsword. "Come and fight me, Morgeld. Fight me for your life! Come on! Come on!"

"What is this yammering?" growled Morgeld. Angry color touched his waxy cheeks as he shifted his deadly sword. "In all the ages of my captivity have they done nothing but breed fools? So, you'd stand against me, my fine hornet? Hear me out before you buzz so bravely in my ear. Lay down your sword or I'll kill the girl here and now, then kill you as well."

"Did you expect a welcome for your return, my lord? Bent necks willing and ready for the yoke? Let the mortal alone. Face me, Morgeld. I'll give you a memorable welcome!"

White splendor blazed across the quiet plaza. The red lantern over the tavern door bobbed in a gust of fresh arctic wind. A young man clad in white and silver, with hair whiter even than Mizriel's, stood enveloped in his power beneath the sign of the Merrie Manticore.

"Ayree," breathed Morgeld, in a voice that contained great hate, and greater fear.

Ayree raised his arms, sending arcs of endless power curving through the night. His cold blue eyes pierced Morgeld and seemed to melt him away. The dark one grew thin, a spider shriveling up in a candleflame, then vanished utterly.

"You've destroyed him," gasped Lymri. Mizriel flew to her father's side, weeping. In death Lord Blas looked old.

"I wish I *could* destroy him," said Ayree. "This is only a strategic retreat on his part. It means that he is not yet strong enough to face me in open combat of power. Morgeld is not one to risk battle unless he knows he can win. He's buying time while his servants burrow beneath the surface of our world like moles, weakening and undermining where they can. Then, at the appointed hour, he will do battle."

Ayree's handsome face was grave. In his words Lymri thought he heard a far-off tramp of many feet marching on a grim errand, the sound of a host of swords ringing out one against the other, the thirsty hiss of clouds of slender arrows. Then the white one smiled and the illusion was dispelled.

"Come with me, mortal," he said. "I'd like to reward one brave enough to challenge Morgeld."

"Stupid enough, you mean," mumbled Lymri.

"Brave," corrected Ayree. "Never confuse the two. Enter this tavern now and drink with me."

Lymri took a step toward Ayree, then hesitated. Mizriel's weeping held him like a chain.

"I have not forgotten her," Ayree said softly. "Look."

From out of the dark, spice-haunted streets of Cymweh there came a pale procession. Twelve maids with golden hair and eyes of northern blue rode twelve white stallions at a slow, majestic pace through the nighted lanes. The tallest, the eldest, dismounted at Mizriel's side, and gently led her away from the fallen lord. Then the girls formed a ring of brightness about Lord Blas's body. Faintly at first, there arose an airy melody that wove itself into a flowing veil of mist and twilight. Softly as a falling flower petal it drifted down, then melted like an April snow. Lord Blas was gone. The twelve ended their song and vanished.

"They are my sisters," said Ayree, "the daughters of the lost sorceress-queen Charel. They hold these Twelve Kingdoms in their keeping. Someday, when all of them are grown and their powers have matured—" He cut off his own words. Even the great witch-king shared the peasant's superstition that to speak of *someday* could turn it to *never*.

"Where have they gone?" asked Lymri. "Morgeld rules the dead . . ." He pressed his fingers to his mouth, ashamed of what he had said, praying that Mizriel had not heard.

Ayree smiled at the little poet. "That is what Morgeld likes to think, and he reaps many ignorant souls who share that belief. If the Lord of Helagarde is so all-powerful that the dead are his, why not serve him willingly since you must serve him eventually? But that is a lie. When the gods departed, they did not abandon mortals so completely. There were too many bonds of love between them. No, Lymri. Amethyst Helagarde holds some dead, but only those who could not believe that there is always light-in-darkness."

"Ambra," Lymri said quietly. The loveliest goddess of them all ruled light-in-darkness, and all true love and mercy filled her name.

"You believe, I see," Ayree said. "Then you will believe me when I tell you that my sisters take Lord Blas to another realm than Helagarde, a realm where Ambra rules and waits to comfort her children. Any man who can walk far enough can reach Helagarde, but Ambra's realm lies far from these Twelve Kingdoms. That is where Lord Blas now goes to dwell."

Mizriel stopped weeping. The truth of Ayree's words and the beauty of Ayree's twelve sisters calmed her grief with a promise.

"My lord," Lymri said timidly. "My lord, you have saved us. We are in your debt already, yet may I . . . may I ask another favor of you? It is bold of me . . ."

"It will be done without your asking," said Ayree. He beckoned Mizriel near and touched the thrall collar. It fell from her neck and shattered like glass on the cobblestones.

"And now let us enjoy the evening," said Ayree.

They passed beneath the swinging sign of the Merrie Manticore. The beast on the signboard, limned in fearsome reds and yellows, carried a foaming mug in each claw and wore what looked like a lantern shade on its head.

Inside the tavern, Lymri and Mizriel soon forgot the chill of the sea air. A yellow smoke hung over all the room and obscured the other patrons, but the tavernkeeper himself came forward to steer them through the fog to a table. He made a great show of reverence to Ayree. As Lymri's eyes grew used to the hazy atmosphere, he saw that those who frequented the Merrie Manticore were not the regular complement of Cymweh seafaring men, nor even the barge-men and fishwives who came down to the port to trade. Rather than greasy cap and tattered shirt, worn shawl and nubbled skirt, he saw men splendid in velvet and brocade, women delectable in samite and silk, cloaks broidered with gold and trimmed with miniver, the gleam and glow of many jewels, any one of which might conjure up a history steeped in greed and glory.

Even the wenches who served at table looked to be princesses in training, working out the last few years of some random curse while they waited for a selection of glorious princes to bumble across them and take them away from all this. The girl who brought green wine to Ayree's table gave off an aroma of sweet rushes, and her slightly slanting eyes were the dappled bronze of a forest pool. She leaned rather closer to Lymri than was really necessary when she poured his drink.

"I trust you will enjoy the bouquet, my lord," she murmured in his ear. "If not, you have only to have a word with me . . . privately. Just ask for—"

"Ask for trouble and you'll get it, girl!" Mizriel snapped at the forward thing. The wench shrugged bare shoulders above a foam of lacy blouse that *could* have been less transparent, and rippled away.

Ayree could not help chuckling. "Don't take Potentilla seriously, my lady Mizriel. She has designs on every man—and none. I warned our host against hiring one of the waterfolk to wait tables. An ondine can rise above everything but her own nature."

Mizriel did not look mollified. Lymri's eyes were still on the ondine's rolling wake and he had not blinked for much too long, given the smoky atmosphere of the tavern.

"Fit for the gods," Lymri mumbled.

"What did you say?" came Mizriel's sharp inquiry.

Quickly Lymri rephrased his thoughts. "I said . . . I only said that this is no tavern for any but the gods."

"Not gods, Lymri." The white-haired sorceress sat back in her chair and tried to look knowledgeable and mysterious. Much as she was enjoying the sights and smells of the Merrie Manticore, the sight she'd prefer now would be Lymri squirming, and the smell she'd favor would be Potentilla roasting over a slow fire.

"Not gods? But—" The poet's hands encompassed the tavern's exotic clientele with a gesture, not excluding the man of wonder now sipping wine with them.

A burst of laughter made him look to the table nearest the hearth. There a party of four imp-faced maidens were engaged in a loud discussion of what made the perfect man. Tiring of words, they began to conjure up more tangible arguments until there were soon four varied and generously favored specimens of manhood sharing the table with them, entirely naked and none the worse for it.

Potentilla decided that even though it was not her table, she would go over and make sure the gentlemen liked the wine.

"They . . . they just *made* . . . ." Lymri was flustered to the point of utter helplessness. "Mizriel, if these folk are not gods, then what are they?"

Mizriel of the White Hair was satisfied that Potentilla would be a minor distraction from this point on. Quietly she answered, "They are not gods, Lymri, I swear it. Oh, we are protected while we stay here, almost as safe as if the gods did have us under their eyes. I've heard of this place, never imagining I'd visit it. It is the Merrie Manticore, the tavern of the hidden arts. Customers here are either witches and warlocks of the enchanted blood or sorcerers and mages who have acquired their magics through study."

Lymri lowered his voice to a whisper. "And Ayree?"

"Ayree, Prince of Warlocks! Ayree, whose veins run rich with the true blood of the goddesses Sarai, Ambra, and Elaar. While he lives, and his twelve sisters with him, there is hope for these lands."

Mizriel had not spoken; the words came from a man robed in plain black velvet. A wild black beard like a stormcloud bristled out from his face. Lymri thought he had seen him before, but perhaps it was only in a song.

"Welcome, Paragore-Tren," said Ayree. With a wry smile he added, "A double welcome for speaking so highly of me."

"Highly?" The wizard's brows rose. "Just giving facts. A man gets no credit for his ancestors. You were simply more fortunate than most." Laying one hand on his breast and the other on Mizriel's shoulder he declaimed, *"Some* of us had to study to gain our powers."

Ayree stood and made Paragore-Tren the smallest bow, but with the warmest smile. "Then join us and study this wine. Join us and hear these mortals tell their tale as well. We may learn something important from them of Morgeld."

"This one will tell me all I need to know," said the wizard, pointing to Lymri. "My chosen charge is Prince Alban, and he knows the prince. He is called Lymri."

"Ah," said Ayree. "Well, Lymri, can you tell us where the prince is now?"

"That's all part of the same tale," said Lymri, and as briefly as possible he recounted all he knew of Alban and Ursula.

When he had done, Ayree said, "There you see why your scrying spells could not find him, Paragore-Tren. He's become Krisli's Fool, as Lymri tells it. Krisli shares some of his half-brother's traits. He is extremely jealous when it comes to protecting his own."

"Hmmm." Paragore-Tren stroked his mossy beard. "And it may be that Krisli shields Alban for other reasons. He's not exactly fond of Morgeld. To thwart his half-brother might amuse him enough to make him work for our cause."

"He would work tirelessly to put an end to Morgeld . . . if he could."

Ayree drank the last of his wine and set the crystal goblet spinning in the air above the table. Without warning, he let it fall. Lymri lunged for it, fearing that the fragile vessel would shatter on impact with the thick plank table. His frantic dive was needless. Mizriel of the White Hair had already netted the falling goblet with a minor spell.

"There you see the reason why Krisli can't interfere," Ayree said. He sounded resigned. "The reason, too, why Paragore-Tren and I can't engage Morgeld openly. Whether our magic came to us by birth or study, it is still our magic, and only mortals who have been cut off from all knowledge of spells and enchantments can forge Morgeld's final doom."

"At least we can do something to help our magicless mortal friends every now and again," said the wizard. "So, Lymri says that Alban and Ursula are heading for Sombrunia. I would not have it any other way. More vital matters need my attention in the northern lands. Once they reach Sombrunia, the Council will tell Lord Prince Alban of his father's death soon enough."

"His father's dead?" asked Lymri. He pictured his friend receiving that heavy news bluntly, heartlessly, from some old relic on the Council, and shook his head vigorously. "No. It's not right. They'll hustle him off the ship and onto the throne without time for a tear. He must know sooner. And gently."

"Why should you care how he learns the news?" demanded Paragore-Tren.

"Because, sir," Lymri replied stoutly, "I never had father or mother, and I know the full measure of sorrow. I'll take ship tomorrow and find my friend. He can call me a bird of ill omen for the sad news I bring him, but he can also have my comfort, and my heart ready to share his unhappiness.''

"Well said, Lymri!" Ayree thumped him on the back. "A true friend deserves a swift ship. You'll intercept the *Elaar's Eye* at Malbenu Isle.''

"And I'll go with him," said Mizriel.

"No." Lymri was firm. "You must return home. The sea lanes are dangerous. I have a mission; you have none. All I was supposed to do was say goodbye to you from Ursula. That's done, so go home.''

"And who are you to order me around, little poet?" snapped Mizriel. When she grew angry, her white hair seemed to grow brighter, like slowly heating metal, until it fairly blazed with the burgeoning strength of the uncast spells gathering within her. When her temper broke and she finally flung out her witcheries, their freed fury would be awful to see. "I'll go where I like!"

"Not with me, you won't. You'll slow me down. Lord Ayree, as a man with twelve sisters you know how difficult it can be to travel with a woman. Convince this stubborn girl she belongs safely home.''

Ayree shook his head. "My sisters are a special case. I don't think Mizriel will be convinced. The best I can do for you is this." Ayree touched Lymri on the brow, almost casually, and the little minstrel vanished.

"Where is he?" Mizriel gasped in rage. "What have you done with him? Ayree, you are my master in the hidden arts, but you offend me in this. Haven't I a greater claim to your favors, being a sorceress? And I learned my witcheries by study, my lord! I wasn't born into them like you!"

"Peace, Mizriel," Paragore-Tren intoned somewhat stodgily. "It is not your place to contradict the judgment of the warlock prince.''

"I am sick and tired of being told what my place is!" Mizriel exploded. "First Father, then Ursula when she was old enough, then Morgeld with his leaden collar, then that minstrel boy, and now the two of you! Well, my lords, know this: I have the deeper magics in me. I felt them rise on a distant morning in my little garden. Now I mean to use them, and use them against the next person who dares to tell me my *place!''*

Her snowy hair whipped into a furious blizzard. The tavern door behind her burst open with a howling gale that whirled itself around the sorceress and snatched her up in its frozen heart, then bore her away into the night.

"Well," commented Paragore-Tren. The tavernkeeper closed the door wordlessly. He was used to many such dramatic exits, considering his clientele.

"Well," echoed Ayree. He took the crystal decanter and poured them a thin green wine, then lifted the jeweled cup in a toast. "To my lady Mizriel of the White Hair, and to the little Lymri. Like steel and flint together, may they strike light between them and cheat the darkness."

Chapter VI

AETHELSTAN AND GREL

"I tell you, Grel, it's easier than learning swordplay and sweeter than drinking wine!"

The speaker was a tall, blond-bearded giant, his glorious whiskers disguising his youth. He leaned closer to the doubtful face of his drinking companion and refilled the latter's horn.

"My father has given me a good longship and a crew of slaves to man her. Snorri and his brothers have agreed to join me, but a captain needs a trusted friend always with him to keep jealous blades from his back when the plunder's to be divided. You are my best friend in all Braegerd, Grel. I don't wish to sail without you."

Grel looked pensive—his usual look. He always appeared to be inwardly debating some weighty matter and always misplacing the answer. He was no fool, merely a simple soul, and like his companion he nurtured certain hidden dreams.

"I accept," he said at length, and shook Aethelstan's hand. "What's the prize and what's the profit?"

"We prowl the Opalza Sea and take what ships we find. We'll ravage the coasts of the southern lands, if that pleases us. We'll take the ships of Vair bringing jewels to Cymweh and the ships of Cymweh bringing gold to Vair."

Grel poured another measure of wine. "Jewels," he said. "I like jewels. There are other prizes I like also, Aethelstan."

Aethelstan winked. "Women." He grinned. "I agree with you. There are times I find our Braegerd shield-maidens too boisterous. My tastes run to something softer. Well, we'll find more than a few

58

women on the ships. And if we don't find enough that way, we'll sail up the Koly to see what King Egdred's court can provide.''

"Agreed," said Grel, rising from the table. Aethelstan's teeth flashed as he flung his arm around Grel in a bearhug. Together they left the tavern and staggered down to the docks where the Braegerd longships waited.

The demon-crested Braegerd ship sailed with the wind behind her. Bank after bank of sweating slaves strained at the oars, and if it was not the wisest seamanship to waste your slaves' endurance with a good wind in your sails, the folly might be put to Aethelstan's over-zealousness on his first voyage of plunder. Aethelstan's father, the warlord Havnir, had spared no expense. The slaves were strong and could take more abuse than this. Moreover, Havnir had had the finest shipwrights of Vair and Malbenu kidnapped to build the sea-thane's craft.

Aethelstan stood in the prow, scanning the horizon. There would not be much to see until they rounded the eastern horn of Braegerd. The crescent isle's convex side presented an unbroken line of faceless cliffs plunging straight into the sea, with only gulls to answer any summons to battle from the north. Braegerd men never shunned battle, but they preferred it on their own terms. The only settlement large enough to be called a town lay dead center on the isle's southern coast, and no northern captain was foolish enough to lead an invasion into that well-sentried bay.

Once around the horn, Aethelstan saw the shipping lanes of the Opalza Sea set out before him like a strangely deserted bazaar. The waters were more traveled in spring, but spring was also the season of armed convoys out of Cymweh. There might be fewer ships in autumn, but they went unguarded. *It all balances out*, thought Aethelstan. He could pick and choose his prey.

"Sail ho!" sang out Snorri from the masthead. The azure sail of the *Elaar's Eye* cheated Aethelstan's vision until the little merchantman hove nearer.

"A ship of Cymweh," muttered Aethelstan. Grel joined him in the prow to study the vessel.

"Do we take it?" he asked.

"Yes," said Aethelstan. "Give orders for pursuit. It's a good omen to take our first prize so quickly, no matter how small. All men to arms! Quicken the rowers' stroke!"

Aethelstan's men raised their swords high and bellowed the battle cry.

Alban sat on the deck railing of the *Elaar's Eye* and pretended to tune his lute. Ursula stood further forward, leaning so far out over the foaming waters that she resembled a second figurehead. The sea-witch Elaar has skin as white as narcissus blooms, and hair deep green as the sea, but Ursula was a golden creature, like the sun above the ocean.

They had traveled many days and many miles to reach Cymweh. Once safely away from the environs of Dureforte Keep, Ursula seemed to lose much of her fear of pursuit, although it was a constant worry for Alban. Even though he felt grave anxiety to put as much distance as possible between the lady and her rejected bridegroom—and quickly—he had bowed to her wishes.

"I am free for the first time in ages," she said. "Let me enjoy it, my friend."

So he had. They had walked through meadows and forests, sailed down the Carras on a wool barge, strolled the marvelous streets of Cymweh, and boarded the *Elaar's Eye* together. And for all that, and for all their lack of haste, they had not so much as scented anyone on their trail.

It struck Alban as very odd.

Sometimes—especially when they were on the wool barge—Alban felt as if the old songs about lovers and time were true. A moment without the one you loved became a hundred years, a hundred years with your beloved became a moment. Was his love alone enough to make a sluggish barge convey them to Cymweh as swiftly as it had? The bargewife put it down to freakish currents favoring their trip and refused to question her good fortune, but Alban wondered.

Was it love that made a wool barge fly over the waters, or some other enchantment? A parting gift from Mizriel? Alban knew all about the sorceries of Ursula's little sister.

He tried to shrug off his doubts and be like the bargewife, accepting the gift of time without questioning its source. Questions only led to more questions, and if love did take the credit for the speed of their flight, it was love from only one side. All the time he had spent in her company made no apparent difference. Alban felt no closer to knowing the lady Ursula than that first night of their meeting at the campfire.

" Ah, I love the sea," sighed Ursula. Her words went out over the waves.

"Do you, my lady?" he asked. She looked at him directly only when spoken to, and then not for long. "You lived far from the sea."

"But I dreamed of it. In dreams I was a white bird that slept on the waves. I rather wish Mizriel's spell had turned me into a gull instead of a bear." She laughed and looked away.

"Why did your sister do that?"

The salty breeze from the bow sprayed Ursula's hair with jewels of brine and set her tattered cape flying out behind her. "An argument," she replied. "We were both very young. I was envious of her, because she had a talent for witchcraft and I was so . . . ordinary. I was certainly as cantankerous as a bear whenever I spoke to her, and I made it worse by playing the dignified, grown-up lady who just *has* to correct her hoyden little sister. I told her she was disgracing our family and the device on our shield . . . which happens to be a rampant bear." She smiled at the irony. "Mizriel said that if our device was so important to me, I could have it. So she gave it to me." She glanced sideways at Alban and added, "You have been very understanding about my problem, friend."

"It's had its moments," chuckled Alban. "Remember the time you turned bearish on the barge? And I convinced the bargewife it was only an illusion cast by pixies? Or our last evening ashore when you grew shaggy in the tavern?"

"By the time the innkeeper came to see what had sent his customers stampeding into the street, I was myself again." Ursula smiled reminiscently.

"Perhaps he thought they were mad with drink, and watered down his wine more than it was already," said Alban. Their laughter blended and Ursula leaned closer to him. Suddenly she drew back, as if catching herself at something forbidden, and regained her old icy distance.

That's how she always is, thought Alban. *Beautiful, but like the hard, perfect rind of a golden fruit, guarding an inner sweetness. Why doesn't she let herself smile without thinking it over first? Why—*

"Pirates!" The dreaded cry shivered the calm. "Braegerd pirates!"

In an instant the peaceful ship was transformed into scurrying confusion as the barefoot ship's crew thundered across the decks. They swarmed up the rigging like monkeys. They threw themselves down beside the oar-slaves to add their strength to the rowing. The *Elaar's Eye* had few sails and only one rank of rowers.

The captain watched in despair as the pirate longship easily overtook them.

"My lady, you must go below!" cried Alban. "We will be fighting for our lives."

"I too can handle a sword," Ursula said calmly.

Alban gave her one quick look of astonishment. "Very well. If the master-at-arms will give you one, take it and defend yourself. But expect no favors. Braegerd men have no qualms about fighting women. Their own females are often shield-maidens. You'd do better to go below."

Ursula gazed steadily at the ever-nearer longship. A horde of bearded faces crammed the rails, leaning forward eagerly toward their prey. The *Elaar's Eye* was a smaller craft, with a much smaller crew.

"You'll need me abovedeck for this fight," Ursula said reasonably. "I will not—*Oh!*"

"My lady! Are you hurt?" Alban embraced her, his hands searching the smoothness of her back for the shaft of a Braegerd arrow.

"No! Oh, no!" she wailed, pushing him away. She lifted her gown and showed a bruin's paws. "My hands will soon be paws as well," she groaned. "Then how can I wield a sword?" Her sorrowful cries became bearish bleats and she scuttled down the hatch just as the first grappling hooks of the Braegerd men found their nests in the rigging.

The barbarians boarded the *Elaar's Eye* with chilling howls and battle cries, swords shattering the sunlight. Alban was unarmed when the Braegerd men boarded, but soon he took a dead man's sword and waded into the fiercest part of the fight. The smell of fresh-spilled blood drowned the reek of the barbarians. Alban fought well, staring down eyes blue and cold as his own, that returned his look with hate or mockery before filming over in death. A sword pierced his defense, scoring his left arm with fiery pain. He repaid the stroke with deadly interest. Then the flat of an unseen blade struck him hard across the temple and sent his senses spinning down into blackness.

As the light returned to his eyes, he was aware of a gentle rocking motion, then a tightness across his chest and the dull throbbing of his arm. He opened his eyes to grayness. Sunshine filtered through a hatch cover and cast a checkerboard design at his feet. The little squares of light and shadow moved and two Braegerd men dropped lightly into the hold.

The first, a red-bearded blond, examined Alban roughly. "This one'll live," he told his partner. The second man was giving the same brusque treatment to a dim bulk sprawled against the other side of the hold.

"Good for him," growled the second. "This one won't. He'll be dead by sunset."

The first man snorted and shrugged. "We'll check on that later. What'll we do with the live one?"

"Nothing's down here but these two," came the reply. "Untie him and lock the hatch cover."

"Are you mad?"

"Not mad, just practical. He'll be in better condition for sale if he has a little freedom. Besides, he can care for the other and tell us when he's dead. You'd do that much in exchange for having your bonds come off, eh?" The barbarian addressed Alban with a yellow grin.

"I make no bargains with you."

It was the second man's turn to shrug. "As you like it. Stay trussed, then." He began to leave.

"Wait!" Alban called. The man dropped into the hold again. In a low voice Alban agreed to the barbarian's terms. "I'll care for him. It would be wrong to let him die like this. Untie me and bring me water and clean cloths."

The red-beard cut Alban's bonds with a horn-handled knife, then kept the blade close to Alban's throat while his friend got the supplies. They left him with food, water, and bandages. Above him, Alban heard an iron bolt shoot into place across the hatch cover.

A weak moan came from the dying man. Alban went to him, carrying water. In the faint light he recognized the captain of the *Elaar's Eye*. He had been a fat, cheerful, prosperous merchant when Alban last saw him, sword in hand, ready to defend his ship but not about to die for her. His wounds were still fresh, not relics of the sea battle.

"You were hurt after the battle!"

"Battle?" repeated the dying captain. "It was too brief to be called a battle. I'd call it a joke if I hadn't seen my men cut down in front of me. Braegerd men are brainless! One of them stove in my ship below the waterline with his ax and the others had to scramble back on board this vessel, carrying anything that looked good. You and me they took because they could sell us as slaves. Our cargo wasn't much, but they took that too." A spasm of pain creased the captain's face. He forced himself to turn his groan into a laugh. "Their captain's young," he went on. "Wet my lips, son. My throat's too dry for telling."

Alban moistened a rag and dribbled water between the man's cracked lips, then washed his wounds as well as he could. He would have bandaged them, but the captain's hand stayed him.

"Don't bother, boy. It's no use. Let me finish what I'm telling you. Like I said, the captain's a young barbarian. He took a fancy to make me his personal slave. A captain to wait on a captain. Made me pour his wine while we watched my pretty lady sink into the sea. May Elaar avenge her! Then it was time to split the booty.

"It was all ranged very neat on the deck, and that's when I saw her. The lady you voyaged with, boy, she's still alive. I wish she were not. No, don't ask questions. Let me speak. While I can still hear my own voice, I know I'm still alive.

"She was there, as I said, looking hard and sparkling as a diamond. The captain goes to take his pick when this big Braegerd dog steps up and says, 'I want her.' His name's Grel, and he's the captain's closest friend, you see. No ceremony with him. The captain looks at him funny, but Grel just says, 'I want her, nothing else. Keep the rest of my share, but give me her.' The captain smiles and says, 'Done.'"

The dying man drew a breath that echoed with the rattle of bones. "That was when I went mad, son," he said. "I couldn't have that sweet, brave lady made some barbarian's bride. I was the captain of the *Elaar's Eye,* responsible for the lady's safety, and they'd have to do more than sink my ship before I'd forget it. I seized a short sword from the booty pile and lunged for Grel." He took another painful breath. "You see what happened."

"And the lady?" demanded Alban. But the captain was dead. Heavily, Alban called for the two barbarians to carry the body away. Soon he heard a distant splash and knew that the gallant captain had returned to sleep with his good ship forever.

Chapter VII

KRISLI'S FOOL

In a small chamber belowdecks, Ursula sat ripping long shreds out of a priceless tapestry and thinking her own thoughts. All around her were the spoils of the *Elaar's Eye:* celadon bowls, glazed vases of buttercup hue, tapestries from the Kestrel Mountains, and a few chests of semiprecious stones. Not much of a haul. This was only Aethelstan's share, a tenth of the total.

Grel came in, locking the door behind him. Ursula pretended not to notice him. Carefully she palmed the little silver knife she had been using to tear the tapestry.

"My lady," he said uncertainly, coming toward her. She set her mouth firm and waited. "My lady and my bride," he said, strongly this time. His arms were around her, smelling of fur and steel and blood. She struggled free and struck out with the silver knife as hard as she could.

It was a good knife and might have done the job, had Grel not been a Braegerd man. Thick pelts protected his chest, the fur robes that no ranking sea-thane would ever be without. The knife nicked the fur and stuck in the hide. He plucked it out like a mosquito and tossed it away.

"You will not fight me," he stated. "You are my bride."

"By my life, I am not!" yelled Ursula. She gave him a lusty kick in the shins to emphasize her point. Grel hardly flinched, feeling nothing through his sheepskin leggings. If he loosed her and fell back a pace, it was only to regroup his thoughts in general, and those on marriage in particular.

"You're a strange one," he said. "I am not ugly. I am strong.

My father is the mighty Braegerd lord Aareg. If I have a northern bride like you in my house, I swear to take no concubines. You are fair. I have always dreamed of a fair wife. I will treat you well. And you are mine."

Grel's speech was bumpy as a ride over rutted roads. Ursula ignored him and scanned the chamber for a solid argument to change his mind. The bowls and vases were too fragile, the chests of semi-precious stones too hard to throw accurately. This was Aethelstan's cabin, and the furniture was of the heavy, serviceable Braegerd sort that was scarcely movable.

"Come," said Grel, seizing Ursula again. "I will declare you my wife before the crew. We have no ceremonies on Braegerd Isle."

"You'll have to get me up on deck first!" screamed Ursula, wild with fury at the way this barbarian simply dared assume she would consent to marry him. She broke his hold and clutched the thick headboard of Aethelstan's bunk as if it were a long-lost friend. "If you want witnesses to this so-called marriage, you can bring them down here!"

"They won't fit," said Grel, marveling at the wench's crazy ideas. He shook his shaggy head wonderingly over the antics of these highborn northern women. Unfathomable creatures. Didn't she know the entire crew must witness his declaration if it were to be a valid marriage? Didn't she want her full rights as his wife? He'd always promised himself a refined northern bride, a real lady, trained, educated; but this one needed looking after. He'd have to marry her properly for her own good.

A happy thought struck him. "It's all right," he said. "On Braegerd Isle we have another way for you to be my bride."

Ursula watched in horror as Grel's strong hands casually unbuckled the iron clasp of his sword belt and let it fall to the floor. He lumbered forward and swept her onto the bed without troubling to make her let go of the headboard. Throughout it all he maintained the look of a man who does what he must, but regrets it.

Ursula struggled and squirmed beneath the full weight of Grel's body. Screaming would be useless. She imagined the barbarians on deck, listening to her cries and laughing, making rude jokes to each other. She grabbed the gold chain around Grel's neck, twisting it, trying to choke him. He only sighed and pinned her hands beneath her.

"My lady," he said slowly, "I do not relish this. But I am Grel, and I have sworn to have you. What I swear, I do. You are mine."

"I am not! I am not! I am not, *not, NOT!*" shouted Ursula, and then the logic of Grel's small world broke.

Gentle maiden's face growing long, small white nose growing black and wet, flowery mouth opening with a roar to show fine, white, slashing fangs. The bear's eyes twinkled with unbearish delight. Chuckles rumbled in the hairy throat as Grel leaped up from the bunk with a choked scream and backed rapidly toward the door. He groped for his fallen sword, but the bear pinned it down with one huge paw and grinned.

"So," said the bear with a merry snarl, "I am your bride, am I?"

Grel shrieked a prayer to Elaar and streaked from the cabin. The bear came loping after.

On deck, Aethelstan had just received the welcome news of land sighted. "Malbenu Isle! The gods favor us. Shall we raid, or shall we stop to barter?"

"A few more battles first," suggested Snorri. "Let the men hone their fighting skills at sea before facing a land raid. We lost too many men when we took that small ship."

"That's so," said Aethelstan gloomily. "What shall we offer for sale to the Malben?"

"Weavings," grunted Snorri. "That ship was loaded with 'em. We've no use for them ourselves. Let each man sell his share for gold, and let's rid ourselves of the slave we took as well."

"He fought well," said Aethelstan, although it hurt him to recall the men that Alban had slain. "Might he join us?"

"He has the look of a Sombrunian," Snorri said quietly.

Aethelstan nodded. No Sombrunian would ally himself with Braegerd men.

Grel burst from the hatchway like a sudden winter storm and twice as white. He rushed at them, panting, and gasped, "Swords! Draw your swords, all! We are bewitched!"

"Grel, friend, what's this?" asked Aethelstan. "How's the wench? Don't tell me she's driven you mad for love. You look right mad enough."

"No wench . . . not human . . . help!" shouted Grel, pointing with a trembling finger to where a shadow stirred in the hatchway.

A golden head appeared tentatively out of the darkness and the lady Ursula, quite human, stood on the gently swaying deck. Aethelstan gave Grel a good, long, hard stare.

"She is not my bride," grumbled Grel under that gaze, his stolid face bright red. "Sell her. I'll take my share in gold."

"Koly!" called Snorri's youngest brother from the masthead. "Koly, ho!" A smell of pine trees blew over the faces of the men on deck, first sign of the sweet green isle of Malbenu.

The longship sailed grandly up the southern mouth of the Koly, the sole river of Malbenu Isle. It was no true river, for in forgotten days the island had been shaken with a massive quake that rived out a channel for the sea. The Koly ran salt, excellent for on-land sea fishing. Wells and streamlets gave the Malben fresh water. The tides and the twisting course of the Koly made navigation perilous. Aethelstan studied his charts as the ship passed between steep banks covered with wildflowers.

"This is what we must avoid," he said, stabbing the scroll with one finger. "Eddystone whirlpool, just below King Egdred's castle. The southern Koly's safer than the north; the docks lie farther from the whirlpool. We've done well. Fetch up the goods for sale."

Aethelstan's men hastened to obey. Ursula—unmolested since Grel had given up his claim—wandered the deck and took in the glorious Malben landscape. The land was small, but charming. The Koly ran wide and smooth, carrying the Braegerd men past other ships as she flowed northwards, obeying the call of favorable tides. Then they rounded a bend and trees gave way to a cluster of gaily colored wooden houses, painted with rough designs of blue and white and yellow: Kolytown.

A familiar voice calling her name made her turn from the rail. In the midst of a pile of heavy rolled tapestries and a scattering of pottery stood Alban. A white bandage stained red bound his left arm.

"Oh!" cried Ursula, running to his side. "Oh, I thought you were dead!" Gently she caressed his face and added, "Praise Ambra you're alive."

"And I praise all the gods together that you are well and safe," he replied. "How is it that I don't see Grel's collar on your neck?"

Ursula giggled. "My prospective husband had second thoughts when he saw my other side," she confided. "He was the first suitor I was glad to scare off."

If a gesture can have an echo or a ghost, then Alban felt something very like that on his cheek where Ursula had touched it. Now was the time to speak, now when he knew that she cared enough for him to be glad that he was still alive. Now it was safe to tell her that he loved her. He opened his heart to speak.

"Oh, but minstrel!" exclaimed Ursula. "Your lute is gone! How will you play me your songs now? How I should have missed your music if you'd been dead!"

Alban's face froze. So that was the full measure of his death and her sorrow. She would have missed her minstrel's music.

"My lady," he said hoarsely, "I am sorry if you must do without my music. I am doubly sorry, for Sombrunia is a land of music and now I shall not be able to take you there."

"Why not?" asked Ursula. All about her the barbarians bustled to the job of docking and mooring the ship. Already the Malben traders were coming down to inspect her. The peace-flag fluttered from the mast.

"No love lost between Braegerd and Malbenu," Aethelstan's voice sounded above the row. "But when we come calling to trade, they don't turn us away. They'd be sea raiders like us if they only had the ships for the job!"

"Because, my lady," said Alban, "I am to be sold as a slave with the rest of this jumble. And maybe so will you."

"Me, sold for a slave? Can't you—"

Alban turned from her, helpless. The crowd was thick on the docks, and in the trees beyond the town he saw a cloud of white dust tracing the zigzag path down from Eddystone Castle. Then there were no more trees, and a royal coach drawn by eight Malben kurocs thundered into sight, their antlers gleaming silver in the sun. The conveyance sliced a neat path through the massed people and stopped beside the ship. A crown glinted gold as the coach door swung open.

"King Egdred himself coming to buy slaves," said Alban, half aloud. In his heart he rejoiced. Sombrunia and Malbenu had a grudging friendship. He had only to reveal himself to King Egdred and he and Ursula would be free. But Alban had one regret. The love of a simple minstrel was one thing, that of a prince of Sombrunia was another. It was always easier for a woman to give her heart when there was a crown to be had in exchange.

I wanted to be loved without my crown, thought Alban.

Aethelstan ordered the merchandise to be arranged on the dock; the bargaining began. Ursula and Alban disembarked and stood where they were told, a little to the right of the crockery.

"I saw more of Malbenu from the ship," she whispered. "All I can see here is hats.'' Then she added, ''You'll get a good position, for a slave, Minstrel. They always treat performing slaves better. But I, alas, have a tin ear. Well, cheer up. It isn't the end of the world.''

The crowd in front of them was receding like a tide. It broke away at last before a woman robed in scarlet and a man who wore a crown.

All Malbens are of a single physical type, blond and blue-eyed, with skins so fair that on other men they would look unhealthy. The woman was not pure Malben. Green eyes glittered beneath her blond bangs, and the hood of her cape cast deep rose shadows over her high cheekbones. Alban gave her only a glance. His eyes were riveted to the face of the man with the crown.

''How young he looks,'' wondered Ursula. ''But I thought King Egdred was born in my father's time. What magic is this?''

''Bad magic indeed,'' said Alban. ''That is not King Egdred. It is his brother, Prince Phalaxsailyn.''

''Ah.'' The tall, lanky prince turned at the mention of his name, and leered wolfishly. ''Alban. Alban of Sombrunia.'' His white Malben skin had the pasty hue of a lizard's belly, and all his royal finery hung poorly from his scrawny frame.

''He knows you!'' cried Ursula.

''Know him?'' echoed the Malben prince. ''Lord Prince Alban and I are old friends. We've shared many a trial of arms, haven't we, Alban? But you were always the lucky one. What's changed your luck, Your Highness? It's quite a drop from being champion of the field, with my brother holding you up as a model for me, to being sold on the Kolytown docks as a slave. Why aren't you safe at home?''

''Phalaxsailyn,'' replied Alban, ''those were the contests of children. In the name of hospitality, take us to your brother. We seek his aid.''

''We!'' Phalaxsailyn's derisive laughter was loud. ''So the lady holds the answer. As always. Who is she, Alban? A pretty thing. Your light-o'-love, perhaps? Your sweeting of the moment?''

Alban's hands were free, and he dealt the Malben prince a blow that sent him reeling to the ground. The crowd gasped, horrified, eager yet fearful to see what would happen next. There was a touch of red staining the corner of Phalaxsailyn's mouth when he got up.

''My brother,'' he hissed, ''will not see you. He sees no one, a captive in the southern lands, prisoner of the men of Vahrd. He launched an ill-timed war against them and he may yet pay for it with death. *I* rule Malbenu now!''

"Then this man is truly a prince?" asked Aethelstan. "A Sombrunian prince?" The big barbarian looked troubled. "We don't want bad will from Sombrunia. We'll set him—''

"Which do you think worse, barbarian?" the prince asked through clenched teeth. "Future trouble that may never come, or trouble now? My archers ring the docks from every rooftop. A word to them from me and your ship loses captain and crew."

Aethelstan gazed up. The ornate roofs bristled with Malben archers, best and most feared of civilized fighting men in all the Twelve Kingdoms.

Phalaxsailyn smiled. "You see I don't lie. Well, you came here to sell slaves, didn't you? Sell them! I could use a sweet-faced wench like this in Eddystone." He indicated Ursula. "As for the Sombrunian, let me present Runegilda." He bowed slightly to the hooded lady. "Runegilda, high priestess of Krisli. Once there was a great cult of Krisli on this island, gentlemen. But with the years, the faithful have diminished. Only Runegilda is left to see that her god receives his chosen sacrifice. Tell me, Runegilda, will he do?" The prince pointed to Alban.

Runegilda nodded.

"Good. He's yours. My men will escort you to Krisli's Point and oversee the rites. Had my dear brother kept more faith with Krisli, he might not languish in Vahrd now." Phalaxsailyn tossed a purse into Aethelstan's hands. "Your payment."

The Braegerd sea-thane glowered at Phalaxsailyn, but the Malben prince merely turned his back on Aethelstan and ambled back to his waiting coach. The big barbarian spat strongly into the leather nest of gold pieces. The avidly watching Malbens set up a scandalized buzzing. They had always been taught that the Braegerd barbarians worshipped gold with a passion other men retained for their mistresses.

Aethelstan looked around and addressed his men. "Who will have this princeling's gold? I give it freely!" He poured the coins into the palm of one huge hand and held them high, glittering in the sunlight. The price that Phalaxsailyn had paid for his slaves was at least triple what they were worth. Coins enough, in the little hoard, to buy a man a fine farmstead on rocky Braegerd Isle.

Grel stepped up first. His friend and chief offered him the gold. Without a word, Grel too spat on the slave-price. One by one Aethelstan's crew did the same. It was no empty gesture for them, nor easily afforded. There were many poor men among them, many sons whose fathers could not provide for their futures. It was more often necessity than the joys of blood and battle that made pirates and sea rovers of Braegerd men.

When the last of his crew had scorned the prince's gold, Aethelstan gave a grimly satisfied smile. Again he raised the fistful of coins and bellowed, "The honor of Malbenu Isle!" Then he flung the gold into the churning sea just off the dockside. A murmur of shame passed through the crowd of onlookers.

If Prince Phalaxsailyn saw or heard any of this—if he even cared—he did not show it. His orders concerning the slaves he had bought were being carried out; what the previous owners did with the price was their own affair. Really, these Braegerd barbarians were sometimes so childish. What quaint notions they had. The honor of Malbenu Isle! As if anything mattered but the crown of Malbenu Isle. From the coach window he gave a sign to his men to make haste in clearing off his purchases.

Four men-at-arms marched up to lead Alban to the priestess's dark horse. Ursula flung herself into his arms when the first heavy hand touched him, but it was Alban himself, not an impatient soldier, who coldly removed her clinging hands.

"Don't be sad, my lady," he said stonily. "It's only a poor minstrel they'll sacrifice, and his curse dies with him." Flanked by the armed guard, Alban submitted as the ceremonial halter was place around his neck and tied to Runegilda's saddle.

Tears blurred Ursula's sight. The kurocs were crying their high, mournful, piercing cry in the royal coach traces as Ursula felt herself boosted up behind a mounted horseman, who galloped off with her toward the cold, cryptic towers of Eddystone.

Chapter VIII

AGVAIN

Eddystone perched on top of a sheer cliff above the Koly River. The horseman flew across the lowered drawbridge, bearing Ursula into the blue-shadowed courtyard. They dismounted and entered the keep.

There was water everywhere, even up so high above the river. It seemed as if the Koly could soak through the walls of solid stone as easily as through a sponge. Water left a shimmering dark trail down the passageways. Tiny streams puddled in the halls. The air was frightfully damp and clammy, and held a chill that went to the bones.

Ursula plucked the hem of her skirt high out of the water. Her slippers were soaking. The horseman walked before her through the drizzly corridors, and ahead of her she saw the glimmer of torches. She almost believed they had walked past sunset, seeking the heart of Eddystone, until she realized that it was a virtually windowless castle where torches must light the day as well as the night or the castlefolk would live in darkness. She recalled the little history she'd read—the tales of how the first settlers on Malbenu Isle had had to fight off assaults from northern and southern kingdoms, besides repulsing raids from Braegerd Isle. The central keep of Eddystone likely would have only a few slender windows, just wide enough for defending archers to fire through.

Ursula saw that she had guessed correctly when her guide brought her to their goal at last. The flambeaux lit a chamber larger than the great hall of Dureforte Keep, only darker. Some daylight did come in through a row of high-fixed lancet windows, but they could pro-

73

vide only scant parings of brightness. If there were any wider windows in Eddystone, they would be in the newer sections of the castle, added when the Malben kings felt more secure on the throne.

As for that throne, it stood under a canopy of silver brocade held taut atop four columns of gold-studded crystal. Carved of black oak, it was cushioned in blue velvet embroidered with silver threads. The servants likewise wore blue livery and silver hose, silver chains around their necks.

The throne was empty, but a woman of some thirty years sat beside it on an elegant low stool. Like all Malbens she was fair, but with warm eyes and the blooming skin of a northern country girl. The guard bowed before her. Ursula curtseyed, wondering who she was.

A door behind the throne opened and Phalaxsailyn entered. Agile as a monkey, he placed himself before Ursula so it looked as if she were curtseying to him as well.

"Thank you, my dear," he said, enjoying her anger. "You curtsey well for a common light-o'-love. And what is your name? You do have one?"

"Dogs have names and so do you," returned Ursula. "It's a common honor. But unlike you and dogs, my parents were married when they gave my name to me."

A young knight in the assembled Malben ranks chuckled. The prince's eyes darted out sharply to catch the culprit—too late. Now respectful silence was absolute.

Then a laugh, loud and beautiful, soared up from the crowd to the left of the throne. It died, and the scandalized whispers—*who?*—*who?*—*who?*—rustled through the peacock throng of courtiers and servants.

Whoever laughed so loud, thought Ursula, must be powerful. No one else would dare laugh aloud at this crowned jackass.

The laughter surprised the anger out of Phalaxsailyn's face. Deliberately he resumed his old air of languor and sardonic smile. "Sweet lady, I seek to learn your name only to do you all the honor you may deserve," he said blandly, in the best courtly style. The words cloyed.

"I am the lady Ursula of Dureforte Keep, daughter of Lord Blas, son of Blan, vassal of King Elberd Far-Reach," Ursula recited proudly. There was an appreciative murmur from the Malben nobles. "Did you really think any man's light-o'-love would go as richly dressed as I? You are twice as big a fool as Votan the Witless, and he was our court fool, my prince."

"Dear Lady Ursula," gushed Phalaxsailyn, lounging against one arm of the throne, "forgive me! Your face alone proclaims your high birth. The dirt upon it put me off. But however did you come to be the plaything of the Braegerd barbarians? Sit here beside me, love, and tell your tale."

"I prefer to stand, Your Highness," returned Ursula. "My ship was captured by the Braegerd men out of Cymweh, bound for the southern lands, and that is all. You see, it is a short tale."

"Pray, child," said the woman seated beside the throne, "rest beside me now. You look tired. Bring refreshments for the lady!" She raised her arms to command the servants and Ursula saw by the gentle swell of the plain wool gown that this lady would soon be a mother. Now the woman smiled kindly and said, "I am Queen Renazca. Welcome to Malbenu Isle."

"Your Majesty," said Ursula, kneeling at her feet, "if you are queen of this land, help me. As we speak, the man my father sent to protect me in my journey is about to die, a sacrifice on Krisli's altar. He is no slave, madam. Please, you must save him!" She clasped the queen's hands in supplication. Renazca felt the warm drops of tears.

"Since when," Phalaxsailyn croaked, "do northern lordlings send royal Sombrunian princes to chaperone their daughters? You're a fine-spun liar, my lady!"

Ursula dashed the tears from her eyes and gave the prince a look of supreme disgust. "May I finish, Your Highness?" she asked scornfully. "Lord Prince Alban is to marry my sister, the lady Mizriel of the White Hair. The day was fixed, but she fell ill, an illness to be cured only by a potion distilled from a flower found solely in the southern lands. We could not entrust her life to a servant! Lord Alban and I, her lover and her sister, offered to go, but on our way to Vair, the barbarians overtook us.

"Now please make haste, Your Majesty." Ursula returned her pleas to the queen. "Send messengers to the priestess and save Lord Prince Alban!"

"My poor Lady Ursula," drawled Phalaxsailyn before the queen could reply, "what a piteous tale of woe. A languishing sister, a gallant bridegroom, a noble mission . . . are you certain you have it all right? Would you like to change any detail? No? Fine. I love a polished liar with all my heart." He clapped his hands together four times and the door behind the throne swung back to admit a strange caller.

The man was tall and heavily muscled, all hardness. A brimmed helmet concealed his eyes. Gray armor, cold and cunningly made as a lizard's scales, shelled his torso, leaving his arms bare. No hood shielded his face, yet that face itself cast its own obscure shadows.

"Captain Tor," said the prince with a low bow.

The veiled eyes beneath the gray helmet slid like twin snakes across every face in the hall, to rest at last on Ursula. "Prince Phalaxsailyn," Tor said quietly, "your court enchants me."

"Oh, I *am* glad. And would your, ah, master like it as well, do you think?"

"Very well," said Tor, keeping his eyes on Ursula.

"Excellent," said the prince. "You see how highly I value your master's favor. Tell him what I've done for him, and assure him of my never-failing loyalty."

"I shall," Tor's hollow voice chimed deep. "And the other?"

"The other is Krisli's by this time," the prince leered. "A service I was quite happy to perform. As for my reward—"

"You shall have it," replied Tor. Almost reluctantly he looked away from Ursula. His boots of black leather were thick and heavy, yet he made not a sound as he strode from the Malben throne room.

"The other is Krisli's by this time," Ursula repeated in a whisper, and the full grief of it crashed over her like a wave. She buried her face in her grimy hands and sobbed, shuddering with misery.

Queen Renazca bent over her, stroking her trembling shoulders, whispering comfort. "Child, it is wrong to believe everything that comes from *his* mouth. Hush. My own men shall ride to the sanctuary to save your friend if they can. For now, show no weakness. He fattens on it."

Ursula slowly lifted her face. "Your Majesty—"

"You must call me Renazca," the queen said kindly. She rose to her feet and addressed the court. "The lady is exhausted. Take her to our finest chamber and give her all she desires. She is my honored guest, and she shall have my own best robes to wear, and my protection so long as she consents to stay."

"Your protection," mumbled Phalaxsailyn with sour disdain. No one heard him.

"Well said, Renazca!" boomed a voice from the left of the throne. "Teach the little sea slug his place!"

A gasp shot through the courtiers. They drew away from the

speaker, as if fearing contamination. Their hasty retreat revealed a tall young woman of wild beauty, skin like polished maple, features sharp as a cat's. Even the dark red lips seemed pointed. Thick black hair hung straight and gleaming down her back to her hips.

"Agvain," Renazca chided softly. "Agvain, dear, you must show a bit more restraint at court, you know."

"At least you have taught her to dress like a civilized woman," yawned Phalaxsailyn. A simple blue dress drooped from Agvain's shoulders in ill-fitting folds.

Agvain's strong brown hands reached up and ripped the blue dress wide, discarding it like an empty chrysalis. A costume of barbaric magnificence blazed forth, taming the rainbow. Pure silk the color of claret loosely sheathed her lithe body, the skirt slit high in front to let her legs swing free. Supple leather boots laced to the knee with silk and dyed to match the dress shod her small feet. Heavy bracelets of garnet and silver held the billowing sleeves in at the wrist. Over all was a sleeveless coat of strange design, with tiers of multicolored satin flounced to the waist, each tier trimmed with tiny silver coins. A silver girdle ringed her waist, substantial enough to turn aside arrows. To the left of the girdle hung an empty iron scabbard.

"I am Agvain, Princess of Vahrd," she declared proudly, shaking Ursula's hand. "I like you. You look soft, but there's something underneath. Can you handle a sword?"

"When there's something worth slaying, I can," said Ursula, looking at the prince meaningfully.

"Charming talk for ladies to have," said Phalaxsailyn. "The Princess Agvain is our prisoner. Note the golden thrall collar she wears." He laughed and sang an old Malben nursery song:

> "The men of Vahrd
> Work mighty hard
> At swilling wine and cheese.
> The girls of Vahrd
> Are stooped and scarred
> Forever scratching fleas."

Agvain shrugged off the insult and replied with one of her own:

> "The men of Vahrd
> Fight long and hard
> Till buzzards come to dine.
> The girls of Vahrd

Are battle-scarred
From slaying Malben swine."

She turned her back on the prince and confided to Ursula, "I was
taken in battle by some Malben pigs. I got careless, let them sneak
up on me. I was too absorbed in watching the bold Velius skewer
three men with a single sword-thrust. Lunge! Guard! Parry! Feint!
Lunge! Parry! Lunge!" She danced around Ursula, fencing with
phantoms.

"They brought me here, the mangy knaves, to hold me for ransom," Agvain went on, barely breathing hard. "We have their king
and they have me. Fair exchange. But that pimply toad on the throne
there lives in hope of keeping me here as his wife. I think he has not
even sent word of my capture to Vahrd. If they knew, the men of
Vahrd would come in such numbers that this cursed isle would sink
back into the sea."

"Sister of my heart!" cried Ursula, embracing the savage princess. "Your desires are mine!"

A knight entered and handed the prince a folded scrap of paper.
Phalaxsailyn read it swiftly, then smiled before addressing the
ladies.

"Charming, both of you, utterly charming. Really, Renazca, we
should change Malben law and let me marry them both."

"You will use my proper title when you speak to me," Renazca
snapped. "As to Malben law, King Egdred is our chief justiciar."

"But he's not here now, is he? And I am his regent. Your Majesty likes our new guest, I see. You promised to send your men to
Krisli's Point to save her friend." He leaned back and fanned himself languidly with the paper. "As regent, I could prevent that. I
could countermand your order."

"You will not dare." Renazca's eyes were hard, challenging.

"No," Phalaxsailyn said a bit too easily. "I won't bother. There
is no need." He opened the folded paper and read aloud what he
had so recently read to himself. "The sacrifice is finished."

Ursula fell senseless into Agvain's arms.

Chapter IX

RUNEGILDA

Krisli's Point is the northernmost part of Malbenu Isle, a point in shape as well as name, a sharpened tip of land that looks as if the gods sliced it out cleanly with their swords. The treacherous Opalza Sea surges around it without wearing down the keen wedge that has punctured the side of many a stout sailing vessel. Steep gray cliffs rise out of the sea there, and there is no beach at Krisli's Point.

Alone, feeling the salt wind ruffle his hair, Lymri lay on his belly and looked down over the sharp precipice at the smashed and shattered remnants caught on the rocks. Ships large and small had met their journey's end there.

" Do you enjoy the view?" a familiar voice inquired sweetly. Lymri flipped onto his back in alarm and nearly rolled over the edge. Mizriel seized his wrist and righted him. "Be careful, friend. My hello was almost your goodbye."

"How did you get here?" Lymri blinked.

Mizriel stood over him like the spirit-figure of a goddess of the sea. A wild wind blew in across the cliffs and whirled her cape behind her like a flying sail.

"You forget I'm a sorceress. Truly, I forgot it myself for a time. I'm in your debt, Lymri. You've taught me that I have more magic in me than words."

"Words can hold power enough," said Lymri, getting to his feet. He wondered if the lady would laugh, should he confess that he wrote poetry.

"Not enough for me. Come, let's take care of your mission here. Where's Alban?"

Lymri shook his head. "I don't know. We were told to meet his ship on Malbenu, but this isn't the port. It's called Kolytown, if I recall my map studies correctly."

Poet and sorceress walked into the forest that sprang up just south of Krisli's Point. It was all oak trees, silent with age and hidden knowledge. The farther they went into the grove, the closer the trees grew. Moss thrived on the gnarled trunks, and above their heads they saw the ghostly gleam of the mistletoe's waxy white berries. Bright orange and scarlet fungi flourished in the shape of mute elfin trumpets at their feet.

"I am tired of this forest," complained Lymri. "If we were to meet Alban at Kolytown, why couldn't Ayree have magicked me there directly? We can't even find the river. I hear no birds, see no animals, and there's not a sight of man." He plowed on in grim silence. The oaks gave way to birches, leafless in the autumn chill, like rows of thin, pale, hungering ghosts watching the wanderers pass. The birches ended and they walked through oaks once more.

"Have you led us wrong?" demanded Lymri suddenly.

"I have not!" Mizriel was indignant. She opened her palm to show him a small rock the color of fresh water. "This is a way-stone," she explained. "You lay your spell of going on it and it grows warmer if you near your path, cooler if you go astray. I have a waystone for each of the Twelve Kingdoms. Few sorceresses have a complete collection," she added proudly.

"And suppose you have the wrong stone for *this* kingdom?" countered Lymri. "You might have them mixed up."

"Don't be sarcastic with me, Lymri. I'm as sick of this forest as—" Mizriel stopped. Lymri opened his mouth, but she hastily laid her hand to his lips. *Listen,* she told him with her eyes. *Listen.*

Lymri listened and heard nothing. But Mizriel's head was back, her eyes darting about the forest shadows, every sense—mortal and magical—attuned to the wind.

Lymri listened again. Now he thought he heard something, a whispering sound that wove its way in and out, above and below the song of the trembling leaves. Mizriel beckoned and he followed, lightfoot.

The oaks ended in a tangle of underbrush. Beyond, a wide turf led down a hillock to the eerie ruins of a marble temple. It looked like a rosy bubble set on twisted columns, their bases entwined with fantastic beasts and a splendor of stone flowers. But the top of the dome was broken, cracks ran up the pillars, and creeping vines tore away the life from the stone.

Past the temple was a formal garden gone to seed. Curious paths of particolored gravel swerved and dipped and laced through it, all leading to the statue that dominated the scene. The young moon had already climbed far that night and was beginning its slow descent behind the temple. It showed as a ghost's smile through the shattered dome. Still, the golden crescent was bright enough to cast waves of loving light upon the statue's marble face.

Lymri shuddered in his skin; the moonlight seemed to give the carven features weird life.

The statue portrayed a tall, slender man, long of face and long of limb. His eyes were soft with honeyed promises and his right hand beckoned gracefully, gently. But his smile was cold with mockery, and his left hand clutched an ivory heart cruelly tight.

The dry whispering that had drawn them came from the dilapidated fane. Now it grew louder as a woman stepped from the ruined temple into the moonlight. She was clad in emerald green, like the statue, with a golden girdle and tiara, holding a golden dagger with an apple-shaped pommel. A second figure followed her, bound to her girdle by a jeweled rope and swathed in a dusky hood that hid his features. Four heavily armed men came after.

They traced the curving garden paths, pausing at each turn while the woman sprinkled something on the earth from a flask at her belt. At length they reached the center, where she knelt and tied the leading rope to the feet of the statue, then arose and uncovered the victim's face.

"Alban!" The name exploded across the garden like a fireburst.

Lymri gave another shout and raced from the shelter of the trees. The woman and men-at-arms watched him come as if they saw an apparition. Mortal or monster, the soldiers were well trained; they drew their blades.

Lymri ran with his hands outstretched, empty. He would have run onto the naked swords in his headlong dash to stop the sacrifice. Suddenly he felt a chill in the palm of his right hand, and it closed around the hilt of a glittering sword. The surprise made him pull up short and strike a challenge, ready for the four guards.

Elaar, I've done it this time for sure, he thought. All four guards were closing in at once. *What did I expect? That they'd be polite and take turns? I'm dead and good as buried.*

"Save your self-pity and hold your blade higher," said Mizriel in his left ear. She had torn her skirts and bound them at the waist to free her legs. A thin, pale, smiling sword shone in her hand.

"You can't fight armed men!" croaked Lymri.

"I made the swords, I can fight with them," returned Mizriel. "Shall I show you another trick?" She carved the air with her sword, leaving a twinkling design of slashes that sparkled like hoarfrost before falling away.

The priestess gasped. Alban was free, his jeweled rope lying in molten drops on the ground, a third sword of Mizriel's devising in his hand. Runegilda pressed herself against the base of Krisli's statue.

"Three against four!" shouted Mizriel. "Better odds now. Strike, Lymri! Strike true!" The white-haired girl charged joyously to meet the soldiers, her hair like a comet's tail.

"All ye gods," mumbled Lymri, "help me remember my fencing lessons." He joined the fracas.

The battle wavered, neither side holding the advantage for long. Surprise and enchantment were on the side of the three companions, but the soldiers had superior strength. Mizriel took one man out of combat with a lucky blow to his sword arm, then flew to Lymri's aid. Alban's man met an easier defeat, a clubbing blow to the side of the head. He would awaken sore, but glad to be alive. Alban's wounded arm still pained him, every twinge making him glad it hadn't been his fighting arm he'd injured.

Two men fought Lymri by pure chance of battle, and it was more than the little poet could handle. He was on his knees when Mizriel and Alban came to his rescue. Three to two, the odds had changed. Then a broadsword turned Mizriel's guard and slashed her hard in the shoulder. She toppled, and Lymri abandoned the fight to hold her close. Alban battled alone against two seasoned fighters.

"Stop! No further blood must defile Krisli's sanctuary!" Through the sweat that blurred his vision, Alban saw the two soldiers lay down their swords. He held his own firm, suspecting a trap. "Throw yours down also, or your arm goes with it! I swear by the power of the gods!" shrilled the priestess. Alban's magic-forged blade clanged down on top of the others.

"Krisli bless you," Runegilda said sweetly. "The ruler of the human heart desires peace."

"Lady," protested one of the men, "what of the sacrifice?"

"It is finished. Look at the moon. She rides low in the heavens. It is too late for a sacrifice now. Krisli will be displeased. Let them go, whoever they are, and see to your wounded comrades. Bring the girl, too. She is hurt.''

Obeying the priestess, the two unwounded soldiers stooped to lift up Mizriel and carry her into the temple. "Don't touch her!" barked Lymri. "Alban and I will carry her, not you!"

They bore her through the shadowed portico where heavy, odorous blossoms of nightsweet cast a spell of dreams. Inside the ruined temple, they laid her down on a raised slab of marble the color of blood.

"So young," murmured Runegilda, gazing down at Mizriel's ashen face. "The wound should not have hurt her this much."

"She's been through too much in too short a time," Lymri answered gloomily. "She should have stayed at home, but she wouldn't listen."

"If she had listened," Alban said softly, "I would be the one lying here now." Lymri heard and hung his head. Runegilda busied herself with cleansing and binding the wound, then brewed a herbal tisane over a shallow brazier. The moon and several stars cast their light through the fissured marble.

"Have her drink this," said Runegilda. Lymri sniffed the wooden goblet warily. "If you think it is poison, say so, and I'll drink some myself. But don't just sit there, she needs it!" the priestess said sharply.

"I didn't say a word," Lymri sulked. He propped Mizriel's fair head on his arm and dripped a mouthful of the potion between her lips. Her nose twitched at the pungent steam rising from the cup, her eyelids fluttered open, and she took the goblet from his hand to finish the draught herself.

Lymri never knew how he happened to find himself hugging and kissing Runegilda. Alban and Mizriel were laughing at him. Runegilda was a magnificently statuesque woman, and when Lymri tried to reach her lips he looked like a chipmunk trying to scale a mountain.

"This is a welcome change from being called poisoner," chuckled Runegilda. "Calm down, my dear. I still have important work to do."

She rested her hand on Mizriel's wounded shoulder, a casual gesture of sisterly affection. The white-haired sorceress gasped when Krisli's priestess lifted her hand. The sword cut was gone. She treated Alban's hurt as well, and just as miraculously. Swiftly she examined the four soldiers, curing their wounds with a light, experienced touch. Not a mark was left to show that they had taken part in any combat. Then she addressed their leader.

"Bertram, whose man are you?"

"King Egdred's man," replied the soldier, all his blind loyalty and love on his honest face.

"And the rest?"

"King Egdred's men every one. Or dead men," Bertram said meaningfully.

"Good. Then, as you love King Egdred, help his friends and hinder his enemies. Even if they're his own blood."

"You mean the prince," said Bertram. It was plain he did not care much for his sovereign's brother.

"Yes, Phalaxsailyn," said Runegilda. "There would never have been a real sacrifice here tonight, my friends." She turned toward Mizriel and Lymri. "An illusion of sacrifice, a petty sorcery that is well within my limited powers, like the healing arts. I dispatched a note to Eddystone earlier today saying that I had already slain him. Phalaxsailyn will have read it and swallowed it whole by now. He pretends great devotion to Krisli, but he's either too stupid or too eager for revenge to know that my lord must only be approached by moonlight. The messenger who carried my note would not dare to read its contents, and if our prince gloats over it aloud, the fellow will assume I was as good as my word. The deceitful vision I meant to weave for you and your men, Bertram, would only have served to provide witnesses, should Phalaxsailyn demand them later."

The plainspoken soldier was dumbfounded by all this. "So many plans . . ."

"All of them necessary," the priestess said. "If the prince did not believe I had killed this man, he would have done the job himself, and now there would be one less prince of Sombrunia."

Bertram made the sign against evil. "Sombrunia's our ally!" he protested.

"And we will need our allies in the days ahead." said Runegilda. "Go, Bertram. Take your men and return to Eddystone. Describe the sacrifice if anyone should ask you to do so, and see that all of you agree on a single tale to tell. On your honor to King Egdred, say nothing more to anyone."

The four soldiers took an oath of secrecy on the red altar. Then they departed and Runegilda turned to ask her guests the reasons that had brought them to Malbenu Isle. She heard out Alban and Mizriel, then came to Lymri, who bowed his head and said, "Holy lady, there is little left for me to tell you. But there is something I must tell someone else, a message for my dear friend, Lord Prince Alban.''

''Lord Prince Alban?'' echoed the Sombrunian. ''Why so formal, Lymri? We two are brothers!''

''Then, my brother, I have sad tidings for you. I am the unhappy messenger of the master mage, Paragore-Tren. Your father is dead, Lord Prince, and you shall rule Sombrunia.''

Alban stared at Lymri and said nothing, but the softness and boyishness of his face began to fade before Lymri's eyes. He took on the look of a man—a man who suffers.

''My royal father is dead,'' he said at last, letting his eyes dream among the embers in the brazier. ''How did he die?''

''I know nothing of that,'' replied Lymri. ''It was his time. Surely the wizard would have told me if there was anything unusual about his death.''

''A peaceful death, at least. The final blessing of the gods. Did the mage say anything more?''

''I think he was glad you were going home, but he didn't seem worried about your speed in getting there.''

''True. The Council will take excellent care of Sombrunia.''

''Then I am hostess to a king tonight,'' said Runegilda, curtseying to Alban. ''It has been long since Krisli's shrine welcomed a king. Egdred neglected us. I would leave this place and go south, where Krisli's cult is still strong, but I am the last of his Malben priestesses.''

''Runegilda.''

The four mortals in the ruined temple froze to statues. The voice that called was sweet and slow as honey flowing from a forest comb, deep as sunless seas. Through the open pillars of the temple they saw moonlight on the face of Krisli's statue.

Its lips moved.

''My children,'' it said softly, smiling a loveless smile. ''Do not be afraid.'' On a wave of smoke the statue drifted down from the pedestal, still clutching the ivory heart—which had now turned bloody red. With each step the statue took, crimson tears fell from the heart. And where those droplets touched the ground, poppies blossomed.

As if entranced, Runegilda went to meet her master. The others came behind, not afraid, but awed and amazed, deep in miracle.

The priestess prostrated herself at the god's slender feet and offered up a prayer.

"Runegilda, arise," said Krisli. "You know me, you serve me well, yet you fear me. Is this proper love?"

"You are the master of the human heart," replied Runegilda, her face still flat against the ground. "I have failed you. The sacrifice was not given."

The wolfish smile never wavered. "The chosen sacrifice is already mine," Krisli said cryptically. "I alone know my true victim. They no longer fear me on this isle. Now the prince serves me selfishly, but I will work his undoing for that. A false heart, the heart of Phalaxsailyn." He raised the hand that held the scarlet heart and crushed it against the sky. An icy white flame burned brightly in his open palm.

"Go, Runegilda," Krisli commanded, gazing down at the maiden priestess. "Leave my shrine on Malbenu. Dark things await this island and this world. He they call my brother will have it so. Serve me elsewhere, not by prayers but by prophecy. Thus I grant it." A drop of opalescent light like a milky tear touched Runegilda's head. "It is done," said the god. "We shall meet in my father's house. Farewell."

An autumn wind, loud with owls and swirling leaves, whirled out of the oak trees and whisked the god from sight. For a few moments, clouds veiled the moon; then silver light again bathed the motionless image that stood majestic on its pedestal once more.

"Krisli himself," breathed Mizriel. "I'm surprised. At home we learned that he isn't one of the more forgiving gods. I expected his wrath, not his clemency."

Runegilda arose, a look of celestial peace on her face as she spoke. "We shall see both his wrath and his clemency before the end. In his father's house he shall take his sacrifice."

"Riddles! What house does he mean?" demanded Lymri.

"Krisli's father is Inota, god of battles," supplied Mizriel. "My father, the warrior-lord Blas, was devoted to Inota, but I don't know where Inota's house could be."

"Come, my friends," said Runegilda. "We have far to go before we find that house. There we shall face the gods, and our own souls. Now we must go to Eddystone. A fair lady there is in great danger. The darkness sends its messengers to claim her. The future blurs before my eyes, as if seen through water. We are with her, but I can't tell if we come soon enough to save her."

"Ursula," said Alban. "We had better go. It will be a pleasure to meet Phalaxsailyn again." He touched the side of his belt where he normally wore a sword, but Mizriel's magic blades had disappeared.

Runegilda led them south. "I will go with you and take ship for the southern lands," the priestess said. "Meanwhile, perhaps I can help you. You especially," she told Alban, "are the favored one of Krisli. I know it."

Alban said nothing. He had spoken Ursula's name, but the thrill that once pierced his heart at the very thought of her was no longer there. He recalled her beauty, and it was no longer unearthly. She had become nothing more than another fair woman to him. His heart was dead.

Chapter X

PHALAXSAILYN

For five days after he received the news of Alban's death, Prince Phalaxsailyn was subject to periodic fits of giggles. He summoned Bertram and his men into the royal presence time after time, just to hear them run through their accounts of the sacrifice. Like a master musician, sometimes he would make them tell it slowly, sometimes quickly. Once he had them stop at the point where Runegilda plunged the dagger into Alban's heart, then sent them from the room while he dabbed away tears that had nothing to do with sorrow. Often he would cut off one man in mid-sentence and have the next fellow take up the telling where his comrade had left off. It was a diversion that eternally amused the prince and earned the disgusted soldiers rich promotions.

The five days were not spent only in listening to soldiers' stories. A great festival was planned, ostensibly to honor the visiting lady from the north. The prince's servants and victualers depleted the castle larders, the shops and storehouses of Kolytown, any trading ships in the harbor, and finally the countryside, all in order to provide for Phalaxsailyn's feast.

Four master cooks, six apprentices, twelve scullery wenches (never a steel-nerved lot), and one skittish turnspit lost their minds. Twice that number lost their positions. Gossip said that the kitchen help who did not go mad or drop from exhaustion were likely to be knighted or dead by next court session. Wise wagerers favored dead.

An unbroken procession of supply wagons came into Eddystone and spurts of messengers departed at random, on the trail of further supplies—somewhere on Malbenu Isle was a farmer who still had two pigs, and they intended to find him. Besides the wagons arriving laden with food, there were others packed with Malben nobles who did not reside close to Eddystone. The squeals, squawks, bellowing, and general uproar in the castle's courtyard were impossible to sort out as human or animal.

Toward the end of the fourth day, there came a colorful addition to the incoming train as entertainers of every sort and stripe flocked to the castle. There were minstrels aplenty in Phalaxsailyn's court, but most of their repertory consisted of songs like ''The Prince of Manly Beauty'' and ''Virtue Ought to Wear a Crown.'' The players now arriving in answer to a frantic summons from the major-domo would actually *be* entertaining.

Starveling songsters, mountebanks, acrobats, dancers, animal trainers, and talentless road scum came to Eddystone as soon as they heard the faint sweet jingling of coins and the tempting aroma of free food. If nothing else, their table manners would provide the invited guests with much educational diversion. The clothing of every nation in the Twelve Kingdoms was represented, from northern furs and leathers to southern veils and swathings.

All the entertainers were herded together in a disused guardroom of the castle while Eddystone's decrepit chief steward sent his assistants into the multicolored mob to take down names and specialties and to assign them sleeping spaces in the castle courtyards, stables, hallways, and any place unoccupied by another body.

Amid this confusion, a handsome young southerner who earned his living by his dog's tricks spied a quartet of musicians immediately beside him. He was from Vair, and they looked like they had come from the deserts surrounding that mountain-ringed kingdom. A sudden longing for the sound of a southern tongue made him address them in the patois of the great bazaar of Ishma, a comfortable dialect shared chiefly by those people of the southern lands that lay east of the Dunenfels Plain. West of that, the Sombrunian lords disdained any language but their own.

The animal trainer got no answer.

That is odd, Mustapha thought to himself. He held his wise dog in his arms to protect the small beast from the milling of many feet, and the dog gave him a look that appeared to say he shared his master's bemusement.

Mustapha tried again, introducing himself more loudly to be sure they'd heard him the first time. The tallest of the robed desert players looked him straight in the eye but gave no sign that he'd understood a word.

His eyes were bright blue.

That is odder, thought Mustapha. But he had seen many odd things in his travels, and considered himself likely to see more. He gave his name in the common speech to the harried assistant steward and dismissed the silent quartet from his mind.

At last the night of Phalaxsailyn's feast had come. The last beast had been slaughtered and cooked, the last layer of sweet rushes scattered over the hall floors, the last player given his place in the entertainments, the last tailor sent gibbering away with full pockets and an empty mind.

The torches were anointed with scented oils of flowers. Incense smoldered in footed braziers of bizarre design. Angelic pages crowned with roses passed among the nobles bearing trays of candied rose blossoms and violet pastilles. Older boys in white linen tunics belted with yellow flowers poured long, intoxicating streams of dandelion wine into outstretched cups and goblets.

Prince Phalaxsailyn reclined clumsily on the throne, a wreath of asters in his hair. A petal drooped crazily over his left eye, but he had drunk so deeply that he didn't bother to move a hand to brush it away.

Queen Renazca held her usual place, bedecked with blossoms like the other guests. So was Ursula, who sat obediently beside the queen on the steps of the throne. Only Agvain refused the flowers, wearing a plain white dress with a gold chain at the waist to match her golden thrall collar.

The prince raised his hand imperiously. The herald called for silence. A space was cleared before the throne and a huge carnelian urn was brought in, brimming with rounds of gold. A gold and silver bowl full of gems was placed beside the queen.

"It is the court custom," Renazca explained to Ursula. "We pay our mimes, musicians, jugglers, and bards as they deserve."

A young knight called Sir Kerris also sat on the steps of the throne, one rank below the lady Ursula. He was a pepper-haired fellow who had taken a liking to the lady and volunteered to be her guard of honor. In the first days of Ursula's black grief he had cheered her with eccentric stories and comic songs, praising each smile he had coaxed from her and leaving small trinkets at her door to reward her each time she laughed.

Now Sir Kerris studied the treasure urn near the prince and remarked, "This says more than the fools realize."

"What do you mean, Sir Kerris?" asked Ursula. It was the first time she had seen him so severe.

"I mean, my lady, only a king may pay the players thus. In the king's absence, the task should fall to the queen or the chief steward."

"So," murmured Ursula. "He plays king in his brother's place. Will anyone else notice this but you?"

"They notice it. But they fear him. Our bonny prince has strange servants. A shield-brother of mine once objected publicly when the prince sacrificed to Ambra. That's reserved for the king, too. He disappeared that night. They say that the river knows where he lies."

The merriment began. A succession of minstrels, bards, jesters, tumblers, and other performers filled the hall with their antics. Sweet music alternated with loud laughter. Even the most inept of that great company of players went away a richer man than he had come. (Some unkind souls whispered that it was best to reward the untalented with a generous hand, to make sure they had enough money to buy their passage away from Malbenu Isle.)

The prince filled Ursula's skirt with gold so that she might also reward the artists she liked best. She tossed many coins, forgetting her sorrows for the moment, and laughed when Renazca rewarded the animal trainer, Mustapha, with a large ruby. His wise dog fetched it and made a cunning bow before the throne.

"Isn't he adorable?" The queen smiled and beckoned the little white beast to come nearer. She scratched him behind the ears.

"He is." Ursula giggled at the way the little dog rolled his eyes in ecstasy at the royal caress, yet never loosed his hold on the ruby. "Truly, a very wise dog."

"And a lot of good eating on him, too," said Agvain. The people of Vahrd were noted for their stews, and a pragmatic willingness to make do when it came to the ingredients.

Mustapha's dog jerked his head up and gave the Vahrdish princess a look that made Ursula laugh even more. Prudently the animal retreated to his master's side and hid himself under Mustapha's long robes. Man and dog made an amusing sight as Mustapha retired to the feasting table set apart for the artists, appearing to go there as fast as two feet and four paws would take him. The dog kept himself tucked away in the gauzy safety of his master's clothing, emerging only to accept an occasional tidbit from the table or to give Agvain still another resentful stare.

"A wise dog indeed," said Ursula. "You'd almost think he understood what Agvain said."

Prince Phalaxsailyn called for silence.

"Noble lords and ladies!" he proclaimed tipsily. "I ask your indulgence. I would like to explain the reason for this feast. Have none of you wondered about it? If the ladies Ursula and Agvain will step forward, all will be made clear."

Ursula and Agvain balked until the barbarian princess spied Renazca's pale, sad face. Mutely the queen begged them to obey, not to make a scene. "Her time is near," whispered Agvain. "We must obey the stoat-faced princeling for her sake."

"Are they not beautiful?" the prince demanded of his court. "The loveliness of the north and the grace of the south. What man could choose between them? Not I, my lords, not I. And so I have called you here to make the choice for me and say which lady shall become my royal consort."

Any cries of surprise from the court or of indignation from the ladies were cut short by the din created by armored men storming into the hall. Not of the castle garrison, these were like no men the Malben nobles had ever seen before. At their head marched their silent captain. A sanguine cape draped his shoulders and he carried an iron box in his hands.

At the players' table, Mustapha's sun-browned face paled. A look of deep hatred twisted his features into a silent malediction. He knew that man—no helmet could hide his identity enough, no span of years could wipe out the memory of what he had done to those Mustapha had loved—and all the strength of the animal trainer's heart longed to dye the captain's cape a deeper shade of red with the man's own blood.

The wise dog snarled.

The captain did not remark on the reaction to his entrance. He never even glanced at the players' table. His gray troops moved with the cold efficiency of a machine, drawing black arrows and notching them to their longbows as if they were all merely the limbs of a single brain.

Phalaxsailyn looked content. "Welcome, Captain Tor. You honor me. Will you help me make the choice? How diplomatic if I wed Agvain, uniting Malbenu and Vahrd in holy brotherhood. And how fortunate for your father's house, Lady Ursula, if you became my queen. Set the bowls before them!''

Under Tor's cold eyes a trembling page placed two crystal bowls at the ladies' feet while the steward bound their eyes with folded silken kerchiefs.

"We can't let you see the ballots being cast," tittered the prince. "And now, my lords, choose!"

In her lonesome darkness Ursula heard many footsteps and a ringing sound in her bowl. More footsteps and more ringing sounds followed. *And I can do nothing*, she thought. *Alban is dead! Alban!*

"Unbind their eyes!"

Ursula's blindfold came off and she looked about, first at Agvain, and then at the bowls. Gold pieces filled both, precious ballots. In Agvain's bowl they barely reached the rim; in hers they spilled over onto the floor.

"My lady Ursula," said Phalaxsailyn. She faced him warily. "Or should I say, my bride-to-be?"

Tor's voice rolled through the air like thunder. "O Prince! Will you rob my master of his chosen bride?"

Phalaxsailyn showed his teeth in a dry smile. "I know all about your master's plans, Tor. I've served him long enough to know them. Does it matter so much who *does* wed the lady or who does *not*? Our master's final danger is dead on Krisli's altar and I sent him there. Surely"—the prince eyed Ursula—"I deserve a reward for that?"

Captain Tor knelt and set the iron box on the floor, then slowly opened the lid. Palpable darkness enveloped the hall. The torches blazed with a blue light that cast a glare of death and horror over mortal faces. In the ghastly flickering all beheld the image of a tall, thin, sere man looming over the lady Ursula. Dead leaves rustled in his voice. His awful, skeletal smile never varied a hairsbreadth when he spoke.

"Phalaxsailyn," Morgeld's image said, "you have my thanks; and you shall need it before long." The grisly apparition turned to Ursula. "My wandering lady, how are you? It seems you prefer another bridegroom to me? So be it. But should you change your mind, my captain will abide on Malbenu to bring you safely home to me. Well, my lady, how many lies have you told these good people so far? Your lies will all return to you and bury you in darkness. Farewell." The shadow seeped back into the iron box and Morgeld's captain shut it fast.

"It appears," remarked the prince, somewhat shakily, "that my master has no violent objections to the marriage. Forgive me if I say that I wish the vote had gone the other way." He gazed fondly at Agvain. "Well, princes must sometimes marry for politics, not love. Bring a seat worthy of my consort!" The steward pounded his staff of office on the floor. A boy fetched a queen's stool, like Renazca's, and placed it beside the throne. The prince took Ursula's hand and kissed it with clammy lips.

A strangely robed man had entered the hall. Boldly he approached the throne with commanding strides. Lords and ladies bowed themselves out of his path. Phalaxsailyn hastened to greet him.

"Welcome, sage one." The prince bowed humbly. "Have you read the stars? Do you bring me the news I long for?"

The man was swathed in rich black velvet, trimmed with the skins of foxes. In a low, rolling voice he intoned, "I bring you that news."

"Praise to Krisli," said the prince.

"Honor to those who serve him," replied the man. "Why have you summoned me?"

"A wedding, Maegisthus. You must marry me to the chosen of my heart." Phalaxsailyn took Ursula's hand.

She pulled away from him, trembling with rage. Ursula recalled with dread the name of Maegisthus, one of the most powerful sorcerers in the Twelve Kingdoms. Even his poorest students were feared mages. It was said that Maegisthus could call up visions of the gods—and more than visions.

Ursula fell to her knees before the archmage. "Hail, Maegisthus! I am the Lady Ursula, daughter of Lord Blas, sister of the sorceress Mizriel of the White Hair. My sister lies ill, waiting for me to bring the herbs that can cure her, while this princeling keeps me here against my will. Grant me your protection!"

Maegisthus' eyes shone like yellow ice in the shadows of his hood. "What herb do you seek?" he demanded.

Ursula lowered her eyes, feeling her heart pounding. If she could win over the wizard, he might shield her from the prince, and perhaps from Morgeld himself. The power of the brotherhood of sorcerers was vast and unknown. But she was ill-versed in herbal lore. "I—I forget the name, but it has five green leaves, scarlet blossoms, white berries, and—"

"Enough!" Maegisthus thrust high his hands. They were stained from strange liquids and marked with arcane scars; patterns of twisted veins writhed around his wrists like serpents.

Ursula's heart shrank as she looked into the wizard's eyes. There was no anger there, or hate, or any human feeling; only flames. She gave a small cry and hid her face.

"Ursula," rumbled the wizard. "Ursula, daughter of Blas, you have lied. You have lied and been fool enough to think I would not know you lied. Do you know what becomes of those who lie to Maegisthus?"

Ursula shuddered; even through her closed lids and clamped fingers she could feel the chill amber fires of his eyes burning into her brain. She was lost.

"Maegisthus!" Queen Renazca's voice rang out high and proud, diverting the mage's terrible gaze for a moment. "Maegisthus, remember how well my lord King Egdred and I have always honored you, and forgive the girl for my sake. She has lied, but with a good reason. You can read hearts and minds, but not souls. Forgive her."

"Your Majesty is right," replied Maegisthus. "Only the gods read souls. No wise wizard dares to try. I will forgive her"—Ursula looked up with hope—"and I will marry her to Phalaxsailyn at once."

Ursula's hands flew back to cover her eyes.

Maegisthus gave orders to prepare for the ceremony. Servants brought a tripod, a small ivory table, and a silver goblet. Incense of three kinds was thrown on the coals, while house thralls spread tapestries over the floor and Maegisthus emptied a thin green vial into the chalice.

Amid these ceremonial bustlings, the piteous bride-to-be remained an overlooked detail. The revelers in the hall had business or troubles of their own to preoccupy them. Still kneeling on the floor, afraid to take her hands from her face, Ursula's body shook uncontrollably. By an unspoken agreement that passed as a look between them, Queen Renazca and Agvain left their places to help her. She stood at the touch of their hands, but nothing could persuade her to uncover her eyes. Very tenderly they led her as they would a blind woman to a quiet islet of shadow in the lee of one of the larger braziers on the left side of the throne.

"Open your eyes, child. You are safe now," Queen Renazca said softly.

Ursula's fingers parted. Slowly she lowered her hands and oriented herself. The three women seemed to have claimed the one section of the great hall where there was some bit of calm. The area nearest the throne was lost in the confusion of royal wedding preparations. Liveried servants continued to scurry back and forth, seeing to details, while Maegisthus berated them for errors or clumsiness, or simply glared death spells. This did little to speed things along; the terrorized retainers became even clumsier with fear of a wizard's curse on them.

The farther reaches of the great hall were nearly as chaotic as the smaller part near the throne. The Malben nobles in their flowers and finery squawked and chattered shrilly, nervous as birds caged up with cats. Uneasy hushes and awkward bursts of noise alternated as each courtier did his best to worm as far away from Captain Tor and his men as possible.

Prince Phalaxsailyn was having more wine, oblivious to whatever trivialities occupied the ladies. He did not need to play the vigilant bridegroom; Morgeld's people were there to keep watch for him. With arrows nocked, they merely had to shift their aim slightly to keep Ursula and the others from doing anything rash.

The prince yawned, and blandly asked Maegisthus why something as simple as a wedding took so perishing long to make ready.

In their comparative isolation from the rest of the hall, the women could speak freely, though for wisdom's sake in whispers. "Child," hissed Renazca, "you can refuse the prince. Free consent is required for marriage on Malbenu."

Ursula looked wan. "What's the use?" she sighed. "If I refuse, Morgeld's captain will take me back to the lord of Helagarde. I will marry the prince. But I won't live to be his wife."

"Fool's talk! What will your death buy you?" snapped Agvain. "In Vahrd we don't give up without a struggle. Be valiant, Ursula. Refuse the prince! Refuse Morgeld, too! If I had my sword, I'd fight beside you."

"Agvain," Ursula said with gentle resignation, "my fighting is done. My life is over. They've killed Alban. Now it doesn't matter what becomes of me."

"You loved him?"

"I lived without love so long, Agvain! I stopped hoping for it long ago. Even when I thought he was just a poor minstrel, my heart loved him. My common sense"—she smiled ruefully—"told me it was impossible for a lady to love someone so low."

"In Vahrd we let the heart speak first, and the desert take your common sense," said Agvain.

"I wish I had been born in Vahrd. Now it's too late."

"Why do you tarry, my love?" called Phalaxsailyn from his pilfered throne. Finally everything was set up to Maegisthus's specifications and it was time for the prince to take some notice of his intended bride. "Why are you skulking in the shadows?"

Reluctantly the women came back toward the throne. Renazca and Ursula sat on the stools flanking Phalaxsailyn; Agvain squatted comfortably on the floor beside her sorrowing friend.

The prince made a simpering face. "Charming, charming. What were you pretty dears chatting about? Some motherly advice from our dear sister Renazca about the wedding night? You needn't have wasted your time, my lady. Nothing she could tell you could possibly prepare you for so much joy.

"Well! We are ready to begin. But first, some music! This is a wedding, not a funeral. Bring in the next group of minstrels!"

The steward was an old man. His staff of office was also his cane. With tottering steps he walked to the great doorway. Here there were no rushes underfoot to hinder his passage, and none in the central area of the hall reserved for the performers. Later in the evening's festivities the broad, clear space would serve the nimbler Malben nobles well for dancing.

The aged steward cared little about the pleasures of dancers. He was long past dancing, but he still had a job to do. He leaned his aged bones against the doorframe and pounded his staff four times on the stones.

Four minstrels answered his summons. They looked like people from the southern lands, where women as well as men may choose to wander the roads as troubadors. The men wore long robes of white and saffron. The women went modestly veiled so that all you could see of them was a glimpse of their eyes.

Agvain clapped her hands happily. "Southern music! Desert wanderers, by their looks. This will be the first music I'll enjoy since . . . Oh, I'm sorry, Ursula, I forgot that—"

Her apology went unsaid. Agvain felt Ursula's nails drive deep into her arm and saw a ghostly pallor on her face. Ursula's eyes stared wildly, the eyes of a person gone mad.

"Alban." Ursula's whisper was so faint that Agvain scarcely heard it. "He's alive."

"Ursula, what—"

Ursula pointed to the taller musician. "Look at his eyes, Agvain.

You can dye a man's skin with walnut juice, but you can never change the color of his eyes."

"By the gods," Agvain agreed. "But what does he mean to do?"

"I don't know. Whether he cares for me or not, he'll never stand quietly by while I marry the prince. Oh, Agvain!"

"But he can do nothing to stop it. And he'll be killed if he reveals himself now," protested the barbarian princess.

The minstrels sounded the wailing flutes and clashing bells of the desert, tuned the seven-stringed caringash. Maegisthus signaled that all was prepared. Phalaxsailyn took Ursula's hand. The tall musician watched intently and slowly lowered his instrument.

"Stop!" cried Agvain, vaulting to her feet. The courtiers broke out into a flurry of whispers. "You shall not marry her while I live!"

A swift gesture from the prince silenced the whispers. Captain Tor's men raised their bows a fraction to maintain the peace.

"What is this, my lady?" asked the prince, his thin lips forming a taunting smile. "A prisoner dares to interrupt a royal wedding?"

"A princess of Vahrd dares!" countered Agvain. "You don't know the women of Vahrd, Lord Prince, or you'd realize that we don't allow northern milksops to steal our men so easily!"

"Agvain—" Ursula began.

"Silence, wench!" shouted the barbarian. To underscore her words, she hooked her foot around one leg of Ursula's stool and toppled it, leaving the girl blinking with amazement on the damp castle floor. "If I had my sword, I'd cut out your tongue."

"My dearest lady," Phalaxsailyn said slowly, coming down from the throne to face Agvain, "what a surprise. Can I believe my good fortune? More precisely, can I believe you? Are these the same lips"—he came closer and traced them with the tip of one finger—"that so often cursed me and wished for my death? Is this hand"—he took it in his own chilly paw—"willingly given, that once tried to scratch out my eyes?"

"Prince, wed whom you like," replied Agvain. "I have offered you my love. Take me or free me. The women of Vahrd don't wait long for an answer."

"The women of Vahrd this, the women of Vahrd that. The blasted women of Vahrd sound as if they always work in committee," the prince retorted. "Ah, well. Such fire. My lords, you see that I must overrule your vote and wed the princess of my heart. Maegisthus, proceed. Musicians, a wedding song!"

Although her rump smarted from the abrupt fall, Ursula hardly noticed the sting. Gratefully she watched from the floor as Phalax-sailyn led Agvain to take her place before Maegisthus. Then Ursula stood to right her upended stool, wanting to watch the Malben so-lemnities in comfort. She was sure that Agvain could take care of herself, to say nothing of taking care of Phalaxsailyn. And Alban was alive! Ursula's heart was light.

But her joy fled as quickly as it had come when a heavy hand mailed with steel touched her shoulder. Captain Tor stood at her side.

"Enjoy the wedding—yours will follow soon. Our ship waits at the royal dock. Your chosen lord watches for your return from the towers of Helagarde."

Tor's words deafened and blinded her. The minstrel quartet played while Maegisthus invoked the gods of marriage. They were so close that she might reach out and touch them all, yet Ursula saw them through curtains of mist, moving like beings on a distant star while she watched them from the timeless amethyst walls of Hela-garde.

Maegisthus dashed the chalice into the tripod. A greenish-black steam arose. The wizard frowned. "This is not right," he said. "The omens in the smoke are bad. Your Highness, will you recon-sider this match?"

"Maegisthus," replied the prince, casting covetous eyes on Ag-vain, "omens are for frightening children. Proceed."

Maegisthus grumbled deep in his robes. He joined Agvain's right hand to Phalaxsailyn's. "Bind them in the manner of thy children, O Krisli! Let thy power reign in their hearts. They are wed before thee and before us. May death devour any who speak against this union." He dipped his hand into the cold, wet ashes in the tripod and marked their hands with Krisli's rune. "It is done."

The nobles set up a dutiful cheer that sounded like the bleating of sheep. The prince led his bride to the throne and bade her sit. Egdred, a large man, had made an imposing figure upon that throne; but scrawny Phalaxsailyn took up barely half the massive throne, leaving plenty of room for Agvain to share.

"More music!" the prince ordered. "Let there be dancing as well. Can you play the northern dances?"

The tallest musician bowed and showed the prince that he had a northern lute hidden in his voluminous robes. The other players joined him in a sarabande.

Sir Kerris approached Ursula. "Will you dance, my lady?" he asked, without a glance at Tor.

"Oh, gladly!" cried Ursula, so eager to get away from the shadowy captain that she almost threw herself into the young knight's arms. The dance took them close to the musicians, and although she at last managed to look the masked Alban directly in the eyes, he returned her look blankly.

"What's wrong, my lady? Do you know that desert wanderer?"

"He is . . . I thought . . . no. No, I don't." Ursula continued to dance flawlessly. But she felt pain: it was Alban, it could be no other; Alban her love. She had sent all the desire in her heart to him in her look and he had returned . . . nothing. He did not love her. The stones of Helagarde twinkled like violet stars through her tears.

The music stopped when the prince again called for silence. "My lords and ladies, pray excuse my wife and myself from your company. You understand, I'm sure," he leered. "But let the festivities continue, with our blessing. Shall we go, dearest?" Agvain smiled a tiger's smile.

"Hold!" someone shouted.

The stranger was tall as a young god, dwarfing the Malben nobles, and his voice sounded like the deep, clear, brave note of a battle horn. He wore a light mail vest that left his powerful arms bare; his legs were sheathed in leather to the thigh. Long riding in the desert sun had tanned his face, which was framed by bright hair that looked like it had been cut with the edge of a battle-ax. He carried dagger, shield, and sword.

The scented, bloom-crowned lords of Malbenu shrank back before this giant.

"Hail, Phalaxsailyn!" the stranger said, not bothering to hide his scorn. "Have all your gold ready to reward the good news I bring. Your brother, good King Egdred, lives!"

"We know that," returned the prince coolly. "He is your prisoner in Vahrd. You might have saved yourself the trip."

"Whoever called him our prisoner lied," declared the giant. "He was never our captive. Lord Olian of the desert hosts of Thulain held him. Lord Olian himself told us of the many ransom notes he sent to you, but neither ransom nor messenger came back. You are a poor correspondent, prince. You have left it to the High Chief of Vahrd to redeem your brother, who now prepares for his return. In exchange for our courtesy, King Egdred swears to send us back our princess, the shield-maid Agvain. See to her preparations! I have spoken.'' The man laughed and snatched a brimming cup from the tray of a cowering page.

The prince made a barely perceptible sign to Maegisthus. Like smoke the wizard glided between the frozen dancers and slipped behind the bronze giant, waiting. The Vahrdman strode up the steps of the throne where Phalaxsailyn rose to meet him.

"We rejoice," said the prince, in a tone that bespoke no joy, "that our brother will return soon. As for the ransom, we have been secretly gathering it so as not to alarm our people. We sent Lord Olian ambassadors, but none returned. Doubtless they were waylaid by brigands.'' He gave the mailed man a long look.

"You speak of *we* and *we*, princeling," the emissary retorted. "You are hardly big enough to be one. Where is *we?*''

"Oh, I don't speak royally," Phalaxsailyn said. "That would be presumptuous. I merely speak for myself . . . and my bride, the princess Agvain.''

The smile fled the Vahrdman's bronze face; it became suffused with full-blooded rage. Phalaxsailyn relished the barbarian's impotent fury.

Maegisthus drifted closer, his arms rising like slumbering snakes that strike in dreams.

"No wedding congratulations?" Phalaxsailyn smirked. "Vahrd truly breeds barbarians. By what name shall we call such a refined specimen as yourself?''

"Names are but names," growled the giant. "In Vahrd we do not congratulate the dog who steals our intended bride, nor congratulate the bride who will soon be a widow. My name is blood. I am Velius!'' With a roar the titan drew his broadsword and swung at Phalaxsailyn's head just as Maegisthus sent crackling crimson fires leaping from his fingertips.

Agvain screamed.

Something round and heavy fell and rolled into the center of the hall.

Chapter XI

CAPTAIN TOR

No one moved. Even in death the eyes of Maegisthus were not good to see. There was not much blood—wizards have something else in their veins.

Velius's sword had missed its mark. Although puny, Phalaxsailyn was nimble, and he'd leaped away from the sword's arc. The heavy blade's own momentum carried it around to strike Maegisthus's head from his body exactly when the mage had loosed his magic.

The youngest desert minstrel covered the mage's face with a linen kerchief. Her veil parted as she bent over the fallen one, whispering strange words. A lock of starlit hair brushed the dead magician's cheek.

Agvain stole toward Velius, still standing sword in hand hard by the throne. She touched his brawny arm and his sword clanged to the floor, but he did not move. The barbarian princess embraced him, weeping like an ordinary maiden. He gave no sign of consciousness. Ursula had to fetch Agvain away.

"Hush," she comforted. "He is not truly dead, only entranced. The spell will lift itself in time."

"You are all witnesses!" Phalaxsailyn shrieked from behind King Egdred's massive throne. "You saw how the barbarian swine tried to murder me! How he slew Maegisthus! Tor, you and your men saw it as well!"

"We did." Tor's voice sounded like it came from the the depths of an ancient grave. "To lose a royal wizard bleeds a kingdom in the best of times. When times are less favorable . . ." He showed his teeth in the mockery of a smile. "I would not like to gauge the peril Malbenu now risks until you find Maegisthus's successor. Prince Phalaxsailyn, you have my sympathy. All rulers need the protection of magic."

"Quite so, quite so," the prince said nervously. "Will any man here be fool enough to believe the . . . the fairy tale this assassin brought of King Egdred's return? It was a ruse!"

Queen Renazca rose unsteadily to her feet. "Must an assassin be a liar? You told him you knew about the ransom for our lord king. Since Egdred left Malbenu, the isle has been shrouded in ignorance. Some claim he is free and waging war, some say he is dead, some say he is a captive of Vahrd, some repeat the same story that the barbarian Velius told. What is the truth? Speak! Declare it now, before your witnesses."

"Women know little of politics," the prince replied suavely. "Do you really want the truth? There is none. In my council chamber—"

"The *king's* council chamber!" Renazca said fiercely.

"The regent's council chamber, now," the prince compromised. "In that chamber, I say, are messages from the southern lands, and all claim to tell the truth. One comes signed by Egdred himself, saying he is well and victorious. One from Vair says he is sick with desert fever. Another says Vahrd holds him in irons. As for the fourth . . ."

"The fourth says he'll return to us!" cried Renazca, taking a few steps toward Phalaxsailyn. "And when he does, there will be an end to your plottings to seize the crown that is not yours; that never *will* be yours while Egdred lives and I carry his son!"

"My lady," murmured the prince, "the fourth message says that our king is dead and sends as proof a little token." Phalaxsailyn delicately opened his hand. A ring set with a star sapphire dropped like a ripe plum and bounced down the steps.

Renazca shrieked and collapsed.

In a moment Ursula and Agvain were beside her. The queen's page rushed over with wine. The lords of Malbenu stood like cattle able only to watch until the queen's eyes fluttered open.

"His ring," murmured Renazca. "The ring I gave him."

"Please, Your Majesty," said Ursula. "If they can take a man captive, can't they also steal his rings? It proves nothing."

"Velius never lies," added Agvain. "King Egdred lives."

The queen clung to Ursula and let herself be helped back to her place. The tension in the hall relaxed like a loosened bowstring. Agvain was grim as she resumed her seat beside the prince. She had seen the unmistakable look in Renazca's eyes. Any moment now. Any moment at all.

The ancient steward said something in the prince's ear. "Of course!" Phalaxsailyn snapped in the old man's face. "Did you think I'd leave them there forever? Lead the barbarian to our dungeons." This was done. "And take *that* away for burial at once." He indicated Maegisthus's severed head and collapsed body. No one moved. "Are you deaf?" he demanded. "Take it away, I say!" Still no response. Phalaxsailyn stamped his foot.

"My lord," ventured a fat duke, "it's a great thing to touch a dead wizard. Your servants fear—"

"My servants had better learn to fear *me!*" screamed the prince. "Take it *away!*"

Not a soul stirred.

Captain Tor's iron chuckle stung Phalaxsailyn's ears. "And he would govern the island!" the harsh voice rasped. "He can't even rule his servants."

"All right," the prince said grimly. "You'll learn. Bring me the pages. All of them."

A reluctant guardsman made the rounds of the hall, herding the children before the prince. Phalaxsailyn gazed at them with false fondness. "So young, and already so cowardly," he said. "We must fix that. Children, you shall bury Maegisthus for me." The children shivered. "You *will,*" the prince went on, "because if you don't, your pretty heads will join his. Or else . . . or else I'll show you all the view from my private balcony. It overlooks the river where the whirlpool rages. A pretty view. Inspiring. Or else we shall go down beside the river to the rocks, one by one. And I'll do the same with each and every thrall and servant in Eddystone until I find one with courage and wisdom enough to obey his king!"

The Malben nobles gasped and chattered like a flock of parrots, brightly plumed but able only to talk. The guards loyal to King Egdred made a tentative reach for their swords, but found the black arrows of Tor's silent host aimed at them. They were outnumbered.

Phalaxsailyn laughed. "My lords, it was but a slip," he said. "Let's not build mansions on a grain of sand . . . or castles. But as for you, my pretty children, will you obey your . . . prince?"

The pages were huddled together; one of them began to cry.

"Let the children go!" cried Alban. He set his lute aside. "I will

bury the man. In the desert we grant decent burial even to our enemies. Where shall I lay him to rest, O mighty ruler?''

"So, we must find courage in the deserts," the prince sneered to
his court. "Show him to the palace burial ground. We use it in time
of siege, but I would keep Maegisthus close to us. At times a nec-
romancer's spirit is more powerful after death.''

Alban stooped to pick up Maegisthus's head and left, followed
by Sir Kerris and two of his brother knights, who carried the body.

Then Phalaxsailyn called for more music, but the three remaining players did a poor job. The pages scattered to hide among the
guests, none of whom looked eager to dance. Silence was the guest
of honor at the prince's wedding feast.

Slowly, under their prince's scowl, the lords of Malbenu formed
the figures of a dance. Fresh rushes were spread over the once-bare
spot where Maegisthus had lain. They were meant to cover any
stains, and so any thoughts of a wizard's fate. For the time being
they were a minor inconvenience, a very small obstacle, easily
avoided with a sidestep or a graceful capriole. But the nobles' feet
were heavy and their ladies would not set a slipper anywhere near
where the rushes lay greenly dreaming. They gave that little heap
of rushes such an awkwardly wide berth that the figures the dancers
formed were like none ever seen, except perhaps in a dancing-mas-
ter's nightmares.

Alban returned, somewhat pale, and took up his instrument
again, but the hall still echoed ominously.

"We will dance, my lády," said the prince to Agvain.

"I am not well," she answered.

"We will dance."

"I will not dance, my lord."

"Then shall we see how another dances? This party is as gay as
a public execution. Perhaps we should have one. It's dark outside,
and cold beneath the gallows, but torches and braziers should make
us comfortable enough while Velius dances his final measure on the
air. Do they dance well in Vahrd?''

"We will dance here, my lord," Agvain said tersely, rising.

"Good," said the prince triumphantly as he led her onto the floor.
"Then we will wait to see Velius dance. For a while.''

The sight of the prince dancing with his bride heartened the nobles, and the feast began to regain some jollity. Merrier dances followed the formal figures, and the steward sent in new jugglers and

tumblers between the dances, Periodically the prince spangled the floor with fistfuls of gold.

"What's the hour?" Phalaxsailyn shouted from his perch high on the throne, as he scattered the last of his coins.

"Three hours to dawn," replied Tor. With a cold grin he explained, "I have learned to know the hours of night very well. We must leave you by dawn, Your Highness, and the lady Ursula—"

"Yes, yes, I know," said the prince. "You shall have her. But now, more music. The night is not yet done."

Huge casks were trundled into the hall and broached with axes. Lords and ladies dipped their cups deep into tuns of white, red, gold, and purple, staining their sleeves.

Captain Tor approached the lady Ursula, and in a morbid parody of gallantry bowed to her. "My lady, there is a trifle I must ask of you before we board our ship."

"Yes?" replied Ursula, avoiding his gaze. "What is it?"

"Oh, a trifle, a trifle. Your free consent to go."

Ursula jumped in her skin. "My consent?" she exclaimed.

"Just that," agreed Tor. "We who serve Morgeld do so willingly. Prince Phalaxsailyn himself is a fine example of devotion to our master. No one comes to Morgeld's realm who does not wish to be there. But I have the honor of being his captain because I am the only one of all his followers who gave himself wholeheartedly to Morgeld while still alive."

"But . . . but you *are* alive, aren't you?" Ursula laid an experimental finger on Tor's cheek and felt the warmth of life before hastily jerking it away. "I thought that Morgeld's servants were all . . ."

"The dead?" Tor found her assumption entertaining. "Many share your misconceptions, my lady. Yes, I live. The living must come willingly to Morgeld. Others have no choice. We are all his, eventually."

Stubbornly Ursula shook her head, "No. I've heard the tale too many times from my old nursemaid when she wanted to scare me into good behavior. *Does* Morgeld rule the dead? *All* the dead? I can't believe it. Men are older than Morgeld. When the goddess Ambra of the light-in-darkness was born, Sarai All-Mother gave her to be raised by the first man, and when Ambra was grown she blessed him with the first woman. Where was Morgeld then? When Inota lay with the fire-spirit, when Krisli was born, there was still no Morgeld; yet there were men! They didn't live forever. If there was no Morgeld, no Helagarde, where did their spirits go, Captain Tor?'' Ursula smiled boldly. ''Your master doesn't rule quite such an endless realm as you think.''

Tor made a short, disgusted sound. ''Believe whatever comforts you, my lady. I have no time to debate with you. I have seen Helagarde, where every argument comes to an end. So, lady, your consent.''

Ursula found the courage to look steadily into Tor's hidden eyes. ''Never,'' she said evenly. ''Never while I live.''

''Never while you live ignorant, you mean,'' replied Tor, unruffled. ''Helagarde is a fair castle, my lady, and say what you like, Morgeld rules a wide kingdom. He means to rule a greater one. There never was such magic held in one place on this plane as Helagarde contains. She's a fire, an amethyst fire that steals all other light from mortal eyes! Once a man has seen Helagarde, his spirit binds itself to her stones. There he bides so long as the jewel castle stands, and her precious walls will stand forever. Yet no matter how many souls enter her walls, the true power lies with the one able to call them out again to do his bidding.''

''To do Morgeld's bidding . . . when the spirit longs to rest . . . horrible!'' Ursula clenched her fists.

''Not so horrible when you are the master and not the servant,'' said Tor. ''But do you know . . . my master often seems to tire of his most obedient subjects. I think he envies his half-brother, who has only quarrelsome mortals to rule. You'd be surprised how many protest and fight when Krisli's spell is on them! That's what Morgeld desires: to command a kingdom of the living . . . twelve kingdoms. Wouldn't that prize tempt you? You could rule beside him. You could grow mightier than the legendary Queen Nahrit of the Older Empire. Wealth and the secret magics of the earth could be in the palms of your soft hands. What could rival that?''

The dance ended. The steward pounded the floor for silence. The prince had demanded a love song, something sweet and simple, and the tall desert player had come forward with his lute. Alban sang a song that Ursula remembered, a song he had sung many times for her alone—on the barge drifting down the Carras, in the streets of Cymweh, on the ill-fated *Elaar's Eye*. The song ended to dignified applause.

Ursula turned defiantly to Tor, her head high. ''What could rival all you offer me in your master's name? That song, Captain! Nothing more or less that that song! I will not go with you.''

Tor shrugged. "Do you intend to live out your life on Malbenu, then? Or return to the north? No matter. Whatever you decide, first I must reward the lad whose pretty song is worth all my master's kingdom." Tor's mailed hand reached for his sword belt.

"You will not kill him?" Ursula seized his arm.

"Kill him?" Tor removed her hand firmly. "Forbid the thought. This is his reward." He plucked a heavy purse of gold from his belt and tossed it at the singer's feet.

Alban made the elaborate southern gesture of thanks and stooped to pick up the bag. As he bent low, he heard Mizriel's voice whispering urgently in his ear, *Don't touch it!* The warning buzz seemed to come from inside his head, and the message was too strong to deny. He left the bag where it lay.

"You refuse my gift?" Tor was indignant. "Miserable desert dog, you dare to insult the captain of Morgeld's hosts? Pick up the gold or you will regret it!"

Stay, Mizriel's voice whispered inside Alban's head. *You will regret it if you touch it.*

"My lord," said Alban, improvising, "I meant no insult. You do me too much honor. Modesty will not let me accept it."

"Modesty forbids what courtesy demands. So pick up my gift while you still have a hand," said Tor, fingering his sword.

"I can't accept," said Alban. "I played that song in memory of a lost love and took a vow never to receive a reward for singing it. Would you have me break a sacred vow?"

"By no means." Tor's lip curled. "So take the gold as a tribute to your lost love, not a reward. Build her a tomb if she's dead or buy her a gown if she lives."

Alban said nothing.

"If you do not take it," said Tor, "then—"

"Keep your temper, my lord, keep your temper," said young Sir Kerris. "We've had enough killing for one night. If the minstrel doesn't want your gold, let me give it to a lady worthy of every tribute a man can give." He knelt at Ursula's feet and swept her white hand to his lips in a gallant kiss. "My lady, I am no wizard," he said pleasantly. "My sword would do little good against the magic of Morgeld's captain, but I swear to you by that bag of gold, I will not rest until I come to the walls of Helagarde and rescue you from him. Accept the gold as a token of my faith and love."

"Sir Kerris, don't touch it," begged Ursula. "There is something evil about it."

"I'm not afraid," he answered. "I must face worse things if I'm to save you from Helagarde, lady." Scooping up the purse, Kerris smiled defiantly at Tor.

It was hard to say what happened then, it happened so very quickly. Sir Kerris was standing there, the bag of gold in his hand, when all around him time began to flow like a river thawing in the spring. First running in a trickle, then faster, faster, racing away with itself, caught up in its own momentum, Sir Kerris's lifetime careened on headlong, broken free from the wintry ice of time. He grew older, wiser-looking, then paunchy, stooped, gray-haired. A woman and children appeared beside him, then the children's children, aging and vanishing one by one. His hair grew white, and before the eyes of the Malben nobles he shrank and wrinkled up like a fruit in the sun. He was alone, the slight, withered, dusty shell of an old man lying dead on the floor. It crumbled to dust and blew away.

In a scrambling of silks and a fall of flower petals the nobles of Malbenu fled in panic, while Tor laughed an empty laugh to see them run. When they were gone, he closed with Alban.

"Fools earn what they deserve," he said drily. "Fools who think disguise can fool Morgeld." He ripped aside the Sombrunian prince's headcloth. In swift succession he then exposed Lymri, Mizriel, and Runegilda. The last unveiling brought Phalaxsailyn to his feet.

"The priestess of Krisli!" the prince shouted. "You told me you slew this man!"

"I did what my lord Krisli commanded," Runegilda said placidly.

"Mizriel!" Ursula exclaimed. She ran to hug her sister. "Mizriel, what brings you here? What's happened?"

"What has happened"—Tor separated the sisters—"is that Lord Morgeld tires of toying with you. Now, prince, if you truly serve Morgeld, deal with these two in a fitting manner." Tor had his men grab Alban and Lymri and drag them to the throne. "As for the women . . . watch out there!"

The air was suddenly thrumming and throbbing as Mizriel of the White Hair loosed her snowy tresses and began to call her magic in. Slowly as waves of heat that shimmer above the burning desert, her arms rose up to cast destruction. Runegilda too reached out to summon her own powers.

Tor acted quickly. A thread of silver whipped through the air like a dragon's tongue and lashed itself around the wrists of sorceress and priestess. The air heaved and settled, calm and empty of sorcery.

"That will hold you," said Tor, tying a knot in the silver cord. "No spells of freeing will unbind it. For ordinary prisoners, ordinary rope, but the silver snake is suitable for you. Conduct them to the ship!"

"What will you do with my sister?" asked Ursula while Tor's men led Mizriel and Runegilda away.

"I couldn't say."

"But you can't take her! You need her consent, just as you need mine!" she protested. Desperately she wished for her shapechange to possess her. Oh, for the claws of a bear, the fangs with which to rend this captain! No tingle in her feet answered her wish. She was only Ursula.

"The silver snake," Tor said, smiling, "has many useful properties. Among others, it can command consent. But if you care to see your sister's fate, there is a way . . . can't you guess?"

Ursula hung her head. "To go with her," she said dully. "To go to Morgeld." She sighed and shrugged. "Very well, Captain Tor. I've fought against my destiny too long. I'll go willingly with you. Only let me say my farewells."

"Do it quickly. Dawn is coming."

Ursula nodded submissively. She embraced Agvain, then Renazca. "Remember me, Your Majesty," she begged.

"Keep heart, child."

"I will slay Phalaxsailyn and lead the hordes of Vahrd against Helagarde," Agvain swore.

She touched Lymri's cheek. "I apologize for the fright I gave you that night. It was a hundred years ago, I think."

"Dear lady, don't despair," said Lymri. "There's hope. I've seen it myself in darker hours than this."

"And last, goodbye," said Ursula, gazing at Alban as if she wished to inscribe his face on her heart. Tears stained her cheeks as she kissed him. He tasted salt and felt a searing coldness pierce him. She turned her back to him and left the hall flanked by Tor's men. Tor himself remained.

"Ha! On her way to Morgeld at last," crowed Phalaxsailyn. "And now, Captain, when shall I have my reward?"

"You are greedy, Prince," said Tor.

"Greedy? I've served Morgeld well, yet not a hint do I have that

Morgeld will keep his part of our bargain. I'm not asking for the crown, Tor. I can get that by my wits. But couldn't you give me just the smallest sign that . . . ?''

"You shall have it," said Tor, and slewed his eyes toward the queen. Renazca gave a groan and collapsed into Agvain's arms, sending the barbarian princess staggering. Agvain muttered a Vahrdish charm against evil and struggled to take the queen out of the hall as fast as possible. Great hate and greater fear shone in her eyes; in Renazca's, only pain.

"Ah," sighed the prince contentedly.

"The queen is too old to bear children," said Tor. "She will die. If the child lives, you can look to it yourself."

"Thank you, Captain. A generous reward indeed. And now will you come and see how we dispose of Morgeld's enemies on Malbenu?" He nodded to Alban and Lymri.

"I haven't the time. Dawn comes. I must go to the royal dock."

"Allow me to accompany you," said the prince with a great show of deference. "You may at least enjoy the start of their deaths, if not the happy moment itself."

Prince and captain, followed by the guards and their captives, left the throne hall. In the high slit windows the sky began to pale. A sudden salt breeze blew in and extinguished the last of the torches.

Chapter XII

VELIUS OF VAHRD

The dungeons of Eddystone are considered the most horrible in all the known world. The legendary Vaults of Tsaretneidos in the northern lands are worse, but they are mythical. In ages past a learned man of Panomo-Midmists decided to compile a history of dungeons in the northern lands. He toured them all, collecting many quaint anecdotes. He ranked the dungeons of Eddystone as truly unspeakable. (The scholar's plans for a sequel on the dungeons of the southern lands was never finished. He did not return from his voyage of research.)

Velius of Vahrd knew nothing of the dead scholar's work. Velius could not read or write, but he could swear that Eddystone's nether regions were abominable. In the upper stories of the keep, the damp merely seeped through the stones. Here it trickled freely down the walls and formed pools that stank of mold. A pile of mildewed straw on a stone ledge just above the water was Velius's bed. The only light came from a window too tiny to admit a rat. But Velius had a perverse faith that rats, like love, would find a way.

The barbarian awakened from his trance to find himself lying in the water. His guards had just tossed him in and locked the door—after they'd robbed him of all his weapons.

Velius did not accept his captivity. He hurled his huge body against the cell door several times before he would believe that the iron-bound wood was too thick to break. He raged back and forth, churning the soggy floor of his cell to mud, trying to rip blocks of stone from the walls. Exhausted, his hands bleeding, the barbarian collapsed onto the straw and wiped his streaming brow with a few damp wisps.

"And what did you accomplish by that?" came a gravelly voice.

"What?" shouted Velius, springing upright and peering about him into the dark. There was no one there. Velius had keen eyes, even by night. He had heard of men who went mad in prison, and wondered if it could happen so fast.

"No, you are sane," the voice said. The barbarian instinctively reached for his broadsword and ground his teeth when his hand closed on air.

"Show yourself!" Velius bellowed. "Show yourself, coward, and die!"

"You are a barbarian and a fool," said the voice. "If I didn't need your brawn, I'd leave you here to perish. Show myself, you say. Very well. Watch."

A weird radiance illuminated the little cell. The shadows shimmered, and out of the wavering light stepped Maegisthus, his severed head tucked comfortably beneath his arm.

Velius tried to hide his terror. Ghosts belonged in stories. He enjoyed telling horror tales to his war-brothers around the campfire and watching the younger ones flinch, but this was something else. The barbarian reached again for his missing sword.

"You want a sword? Take it," said Maegisthus's head. A yellow spear of light flamed in the air between them and solidified into a blade. Velius closed his hand on the hilt in dumb wonder.

"Who are you?" he asked.

"In life I was the sorcerer Maegisthus, cut off from the sun by the sword of Velius," came the somber answer.

"I never struck at you in my life!" protested the barbarian.

"Not willingly," said the head. "I free you of my blood. Hear me now, Vahrdish warrior. They denied me burial. Only one friendly hand in all Malbenu at last put the comforting weight of earth over my body. As we speak, he stands in peril of death. If I free you from this cell by the magic I still command, will you save him?"

"Who is he?" Velius asked suspiciously. "If you mean the prince, leave me here. I wouldn't lift an eyelid to help him."

"The prince deserves your hatred. In the shadow realms where I have walked since my death, I have learned many things about my former patron, Prince Phalaxsailyn. He serves a master whose name freezes the heart. Let him go to his doom! The man we seek is a true prince, Alban of Sombrunia. If he lives, there will still be hope. Will you come?"

The phantom flickered and waned until it was merely a pale blue light the size of a candle flame. It bobbed and swayed at Velius's eye level. The barbarian raised the shining sword to the blue flame and took an oath on the hilt which the spectre's magic had emblazoned with the runes of the Vahrdish god, Twacorbi. "I swear to obey you, O mage. And when Alban is free, I swear that I'll return this sword to you running red with Phalaxsailyn's blood."

"When Alban is free," echoed the ghost-light. "Or if. We may have tarried too long. Dawn comes, and the tide of the river rises quickly. Follow me."

The cell door shattered like glass at the touch of the blue flame. Hot behind the glittering light, Velius's mighty legs carried him briskly through the corridors of Eddystone. The few guards who tried to bar his way never lived to make another mistake.

A gray and pink light stained the eastern sky, casting the shadows of poplar trees against the castle. The shadows had far to fall, for the trees grew on the sunrise riverbank opposite Eddystone—and the Koly's most treacherous stretch of water was wide as well as deep. The castle roots were sunk in the churning waters, blue stone plunging down so far that even at low tide a man could never see where Eddystone's foundations began.

How had they done it, those long-dead architects? Scholars who spent their lives in rooms full of ancient scrolls said that Eddystone was not the work of mortals. Whose, then? Theories abounded. Some said that Sarai All-Mother's firstborn, Elaar the Sea-Witch, had made this sinister castle for her amusement when she was still a capricious child. Others claimed that the deified hero Neimar, Elaar's husband, had done it in the days when he was yet fully mortal.

Wiser men pointed to the three stone pillars of sacrifice that jutted out of the riverbed. These also were too weird a construct to come from mortal craft. They seemed to have sprouted from the Koly, an awful growth watered with blood. Even with dawn lighting Eddystone's eastern face, the castle loomed so high above the pillars of sacrifice that they remained in shadow. South of these the Koly whirlpool churned destruction. What mortal men could have anchored the foundations of those three grim sisters with the whirlpool tugging so hungrily, so constantly?

They said that whatever creatures took the offerings from the pillars were also the ones who had built them, and built Eddystone as well.

They said that the first king of Malbenu Isle had made a sacrifice there in exchange for Eddystone's walls.

They said that through some royal error, a princess of Malbenu had been tied to one of the pillars and taken. The king who bartered his child for a wondrous castle did not live to enjoy his fortress very long. At dawn on a certain day the curious traveler can hear his cries as the Koly rises to cover the pillars of sacrifice.

His wife was a resourceful woman, and a loving mother.

There are three pillars, but the Malben kings never use more than two at a time, out of respect for the royal dead.

This dawn brought no ghosts. In the gardens and meadows on the eastern shore of Koly, living things waited for the light. Even the chaos of the Koly whirlpool seemed muted. The only noise to break the sacred calm came from the men who paced the royal dock.

This structure had none of the mysterious origins of the three blue-gray pillars. It was built by men; not even a whisper of myth touched it. It lay north of the pillars of sacrifice, north of Eddystone's shadow too. Since the whirlpool cut the Koly into north and south branches, with Kolytown harbor receiving all trade that entered the river's southern mouth, it was profitable for the Malben kings to have their own dock above the whirlpool and enjoy the benefits of a monopoly on ships that breached the Koly from the north. Ledgers, not legends, had built it.

Sometimes, however, the royal dock was used for other purposes than to welcome merchant ships. This day a gray boat was moored there, her sails the color of dying embers.

Two women sat on a bench on the afterdeck, their hands tied behind them. A third woman under heavy guard stood in the prow, her eyes to the north. A crew of ten ruffians hustled with the ropes and rigging while a silent mass of gray-armored men stood unyielding watch.

Prince Phalaxsailyn and Captain Tor stood on the dock, wrapped in the white mists of dawn that floated up from the river. The prince pointed to a part of the river where three thin pillars of blue-gray rock stood partially submerged by the swirling waters. Tied to two of them were two men, one tall and regal, one small and showing all the fear he felt. The river water lapped about their knees.

"The tide of the Koly is a convenient device," said the prince. "It rises quickly in the morning. And should they manage to undo their bonds, as some have done before, the whirlpool is right there to suck them down. Ah! But even if that were not enough, Tor, there is a third and final peril. A strong man may burst his bonds, a strong swimmer may escape the vortex, but no one, no one has ever yet escaped the Children of Koly-stream. Go back to our master Morgeld with this comforting news. Lord Prince Alban is dead.''

Captain Tor bowed and boarded his ship without a word of farewell or thanks to the prince. The ropes were cast off and the gray vessel began its slow voyage north, against the current of the River Koly. The prince did not wait on the dock to see the last of Tor's ship. Mounting his steed, he galloped back up the winding road to the castle. On the wind of dawn he thought he heard the faint wailing cry of a newborn babe.

Lymri struggled with his ropes. The knots held. "Well, Alban," he said, "this is what comes of my going off on your mad lover's quest."

"This is what comes of it," Alban answered. "I regret nothing so much as this. You might have stayed at the university, playing your pranks, singing your songs. You always were a merry man, Lymri, and a poet. Forgive me for bringing you to this."

"Brr, this water's cold," chattered Lymri. "One of the drawbacks of being short, Alban. It's up only to your thighs, but it's past my waist already. Don't ask my pardon, brother. If I'm half the poet you say I am, I'm happy to die for love."

Alban said nothing for a while, then answered, "Lymri, we die for nothing. I don't love her anymore, and she never did love me. We die as fools, Krisli's Fools. Lymri? . . . Lymri? . . ."

No cheerful voice replied to his call. The waters were rising faster with the coming light. Inch by inch they crept up to Alban's shoulders, and he realized that the surging currents would already be over little Lymri's head.

"My brother is dead," he said to himself. "And I won't live long enough to mourn him." The waters edged up to his chin, then touched his lips with a kiss as salty as Ursula's farewell. He said a silent prayer and closed his eyes.

The splash of something heavy falling into the water nearby made him open his eyes again. A strong hand was holding his chin above water, a sword sawing at the ropes around his wrists. The blade slipped and cut him. Alban yelled with the pain, but his hands were free. He clung to the stone pillar as the whirlpool sucked hungrily at his legs. Beside him, the bronze giant Velius likewise held on to the pillar for dear life. There was a weird lick of blue fire—Maegis-thus's ghost—hovering near the barbarian's head.

"Where's your friend?" asked Velius, looking around in the dusky light. Fog made it difficult to see, but in no way dimmed the strange luster of Velius's guardian flame. Alban's heart was too heavy with loss for him to care where the Vahrdman had acquired such an unearthly companion.

"Drowned," said Alban shortly. "The waters found him before you came."

"Sorry," said Velius. "May he go to his gods. Now let's get out of this accursed river and claim your friend's life from the man who stole it."

"With all my heart," Alban responded. He watched Velius climb to the flat top of the pillar and measure the distance from his perch to an outcropping of stone protruding from Eddystone's walls. This was the only irregularity in the lower portion of the castle's sheer face.

Whoever or whatever had played with the blue-gray rocks that made Eddystone, the unknown builder had a practical side. Of what use are sacrificial pillars if there is no way for your devout servants to reach them with their offerings? And even the most tightly bound victims do tend to wriggle. What a deterrent to frequent, satisfying sacrifices if the giver and not the gift ends up in the water!

"I could kick myself," Velius called down to Alban. "Like an idiot I dived into the river from one of their damned paltry windows"—he indicated the heights of Eddystone towering over them—"when I could've come 'round to get you *that* way. There's even a little plank they keep on the ledge to bridge over from the pillars to the shore."

"I know," Alban called. "How do you think I got here?"

"Ah, well . . ." Velius crouched and leaped from the pillar to the safety of the ledge. Alban could just see his flight through the fog. It was no great thing for the brawny Vahrdman to accomplish, but Alban wondered whether he should risk Velius's laughter and ask the barbarian to shove the plank back across for him. He had never done well at the standing broadjump. His courses at Panomo-Midmists had not included gap-leaping. Of course if he did *not* enlist Velius's aid, tried to jump to the ledge on his own, and *almost* made it . . . ? Which was worse—being mocked by a scornful barbarian, or being sucked down by a nonjudgmental whirlpool?

Pressing close to the pillar, Alban thought over his choices as he climbed out of the river.

He had his body almost clear of the waters, but something was holding him back. Something had him by the legs and was tugging him down, down, relentlessly down while he struggled against it.

"What's wrong?" yelled Velius. In the twining mists he could hardly see Alban's face below him. Maegisthus's blue flame was gone, vanished sometime after Velius cut Alban loose.

"I can't climb any higher! There's something around my legs!" Alban hollered back.

"Maybe the rope's gotten tangled. Shall I come down again? Curse this fog; if only I could see!"

As if on cue, a wind from the west blew down into the river valley, scattering the threads of haze, and the soft first light from the east shone clear. From the stone ledge, Velius could see the retreating stern of Morgeld's ship, still sluggishly sailing against the current.

"A poor ship," Velius told himself. "If it weren't under *his* protection, it wouldn't last a day, going at that pace. But Morgeld's got all the time in the world." The barbarian spat hatred after the vessel, then looked down to help Alban.

The mist had blown away. The battle-hardened barbarian had a free view of something that belonged to the world of shadows or madness:

No rope held Alban fast. Instead a hand, tiny as a child's but white and wrinkled as a long-drowned man's, held his ankle in its steely grasp. Another hand shot out of the water, seizing Alban by the fleshy part of his calf. Black talons bit deep as from the darkened waters a score of nightmare creatures broke the surface of the foam and swarmed ravenously toward the stone pillar.

They swam and slithered over the surface of the river, crawled crablike sideways over the face of Eddystone's walls. Tufts of yellow hair bristled from their naked, spongy bodies. Nasty yellow teeth gnashed together and black claws scraped the rocks as they gibbered for Alban's blood and latched onto any part of his body they could reach, like leeches.

These were the Children of Koly.

Barehanded, Alban could do little against them. Nausea nearly overwhelmed him as he tried to pry them off with his free hand and felt his fingers sink deep into flesh the color and texture of cave-grown fungi. The bones beneath felt gummy and elastic. He jerked his hand away with a hoarse exclamation. Their sinister titters echoed between the riverbanks.

The Sombrunian prince kicked out the way he'd seen one of his father's stallions do when beset by a pack of chasplats, those small, voracious burrowers of the Dunenfels Plain. Tiny—but they could bring down the biggest prey. Any beast that stumbled across one of their underground warrens was fair game. Each no longer than a lady's finger, they would pour from their lairs and overwhelm their victim by numbers, and the slash of minuscule razored teeth. Alban remembered seeing the bones of cattle, horses, and men strewn over the Dunenfels Plain, stripped of flesh by the chasplats' merciless assaults. Many of their victims simply gave up as soon as they saw what their attackers were. His father's stallion had fought fiercely, and come away with only minor wounds.

Alban knew that his own bones would lie in the Koly's bed and no man would see them unless, like the royal steed, he could kick himself free from the little monsters' tirelessly grasping talons.

Gripping the stone pillar with both hands, the Sombrunian lashed out with his feet. Yellow-tufted bodies went flying. Some landed back in the river, some splatted against the castle wall; but more were emerging from the stream. There were always more.

Alban dared to hold on to the pillar with one hand. He knew what he was risking. If he lost his hold on the rock, he would tumble into the waters—waters where those tiny horrors were at home. Still kicking, he made a fist and laid about him, crushing the leering, wizened faces, smashing the bony fingers that clawed his flesh.

With the battle cry of his tribe, Velius plunged feet-first back into the river and hacked at the abominable creatures with his broadsword, dyeing the blade milky blue with their blood. He let the current draw him to the pillar beside Alban's. There the barbarian made his stand, one foot hooked to a crack in the rock that was all the hold he'd have to keep himself from the whirlpool's waiting maw.

Velius slaughtered the Children of Koly with more butchery than art. For a man whose people loved the song of swords, such methodical killing was not a thing of honor. But what choice did the barbarian have? It was like mowing weeds. He did his best to keep the ravenous things at bay, to draw their number away from Alban. His sword swung back and forth like a pendulum, dripping salt water and strange blood. He stopped its arc only once, to chop at a flaw in the rock. This splintered off in a jagged blade of stone, and he shouted for Alban's attention before tossing it across to the Sombrunian.

Now both men were armed, and Alban was at last able to do more than wage a holding fight. Not having to touch that pulpy white flesh heartened him. His makeshift blade ran palest blue.

Two swords or not, there seemed to be no end to the ghoulish little monsters. The fighters' arms grew weary. Alban felt his fingers getting numb and wondered how long it would be before they uncurled of their own will and sent him plummeting into the foamy waters.

"Velius . . ."

"Take heart, friend! Fight on! We're winning!"

"Velius, there are too many of—"

"*Fight on!* I tell you, there are fewer of them now."

Was it only wishful thinking? Alban stabbed and cut with slackening strength, but through his fatigue he noted that what Velius said was true. The Children of Koly no longer surged from the water in uncountable numbers. Their ranks seemed to decrease as he watched, and one by one they released their holds to sink back beneath the ebbing waters.

"Tide's going out again," remarked Velius. He pulled himself to the top of his pillar and jumped the gap to Alban's. Without comment he hauled Alban up, then wrapped his left arm around the Sombrunian's waist so that his next jump took them both back onto the castle outcropping.

Alban stood on the brink, fighting tremors of exhaustion and relief that coursed through arms and legs. "Going out?" he repeated. "So soon?" He could hardly believe it. The tides that washed the headlands of Sombrunia did not change their flows so swiftly. He was ready to believe in miracles.

Velius saw nothing miraculous in it. "You don't know the Koly. She's not like other waters—not with creatures like *those* inhabiting her depths. The gods alone know what rules her tides, but it's nothing to do with the Shieldmaid."

"Who?"

"Twacorbi's Shieldmaid. The one whose spear pulls the world's waters this way and that." Seeing Alban's blank stare, Velius sighed. "The *moon*, friend, the *moon!*" To himself he added, "And they call *us* ignorant barbarians."

"Well, if the ebb tide's what called them off, praise Ambra for it, and praise whatever caused its coming on so fast, too!" said Alban. "I'd be dead if not for you, dead twice over, and neither a pretty death. Thanks. Now to deal with the prince. Have you a true sword for me, friend?"

"Where's the one I made you?"

"I . . . uh . . . dropped it into the river when we—you—leaped ashore." Alban looked sheepish. More boldly, he added, "Anyway, I can't see slaying Phalaxsailyn with a blade of stone."

It was Velius's turn to look sheepish. He'd had plenty of opportunities to obtain a sword for Alban from the bodies of the Malben guards he'd slain. In a Vahrdman, such lack of foresight was unforgivable. The men of Vahrd were famous for their military prowess, but they were likewise famous for their hospitality. You never knew when unarmed company might drop in before a battle and want to join in the fun. Spare swords were a must.

Suddenly the dead wizard's familiar rough voice sounded in his ear again, and the tiny blue flame reappeared. "Give him yours." Velius, disinclined to surrender his sword, hesitated. Then he felt a welcome weight slap against his thigh; a second sword had appeared in his scabbard. Happily, he drew it and handed Alban the yellow blade.

"Where did you get that?" asked Alban, taking care to balance himself as he accepted the sword from Velius's hand. The outcropping was not as wide as he would have liked in his tired state, and the stone underfoot was uncomfortably slippery, soaked as it was with the saltwater running from both men's bodies. "You didn't have it a moment ago."

"You're a sharp-eyed man," Velius said, with real appreciation for any skill that might prove useful in battle. "You did a good deed last night, Alban of Sombrunia. By the gods, let me look at you! Aye, you were that desert player, the tall one. I wondered how the Desert of Thulain ever spawned a pair of eyes that blue—though Lord Olian's wives' come in all colors. Ha! You're none of Olian's getting, are you? Take the sword, Alban, take it. It's a wizard's gift of thanks."

"A wizard?" Alban studied the blade speculatively.

"A dead wizard." Velius grinned. "You did him a favor. Now lead me, my lord. We have to see Phalaxsailyn; guide me to him. You're more likely to know the inside layout of a castle than I am." As Velius bowed, the tiny blue flame beside him blew out.

"A good sword," said Alban, considering the yellow blade. "Not heavy enough, but limber. Yes, Velius, I know castles, and I know much of Eddystone. We'll most likely find the prince in his private apartments. Do you see that balcony hanging out over the river?''

Velius looked up. The balcony in question hung high on the castle's riverside face, looking so anomalous against the otherwise smooth facade that it had to have been added to the original structure on a whim. It was farther downstream than the pillars of sacrifice, almost directly above the Koly whirlpool.

''I see it,'' the barbarian said. ''It . . . looks funny, somehow. Not right.''

''That is Phalaxsailyn's nature. Not right.'' Alban's lips pressed together grimly.

''Well, let's thank him for it later. We can't come calling at his *front* door. He's given us another way into his rooms, the lizard-faced bastard.''

Velius shifted his sword from hand to hand. Until all danger was past, he would not sheathe it, but would make do with only one free hand. Alban could not have sheathed his sword even if he'd wanted to; Maegisthus's enchantments had not provided him with a scabbard. He had just managed to secure the blade to his belt in haphazard style when Velius called his attention to another gift of the Koly's ebb tide.

''There's some outwashed boulders sticking up from the riverbed. See them? You couldn't when the tide was in. That's our way over, and then we'll find a way up. Come on.''

The men carefully clambered from the ledge to the newly revealed tumble of boulders below. They tramped along the rocks in the cool of early morning, well aware that the salt-washed boulders were slippery and treacherous underfoot. Though the river was lower, the whirlpool was still a danger. The stout Velius skidded once, and would have fallen if Alban's hand had not saved him.

There were clumps of weed growing between the rugged boulders that clung to the foot of Eddystone. The men scuttled over these and found themselves on a small, naturally formed promontory covered with ragged patches of greenery. Not even the continual rise and fall of the Koly's tides could uproot all life. The prince's terrace cast its shade above them.

''Water does good work,'' said Velius, laying his hand on the weeping stones. ''Look at all these holes! Plenty of handholds. We won't need to come calling at the front door to see our friend the prince.'' He unlaced his sandals and slung them over one shoulder before starting his climb.

Alban stared at the castle wall, searching for the handholds that Velius had praised. The tiniest pockmarks in the stone were as good as a marble staircase to the barbarian. In his native Vahrd, Velius could climb a sheer cliff more nimbly than a seacoast ape.

"I can't!" protested Alban. "It's no good for me. I'm no climber, Velius." Velius was already partway up the wall, using one hand to steady himself and carrying his sword in the other.

"Then you're a lucky man!" replied the barbarian. He gestured with his sword to a creeping vine that ran up the side of Eddystone to the prince's balcony. In the summer the vine bore dainty sunset roses. In the autumn only the thorns were left. "It'll hold you. You're thin enough," opined Velius. "Mind the thorns."

Alban looked at the vine, bristling with bloodthirsty prickles, then at his hands. He shrugged, thrust his sword into his belt, took a deep breath, and began his ascent.

For the first ten feet he seemed to grab a handful of fire each time he shifted his grip upward. His legs fared no better than his hands. The next ten feet went more slowly, but not so painfully, and the next ten after that let him pick up a little speed. He thought of a pet squirrel he had tamed in Sombrunia that would scamper up the ivy to his room every day. He was the squirrel now, and he tried to imitate the beastie's limber leaps from branch to branch of the clinging green ladder. That helped a bit, and he made incredible upward progress. He began to feel sure of himself and was about to call to Velius to watch how well he was doing when the vine beneath his hands grew abruptly thinner and suddenly snapped away.

Alban's heart plunged. He swayed backward, out from the wall, in the first cold rush of panic, then flailed with his arms, trying to swing his body back against the wall. His thighs, strong from years of riding bareback across the Dunenfels Plain, clamped tightly around the rose vine, ignoring the briars that pierced and stung. The yellow sword slapped against his legs, throwing him further off balance, until it slipped through the makeshift loop in his belt and plummeted into the river below.

Alban regained his balance in a few seconds that seemed like hours. The sharp tingle of his cheek hitting the castle wall while his fingers dug gratefully into the cracks between the stones was the most welcome pain of his life. For a time he could only cling there, flat as a lizard against the blue-gray face of Eddystone.

"Are you all right?" Velius's urgent whisper came down from above. Alban raised his face slightly and saw that the barbarian was already on the balcony. "Come on! Hurry!" hissed Velius. "No one's in the room, but I hear them coming!"

"I can't," Alban whispered back. "The vine's snapped."

"What are you holding on to, then?"

"A crack, I think. Where the mortar's worn away."

"You can't stay there," Velius snapped. "There are plenty of other cracks all the way up. You haven't far to go. How do you think I made it? Come on, edge around to the side of the balcony and I'll give you a hand up."

Alban closed his eyes and tried to feel his way up the side of Eddystone. Velius made impatient noises above his head. His progress was snail-like until he took the courage to open his eyes and look for likely handholds. Hand over hand, foot by foot, Alban climbed in the manner of the warriors of Vahrd. His breath came in short, shallow gasps of delight at his new conquest. The rising sun warmed his back as he climbed, and at last he felt Velius's sinewy hand reach down to haul him over the railing of the royal balcony. Together they stepped from the terrace into Prince Phalaxsailyn's deserted suite.

"About time," snorted the barbarian. The sound of a nearby door being opened confirmed his words. "We must hide."

They glanced quickly around the room and, as one, dashed for the shelter of a brown and golden tapestry that hung near an angle of the riverward wall. The scene of stags and hunting hounds wavered for a moment and was still, concealing them.

As Alban caught his breath he gave thanks for the gods' favor, as well as for the uniquely soggy nature of Eddystone. The room giving onto the balcony offered no other likely spot to hide two full-grown men, and besides, there was something about tapestries that automatically lured the soul bent on self-concealment. But if this had been Sombrunia, or one of the colder, drier northern lands, the tapestry would have hung closer to the wall. Alban and Velius would have made two bulges that even the most bat-eyed guard could spy. Praising good fortune, the Sombrunian prince smiled up at the long worked-iron braces that held this tapestry a good two feet from Eddystone's oozing walls. The stratagem meant to preserve the expensive weaving would also preserve his life and secrecy.

What was better still, the two companions could peer around one edge of the tapestry and, if they were discreet about it, observe without being observed.

The chamber door opened and Prince Phalaxsailyn came in with

four guards. They were not the ordinary castle men-at-arms, but
looked like the dregs of every ill-famed tavern that Kolytown could
muster. In the elaborate silver and blue livery of Eddystone they
resembled prinked-out apes. Two and two they marched, and between them came the princess Agvain.

Her gown was dirty and her hair was tousled. She had a look of
sullen anger on her sharp face, and she strove to slip between her
guards and escape. Each attempt Agvain made failed. The heavy
door was slammed and bolted, and the armed men took posts in front
of it.

Phalaxsailyn kissed Agvain's hand. She permitted this, then
made a great show of wiping it clean in the folds of her skirt. "Why
did you force me to leave her?" she demanded.

"A birthing chamber is the place for midwives, not for the royal
princess of Malbenu Isle," said the prince. "There are other duties
for you to perform, my dear."

"I want to be with her," persisted Agvain. "I know all about
birth. In Vahrd—"

"Forget your barbarous heritage. This is your home now, and
our customs will be yours. Oh, my lady, I have waited too long to
begin your education. Will you ever forgive me? The duties of a
regent"—he sighed dramatically—"take precedence over the
pleasures of a prince. First I had to see that my dear sister-in-law
was well settled in her chamber, the midwife summoned, the wet-
nurse ready, and my men nigh. Next I had to make certain that my
castle was cleared of the riffraff from last night."

"Your lickspit nobles," Agvain said haughtily.

Phalaxsailyn shrugged. "*I* meant the entertainers. They were all
paid and sent their separate ways before dawn. So were most of my
guests. I prefer Eddystone quiet, and not quite so crowded."

"No witnesses to your evil," Agvain growled under her breath.

The prince went on as if he had not heard her. "Then there were
our more honored guests to be seen off from the royal docks, and
lastly . . . lastly there was *you*, my sweet. You had to be . . . coaxed
from Renazca's rooms. But finally *I* am free, *you* are here, and our
sadly postponed wedding night need wait no longer, even though it
is full daylight now." He clapped his hands three times. The guards
opened the chamber door.

The balcony room was large, perfectly square, empty of furniture, decorated only by thick tapestries on the walls. A chill from
the river made it unusually unpleasant. But in spite of all that, it was

the prince's favorite. Now, in response to Phalaxsailyn's summons, six burly serving men entered with an odd mass of lumber and cloth on their shoulders. They set it down, performed a few strange maneuvers with it, and an elaborate, ornate, comfortable royal bed stood ready. All then departed, the last man returning briefly with a large mahogany chest, which he placed at the foot of the bed.

"It is wiser," said Phalaxsailyn, "for a prince not to sleep in the same room twice in a row. Do you like the bed? A work of my own devising. Now, would you like anything to eat or drink? Name it, my love. I'll refuse you nothing."

"Then let me go back to the queen," said Agvain.

"Anything but that," smiled the prince. He opened the chest and pulled out layer after layer of fine gowns, gleaming with gold and silver, shining with precious stones and pearls.

"Ah! This will do." Phalaxsailyn selected a filmy robe of ivory samite embroidered with silver flowers, the blossoms picked out with small sapphires. "Put it on."

Agvain folded her arms.

"Shy," remarked the prince. He clapped his hands; three hulking peasant women answered. Phalaxsailyn's introduction was brief: "My love, your tirewomen." Then, "Dress her," he directed.

Agvain kicked and struck out in all directions at the hammy hands pinning her. The fight was valiant but futile. Agvain tore the ivory gown to ribbons, but her brutish ladies-in-waiting forced her into a gown of golden silk sewn with pearls. She was gasping and bruised when they retired.

"That's better," smirked the prince when they were alone.

"You will die before you touch me!" spat Agvain.

"My love, I doubt it. Enough joking, Agvain. I *will* be your master. If it means I must call back those delicate handmaidens to help me, I'll do it. Hate me or love me, lady, but I *will* be your lord!"

The guards by the door chuckled. Agvain held her head high, daring the prince to come closer. In a low voice one of the guards made a side bet with his mate on the prince's success.

Behind the tapestry, Alban had to restrain Velius from springing out. Silently he indicated that the four guards were all armed, while between the two of them they had only a single sword.

An insistent pounding sounded at the chamber door. Phalaxsailyn looked annoyed at this interruption. "Open," he ordered the guards. "Let us deal with this quickly."

In the doorway a crabbed old woman dropped a trembling curt-sey to the prince. "My lord," she croaked proudly, "our lady Queen Renazca is delivered of a son."

"A son?" Phalaxsailyn's hand tightened on the crone's scrawny shoulder.

"Yes, Your Highness. A fine, healthy son. He looks to be as big a man as his father someday."

"And the queen?"

The midwife rubbed her reddened eyes. "She named him Ama-dor, gave him a mother's kiss, and then she died."

Phalaxsailyn laughed aloud, then pressed gold into the bewil-dered midwife's crooked hands. In the midst of his laughter he said, "Good mother, you see how my heart rejoices to learn that my brother has a male heir. And I will do my best for the baby. My love for my nephew will be legendary. Urklis, come." The largest of the guards stepped forward. "Urklis, my man, go with this worthy woman to the late queen's bedchamber and take the baby prince into your care. Your *special* care. You *will* take good care of him, won't you, Urklis?"

"As nicely as you'd want it," grunted the guardsman. He sham-bled off after the midwife, closing the door behind them.

"Demon!" blazed Agvain. "He will kill him! You would kill an innocent child!"

"And all for you, my love," purred Phalaxsailyn. "I won't be happy until I see a queenly crown on your raven hair."

Someone pounded at the door again. "What now?" snapped the prince. The guardsmen unbolted the door and Urklis bowled into the room, casting himself on his knees before his master.

"Your Highness . . ." Urklis quavered.

"Well?"

"Your Highness, the baby—" Urklis was pale.

"Yes, yes, tell me. Is it done? Speak!"

"The little prince . . . Amador . . . is . . . gone."

"What?" roared Phalaxsailyn. "Gone where?"

"Lord, I don't know!" protested Urklis. The prince seized his guardsman by the hair and jerked his head back. A steel dagger glinted in his hand, hovering near Urklis's throat. The monstrous man blubbered like a baby. "The queen's body was still on the bed when the midwife took me to her chamber. The other women were gone, except the wet-nurse, who drowsed beside the cradle. She tried to stop me. I made short work of her, my lord! Then I looked into the cradle and saw—nothing.''

''Did you search?''

''My lord, I swear I did! He was not with the other attendant ladies. The baby has vanished!''

''Imbecile!'' raged the prince. ''Here, take the right pay for such *careful* service.'' Phalaxsailyn slit Urklis's throat as calmly as a man might slit a melon.

''Take your own rightful due, prince of demons!'' shouted Velius, vaulting from behind the tapestry. He kicked Urklis's dying body aside. A swash of blood from his victim's throat momentarily blinded Phalaxsailyn. As he wiped it from his eyes, Velius's sword snickered through the air like summer lightning and pierced his ribcage.

''Velius!'' Agvain was at his side.

The barbarian warrior snatched the dagger from the prince's grasp, tossed it to his lady, then relieved dead Urklis of his sword and threw it to Alban's eager hands.

''Alban,'' Phalaxsailyn breathed, his mouth growing thick as the coldness crept into his heart. ''Can no man ever kill . . . ?'' Shades of Helagarde drifting across his eyes silenced him.

''Now for a fair fight!'' cried Velius, avid for combat.

The late prince's men did not care for even odds. They unbolted the door and fled. Velius and Agvain roared with laughter to see them run.

''Wait,'' cautioned Alban, listening. ''They're coming back, and others are with them.''

Alban was right. Armed men flooded the doorway, and at their head a giant of a man with a lush golden beard ramped like a desert lion. Beneath the particolored splendor of an open robe he wore battered armor and Vahrdish riding boots.

King Egdred had returned.

''Your Majesty!'' Alban cast down his sword and knelt. Velius and Agvain hesitated before discarding their weapons, but at last, reluctantly, followed Alban's lead.

The king's eyes slowly roved the room, lighting on his brother's corpse. ''What's this? Who murders my kin in my own house?''

''I have the honor of his death!'' proclaimed Velius.

King Egdred examined the barbarian's proud face. ''You, Velius? You're no casual killer. Why did you do this?''

Alban interposed. "Majesty, look at me and know me. I am Alban of Sombrunia. I will explain . . ."

The Malben king's face was impassive as he heard Alban out, but when the young man spoke of Queen Renazca's death the king's broad shoulders drooped and a wave of pain washed over his face.

"And my son?"

"We know nothing more than what we overheard. Prince Amador has disappeared."

"And all this," mumbled the king, "all this is my reward for seeking battles—glory! My place was here, with my people, with my loved ones. I am punished." He turned from them and strode to the balcony, where he stood for a time silently watching the river below. When he spoke again, he seemed to have shaken off a great weight. "I have no time to mourn," he said calmly. "I must heal my kingdom after my brother's rule. As for you, my friends—name any reward for the service you've done me."

"Passage to Vahrd," said Velius, "for Agvain and me."

"Granted, with gifts to keep you company," said King Egdred. "And I assume you wish passage to Sombrunia, Prince Alban?"

Alban shook his head. "I have other work to do. There's a gray ship sailing north. Three women are prisoners aboard. One of them will be Morgeld's bride."

"Morgeld?" King Egdred scratched his head. "A name out of legend. I thought he was a tale to frighten children. Does he truly live?"

A sudden covering of clouds veiled the morning sunlight and darkened the chamber. Rain began to fall, whipped by the wind into torrents that streamed into the open room. The sea wind howled and wailed, buffeting the soldiers' faces, making the tapestries ripple and billow on their braces like the breast of the sea. Thunder rolled and made the floor beneath their feet shift as lazily as the back of a sleeping dragon. Then suddenly it stopped.

"What storm behaves like this?" demanded Velius, holding Agvain close. Though the rain now fell gently outside, the stormclouds remained, and lightning flashed like a swordsman's challenge.

"Witchery," moaned one of the soldiers. A hard look from his king could not still his trembling. "This is a sorcerer's storm, and nothing natural!"

A knife of white light sheared across the floor from the open balcony, cutting a path through King Egdred's troops and clearing the

doorway. The men scurried out of range, herding themselves un-
willingly into the room. There was no means of escape, unless they
grew so foolhardy as to attempt a leap from the balcony. Brilliance
and livelight blocked the portal to the hall, sealing them all inside
the chamber with a barricade of brightness. The warriors shaded
their eyes and peered into the dazzle. More than one of them now
mumbled of witchcraft.

Light split from light. A fair young man in icy robes emerged
from the radiance.

"I am Ayree," he said.

The soldiers' mumbling grew to fearful conjectures. Ayree's
name was well-known in the Twelve Kingdoms, and many legends
told that the welfare of all the realms was intimately tied to the witch-
king's bloodline. How? The bards of the north and the storytellers
of the southern bazaars could only shrug. As with all legends, there
were some chapters lost, some still left to tell themselves. What they
did know was this: Ayree had the blood of gods and the most powerful of mortal mages mixed in his veins, but he had never used his
spells for evil. Nevertheless, most men feared to meet the cold lord
of Castle Snowglimmer or gaze long into his glacial eyes.

King Egdred was brave enough to come forward. "My lord Ayree, your fame runs before you. Whatever purpose brings you,
Prince of Warlocks, you are welcome in my kingdom." Egdred extended a hand in greeting. It passed through Ayree's body.

The witch-king chuckled drily. "Perhaps I should say that I am
merely a sending of myself; a vision. Other matters hold my body
elsewhere, but *this* man's life demands that I come here and speak
while there is yet time." The vision pointed at Alban.

"Me, my lord?" The Sombrunian had heard wonders of Ayree
from Lymri and Mizriel when they had saved him at Krisli's altar.
Never had he thought to see the face of the young witch-king, or to
hear Ayree speak of him with such apparent concern. "Why me?"

Ayree's voice recalled the thunder. "Do not be so astonished,
Alban of Sombrunia. One man's marvel is another's myth. Egdred
can scarcely believe that Morgeld lives, except as a nursemaid's
tale, yet he accepts my presence without question. I tell you all,
Morgeld does live. He lives, he is free, and he works to make this
world his own entirely. From the day that Janeela bound him, we
knew he would escape and return. So it was prophesied, and so it
was written in the Scroll of Oran."

The vision seemed to smile. In his bodiless flight to Malbenu Isle,

Ayree had spied a northbound ship with two familiar faces aboard whose destiny might someday touch that lost and precious scroll. To others, they looked like just a Vairish player and the small trained animal who earned him his living. But to Ayree, Mustapha and his wise dog were more. As he spoke to Alban and the rest, the witchking's scrying eyes were elsewhere. They searched the heart of Mustapha, and there read hate for Morgeld's captain, Tor. While in the Malben court, man and beast had heard of distant Helagarde, Morgeld's stronghold. There Tor was bound, and there the duo meant to hunt him down. He had blood to answer for—the blood of their friends—and they would have that answer.

Go, Mustapha, thought Ayree. *Go, gentle player. Who knows how great or small your role shall be? How much power you mortals wield, and never know it!*

The memory claimed only an instant. The vision spoke on.

"Yet while Morgeld was still bound, we planned our defense, waiting and working in silence and secrecy—we, the enchanters who serve good, and never weave a spell with evil intent. But we have done all we can. A mortal will defeat Morgeld; a mortal will finally destroy him, just as Janeela the Silver One who bound him was mortal. Our magics are nothing against his. Truly, there are greater forces than our magics working now, forces which will not let us interfere. Still, we can use our powers to a degree. We can use them to aid the mortals destined to overthrow Morgeld."

"By Elaar, my lord Ayree," King Egdred said, kneeling and presenting his sword hilt-first to the vision. "By Elaar, I swear that you shall have all Malbenu's aid against the ruler of Helagarde!"

Ayree raised his hand. "Put up your sword, King Egdred. Make no promises for your realm. Not even I can read all the future holds, but I can tell you this: blood of your blood shall sway the balance in the final battles."

The king blinked, confused by this ambiguous prophecy. Ayree did not enlighten him; his words were for Alban.

"You, Alban of Sombrunia, you above all must be careful. Morgeld fears you most of all. Your death would please him more than even the triumphal moment when he broke Janeela's bonds, the bonds she paid for with her life. My brother in magic, the wizard Paragore-Tren, has been seeking you. He would counsel you to return to your kingdom. I could send you there at once if you would consent to go. Return, Alban! Return to your home and safety."

"No," Alban protested. "I can't, not yet. Morgeld has Ursula,

Mizriel, and Runegilda on a ship bound for Helagarde. I can't abandon them.''

''Three women?'' wondered the vision. ''Do they matter?''

''They matter to me. If I'm Morgeld's enemy, he'll seek me out sooner or later. If I play the coward, he'll find me. But I intend to go after him instead, and all the evil magic in his hands won't keep me from him!''

This time there was warmth in the vision's smile. ''I read love in you, Alban.''

Alban lowered his head. ''Love doesn't enter into this. We need warriors, not lovers; men who can wield swords, not songs.''

''You have much to learn,'' said Ayree. ''Go then, Alban. Follow the ship you seek.''

A thread of light—it might have been a feather—gently touched Alban's brow. Light suffused him, then melted, taking him with it. The vision of Ayree wavered.

''Stop!'' King Egdred still knelt before the vanishing apparition. ''In the name of the gods, mighty one, tell me where my son is! Tell me where to find him!''

Ayree's serene face grew sober. ''Other hands will find him and return him to you, if they live. The future is closed to me. If they survive, you will see your son.''

Outside, the stormclouds parted, and sunlight struck Ayree. Light touched light, and then it was only a patch of morning sun shining before the grieving eyes of the Malben king.

Chapter XIII

ELAAR

Morgeld's ship was mist and fog and exhalations of dark evening air. Unearthly breezes tossed its topmost pennant, and an alien wind filled its sails when other ships lay becalmed.

Ursula stood at the gray ship's prow and dreamed of the day when she and Alban first set sail for Sombrunia aboard *Elaar's Eye*. No azure sails filled the sky now. No kind-faced sea spirit had her runes inscribed on this boat's bow. Ursula gazed ahead, watching the waters of the Koly part before Morgeld's ship, never daring to look back at Eddystone.

The gray ship picked up speed with the turning of the tide. Soon the grim vessel cleared the northern river-mouth and sailed the Opalza Sea.

"A word, my lady." Tor stood behind Ursula. With him was a barrel-bellied roughneck, pig-faced and moody. "May I present the captain of this ship? I have commended you to his especial care."

"Then your master has relieved you of your rank, Captain Tor?" asked Ursula bitterly. "Might I hope to be there when he punishes you?"

"Mistress, you misjudge," Tor replied. "I am a land-bound captain. I wish to introduce you to this man before I return to Helagarde."

Ursula looked out over the trackless sea, then back at Tor, who laughed at the open puzzlement in her eyes. "Even I, his mortal servant, sometimes travel in ways that other mortals don't know. Until we meet again, my lady."

The sun broke the eastern horizon, striking emeralds from the sea. Beneath the healing rays of light the murky timbers of Morgeld's ship faded to a lighter shade of smoke. A cold southern breeze filled the sails and sent Tor's scarlet cloak billowing—and Tor himself dispersed on the wind like mist. Ursula glanced sharply up and down the deck; not a sign of Tor or his men. The silent guards had followed their captain on the wind to Helagarde.

"You'll get used to that," said the sea captain briefly. "The sun's not for them, nor they for it. Go to your cabin."

"I would rather stay here. I enjoy the wind."

"I've been told of you, lady," said the captain. "You're headstrong. I've no time for your quirks. Do as you're told."

"What if I won't?" Ursula stood to her full height and challenged the squat, ugly little man. She toyed with the idea of shoving him down.

The ship's captain shrugged and reached for a nasty-looking bit of equipment fondly called the ship's cat. Nine braided thongs swung lazily from a wooden handle. He spat casually on the deck at Ursula's feet, then said, "Lady, I've got full hands here, running a ship with short crew. I've my own plain way of dealing with women. I can lay this beauty across your back sweet as you please, Morgeld's bride or not."

"I'd like to see you try," Ursula growled between clenched teeth. In her toes she felt a familiar tingle.

The captain swung the cat back and forth idly. "Brave, eh? Well, shall I see how brave your little sister is under the lash? Or—"

A heavy paw knocked the cat-o'-nine-tails into the sea. The bear's hairy muzzle wore a very human grin, malicious and gleeful. And the bear laughed, pinning the captain to the deck, batting his face back and forth with a free paw, then bowling him head over heels down an open hatchway. His cries brought the crew.

The bear gave them her full attention. Singly and in groups they were chased up and down rigging, across decks, through doors and down hatches. The bear took offhanded little bites and patches out of their hides, enjoying herself immensely. At last she returned to the captain, fished him out of the hatch, and played with him like a pup. "Any more threats to make, Captain?" Ursula remarked.

The ship's cook appeared from the galley with a monstrous slab of raw liver in his greasy hand. "Here, bear," he crooned, his rough voice cracking with terror. "Nice meat, bear. Come and get it."

Ursula sat down comfortably on the captain's belly, but the sight of the raw liver was too much for her. "I hate liver!" she roared.

"Cooked or raw I hate it, and I hate stupidity worse than liver!"
She charged the cook, who fell backward down the galley steps,
taking the liver with him. Then she shambled back and resumed her
place on the captain's paunch. "Now, friend, you'll release my sister and the other lady. Because if you don't, I'll see whether I prefer
the taste of raw sea captain to the taste of raw liver."

"Release them!" the captain choked. "At once!"

The crew didn't move.

"When I finish with him, I'll still have room for you!" the bear
bellowed. "Release them!" The crewmen remained stock-still,
subtle smiles on their leathery faces.

"How dare you?" growled Ursula. She raised a titanic paw high
to make an end of the captain—and froze.

At the end of the rough-furred limb dangled a lady's delicate ivory
hand. Ursula was becoming a woman again. The change gathered
speed, racing up and down her body, last of all transforming the
bear's snout to Ursula's angry face.

Then the crew sprang forward and seized her.

"An enchanted bride," groaned the captain, rubbing his bruises
and scrapes. "Better Morgeld than me. Don't try your pretty tricks
on him, though. He'll break you of them or he'll break you. Now
go below!"

"Have a care," Ursula menaced, struggling in the grasp of four
strong sailors. "I'll turn myself into a bear again and kill you all!"

The captain rubbed his stubbly chin. "I doubt you, lady. If you
could control that spell you wouldn't have changed back to a woman
just now. Bring rope, lads. We'll tie her up in her bunk, and if she
turns into a bear again she can do her growling belowdecks."

A brace of crewmen bound Ursula hand and foot with a coil of
rope.

"Release me!" shouted the lady. "Get that filthy rope off me
before I—"

The captain's gnarled hand cracked smartly across her cheek. "I
said peace, girl," he remarked, a satisfied grin showing his crumbling teeth. "You won't surprise us again. You're no sorceress."

"She may not be, Captain Porker, but I am!" Mizriel's white
hair streamed behind her, her arms raised high and free of fetters.
Consternation showed in the captain's face. Flanking Mizriel were
the other captive woman and a chit of a man, sopping wet and draped
with the greenery of the sea.

"Take them!" shouted the captain. Mizriel laughed and frightened a flock of seven seagulls balanced on the rail beside her.

"There are your men, Captain Porker. They are busy learning to be birds, but they'll do better with a leader. Is it loyal to abandon your men, sir? Go! And may the sea swallow you!"

The rope at Ursula's wrists and ankles fell limp as a headless snake. A flurry of white wings caressed her face and she heard the mewling of many gulls. They spread tentative wings and wandered the deck aimlessly, lost in their new bodies. Then a silent command passed through them all and they rose in a feathery cloud that wheeled away north.

They were nothing but specks against the sky when Ursula asked, "Will they be gulls forever?"

"It's not the worst fate in the world," said Mizriel. "In a way, I've done them a favor. I've freed them of an evil master. And as sailing men, they should like the seagoing life I've given them."

"In other words you haven't the vaguest notion of how to lift that spell, either," Ursula commented wryly.

"I've freed you from your bonds and your guards. We can turn this ship and take you so far from Morgeld that he won't be able to recall your name. And all I hear from you, sister dear, are complaints," Mizriel snapped.

"An older sister has the right to give constructive criticism," Ursula remarked with that superior air Mizriel found unspeakably annoying. "But if you want complaints, tell me how you intend to manage this ship with no crew."

"By magic," Mizriel said simply. "You doubt my power?"

"Not at all. Make the ship turn left."

"Port," Lymri joined them. "Starboard is right, port is left."

"Alban's friend!" Ursula was delighted. "You escaped!" She embraced him warmly. "That must mean that Alban—"

"Dear lady," Lymri said gently, "when they bound us to pillars in the river so the tide or the whirlpool might have us, the waters covered me before they took Alban. I struggled with the ropes, trying to hold my breath as long as possible. Then, when I thought it was all over for me, I felt the bonds give way, almost as if tiny hands undid them. I opened my eyes underwater and saw Alban still fast to his pillar, but before I could reach out and undo his knots, the current swept me away.

"All this time I was underwater. It was strange, but I never knew I could hold my breath so long, almost as if I could draw breath from the water. The currents drew me further from Alban until I ran up against something hard, a wedge of wood that I used to pull myself up to the surface. My head broke water and I saw I'd gotten hold of this ship by the rudder, like a barnacle.

"I held on there till we cleared the rivermouth, then climbed aboard. As I began my climb, I thought I saw a most remarkable thing. The sun was just rising, so it might have been a trick of the light, but I saw a maiden with hair and skin green as river reeds raise herself above the waves to smile at me. Then she dove, and slapped the water with a golden fish's tail."

Mizriel drew Runegilda a little apart. "A being like that is more than a trick of light," she whispered.

Krisli's priestess concurred. "So he would say, too, if he were not afraid we'd think him mad. He claimed that tiny hands seemed to free him . . . When he said that, I *did* doubt his sanity. The Children of Koly do not loose one sacrifice and take another; they devour all." Runegilda gave the little poet a thoughtful look. "The waters of the world shelter creatures of good and evil. They have their kingdoms and their wars, just like surface dwellers, or so my studies said. I wonder . . . why should this man be so favored by the waterfolk?"

Mizriel glowered, recalling Potentilla, the ondine from the Merrie Manticore, but kept her own counsel.

Lymri was continuing to tell Ursula his story. "I reached the deck and saw Morgeld's men melt away. I kept to the shadows, sneaked up behind Mizriel and Runegilda, and untied the silver knots. You know the rest."

"No spell could break those bonds," said Runegilda placidly. "Mortal hands sometimes succeed where magic fails."

Lymri took Ursula's hand, seeing sorrow engulf her. "My lady, if I escaped, he might have freed himself too. There is always hope."

"No," answered Ursula. "Not for me. All my hopes are gone. With the gods' help he cheated death twice. Why should they let him go a third time?"

"The gods bestow great things on great men," answered Lymri.

Ursula was not comforted. "I am Ursula the Accursed. I thought I was unlucky when no man loved me, but it was better that way. A young knight died for me at Dureforte Keep. Sir Kerris died at Eddystone for my sake, and now Alban. How many deaths must I cause?"

Mizriel's lips parted, then closed. *It is not the time to speak of Father,* she thought.

Ursula smiled sadly. "I know about Father, Mizriel. Do you think Tor could resist giving me such news? Father too is dead because of me, and how many more? How many more?" Her voice broke into sobs.

Krisli's priestess embraced her and said, "The gods order the world. All of our powers are useless against them. But hope never is. Cry now, then free your eyes for other things. We still have no crew, as you said, and autumn on the Opalza Sea is a deceptive season."

"I have my waystones, but they only work on land," said Mizriel.

"I know some navigation," Lymri volunteered, studying the rigging overhead. "We raced sailboats on the River Salmlis. Steering a ship's easy once you know where you're going. I could plot us a course anywhere."

Ursula dried her eyes. "Take us back to Cymweh, then, and from there we'll go home. Our land needs us."

"Morgeld's probably overrun our land by now," Mizriel said gloomily.

"Then Morgeld will have a fight on his hands." Ursula's face was pale and stern, like the ivory paintings of Braegerd shieldmaidens setting out on their first raids. "Our father was vassal to King Elberd Far-Reach. We'll claim his aid and protection. He may be slow to act, but he must avenge a vassal's murder."

"Then it's agreed," said Lymri. "First we sail for Cymweh."

"*First,* little poet," Mizriel corrected, "we get you a dry change of clothing."

"We should all change," suggested Runegilda. "We'll make poor sailors, hampered by women's robes. Let's see if the late crewmen left any extra shirts and breeches belowdecks to fit us."

The calm weather held while they changed, and it was a more ragtag crew than before that Lymri called to order at the ship's wheel. "Our course is set. Now we'll divide ship's duties and we'll be in sight of land before we know it."

"Is Cymweh so close?" wondered Runegilda.

"No, but the kingdom of Glytch is. We can land there and get a real crew aboard. We'll be all right for now, but the long voyage to Cymweh would be too much."

"We could do it," Mizriel sulked.

"Certainly. With your magic," Ursula sneered.

Mizriel kicked her.

"We'll have shifts of two, one to watch and one to steer," said Lymri. "We'll take turns in the galley. I'll be first to steer, Mizriel first to watch, then she'll take the wheel and Runegilda will watch, and so on in rotation."

"It sounds tiring," Mizriel sighed.

"Tired already! The girl who could sail to Cymweh by herself?" Ursula jibed.

"That's enough," Lymri said. "Let's keep it friendly, even if you are sisters. Here, look at what I've found. One of the crew was musically inclined." He proudly displayed a battered mandolin. "Shall we start our voyage arguing or singing?"

"Singing, by all means," said Ursula, giving Mizriel a hug. "Make it a comical song, Lymri; we need it."

"Then I will sing you the northern ballad of Harmon and Rioja, the incredibly unfortunate and unlikely lovers," he declared, and began:

> "The night fell swift on farm and town
> And on the castle, too.
> That fateful night of ill renown
> When Harmon came to woo.
>
> The lady sat all pale and fair,
> Her casement open wide,
> When Harmon spied her golden hair
> And swore she'd be his bride.
>
> He galloped boldly o'er the moat
> And to her father came.
> 'Oh I would wed your daughter fair
> And Harmon is my name.
>
> As I was riding through the mist
> I saw her golden hair
> A-trickling down your castle wall
> And blowing in the air.
>
> The birds have nested in her locks,
> The squirrels in it sleep,

The villagers cut hunks of it
As straw to feed their sheep.'

'You love my daughter for her hair?'
Rioja's father said.
'You love a lass who lends her locks
To robins for a bed?

Why, you have never seen her face,
My young and foolish knight!
I tell you true, that face of hers
Once put a witch to flight.

Her eyes are red as strawberries,
Her skin is pale as cheese,
Her nose is like a buzzard's beak,
Her breath like buttered peas.'

'Oh, say no more!' Sir Harmon cried.
'I love her still, you see.
Set me a quest to win her hand
Then marry her to me.'

'You are a lunatic or fool,'
Rioja's sire replied.
'Although my daughter's hideous,
She'll be no madman's bride.'

'Oh Father, do not say you so!
Oh Father, bid him stay!
For I'd not have this fair knight go.
I love him, by the way.'

Rioja's words were all in vain,
Her father would not heed.
He sent Sir Harmon forth alone
Upon his swaybacked steed.

A cloak of rosy silk wore he
And hose of Lincoln green,

A cape of wool more white than milk,
A hat of purple sheen,

A satin shirt of ocean blue,
A pair of sandals red;
A questing song was in his mouth
And nothing in his head.

'Farewell, farewell, my own true love!
You *will* return, of course?'
'I swear I shall!' Sir Harmon cried,
And then fell off his horse.

The fair knight's neck did snap in two,
Alike the girl's heart broke.
A warning let this be to you
That true love is no joke!''

''My idea of love precisely,'' said Mizriel. ''First you break your
back for your beloved, then your heart, then the dishes, and finally
your neck. What good is love?''

''What good is love?'' echoed Ursula, though in a different voice.
Ursula has loved too much, thought Lymri, *and Mizriel not at
all.* An eerie longing swelled his throat as he looked at the two sisters. His heart ached for them both.

Aloud Lymri said, ''Let's take our posts. We must be used to the
routine before nightfall.''

They obeyed, taking their places willingly. Ursula went below
and slept an exhausted sleep until Mizriel awoke her for her turn on
watch.

''The sun's almost down, Ursula. You can stand lookout from
the prow or the crow's nest. The view from up there is wonderful.''

''I'm not the climber you are, Mizriel. I'll take the prow. The
sun is down, you say?'' Mizriel nodded. ''And—and nothing has
happened?''

''What should happen?'' Mizriel shrugged.

''Morgeld's men,'' Ursula said. ''They left with the sunrise, and
I was afraid that when it set again—''

''Not very likely. They aren't the sort of creatures to leave solid
land if they can help it. Water's too clean an element for them. If

Morgeld was able to force them to cross water to get you, he's more powerful than I thought."

Ursula went above while Mizriel stretched out comfortably on the bunk. A velvet night had fallen, sweet with breezes unusually balmy for autumn weather at sea. Near the wheel, where Runegilda steered Lymri's course, an orange ship's lantern glowed, but the prow was in darkness.

Ursula leaned far out over the water to feel the cooling spray tossed up by the wavelets. The moon sprinkled silver on the sea, the sea cast shimmering flecks of green and blue to the sky. A thin line of phosphorescent foam flowed along the sides of the ship like a bridal train.

"The veils of Elaar," murmured Ursula. She closed her eyes and was again a child at her nurse's knee, hearing the old stories of the gods. "Seven veils and seven stars she wore when she wed the hero Neimar. Seven sons and seven daughters were their children. Seven blessings on all maidens who believe in her, seven curses on all maidens who refuse." Ursula sighed and gazed across the empty sea. "O Elaar, Sea-Mother, I always threw garlands into the Carras River for you. I believed; I still believe. Why have I received only your curses?"

Waves lapped against the ship. The deep tranquility of night surrounded her. By the light of moon and stars, Ursula saw fat white clouds drifting together to the north. They flowed into high, snowy battlements and towering cliffs of darker shade.

"A storm coming," Ursula said aloud. "Perhaps we'll reach land before it breaks." She looked down at the moonlit waters again. "And if we don't, what difference will it make to me? The sea is lovelier than the land. I think I could even forget Alban if I walked the bottom of the sea long enough. Mizriel can ask King Elberd's help without me. Let her do it. Elaar, my mother, let me walk in your palaces of pearl. Elaar, my mother, let me walk in your coral gardens. Elaar, my mother, let me walk the silent caverns."

It was an old, old invocation. She recalled it from ancient histories that told of days when high-born maidens gave themselves to the Opalza Sea. Gilded ships carried them from then-barbarian Cymweh, past the islets of Neimar's Necklace, onto the open waters. They wore their finest robes, their costliest jewels, then called to the goddess and leaped into the waves.

Ursula wore no jewels. Her clothing was the rough shirt and dirty breeches of a common sailor; but no maiden ever looked half so joyful or eager to plunge into the sea. She used a rigging rope to steady herself and balanced on the ship's rail, a slender shadow against the stars. Letting go the rope, she sprang out into darkness. The waters closed over her.

Coughing and choking on brine, Ursula wiped her stinging eyes with a sopping wet sleeve and refused to believe what she saw. She was sprawled on the deck, dripping and soaked, being pounded heartily on the back by Alban.

"When did you take leave of your senses?" he shouted at her. He was also thoroughly soaked, his blond hair plastered down with seawater. "Are you that eager to die? Can't you wait like the rest of us?"

His angry harangue was drowned in her tears and laughter as she clung to him, hugging him, kissing him, pinching him to see if he was real and herself to see if she was dreaming. He tried to break her embrace, tried to pull himself from her arms to avoid her kisses. He tried to turn his face into a stern shield against her tears, and he failed completely.

"I could almost think you were glad to see me," Alban said, attempting to turn it all into a joke. "I must thank Ayree the next time I see him. He must've told you he was sending me. I only wish he'd told *me* you were planning to take a midnight swim." His voice rasped and dipped like a schoolboy's. She was warm in his arms, so very warm!

"Alban, Alban, I thought that you were dead!" Ursula sobbed. "Three times I've lost you; three times, but none hurt me as much as when you turned away from me on the dock in Kolytown. Do you think I love your crown or your kingdom? Keep them for another woman, make her your queen if that will convince you I'm telling the truth. But take me with you—take me wherever you go! Let me be your lover, or let me be your friend if nothing else. And when I die, let yours be the hand to close my eyes. I love you."

He held her gently, as if fearing a tighter embrace would make her slip away from him and become again the tall, cool, unfeeling woman he had first loved. Words of his own love rose to his lips, but doubts sealed them, silencing him because he half believed he could not trust her now. *Your heart has betrayed you before,* he thought. *Wait, wait and see.*

Lymri found them there in each other's arms when he came to take his turn at watch. Soon the happy sounds of reunion filled the little craft, luring Runegilda and Mizriel forward to see what had happened.

"Shall we change course for Sombrunia?" asked Lymri.

"We might as well," said Mizriel. "Have we enough supplies?"

"I'll go below and check," Alban offered. Runegilda detained him.

"We will not sail for Sombrunia," she stated. It was not a countermand, merely a fact. Krisli's priestess pointed out across the waters. The white clouds that Ursula had noted earlier had changed, their aspect growing more sinister. The northern horizon was as hunched and menacing as the back of a great black fighting bull.

Runegilda said, "The gods command." Then the storm came.

Cat-and-kitten clouds tumbled across the sky to booming rolls of thunder. Waves reared out of the heart of the sea to defy the lashing rains. The wind complained bitterly while the ocean's wicked roar shook the ashen ship. The clouds turned lazy somersaults, riding the madness of winds and waves and rain.

"Not this!" Alban screamed into the swirling sky, sheltering Ursula in his arms. "Not this! Leave us! Leave us!"

A towering wave crested high above the fragile ship. Just before it crashed down, Alban saw, shining with gray light inside the emerald concavity, a familiar face smiling in evil triumph.

He did not have the chance to tell Runegilda that this storm had not come at the gods' command.

Chapter XIV

THE STRAND

Twelve ragged men sat hunched around a small bonfire on a sandy shore. Their cloaks were heavy with damp, their beards spangled with ocean spray. The storm had carelessly tossed their proud ship against the sharp rocks of this desolate coast. All that remained of her lay crackling in their campfire or sunk at the bottom of the sea. For their captain, it was as if they warmed themselves over the burning splinters of his own heart.

"What's that?" one of them shouted, springing up from the fire. The waves brought a dim shape nearer shore.

Their leader stood and peered into the dying storm. "A ship, Osbert," he said. "She looks deserted."

"If only we could reach her before she strikes the rocks!" Osbert groaned. "She'll smash on them sure."

"Ship or driftwood," remarked the brawniest man of the company as he wrapped his cape snugly around him. "We sail her or we burn her. Either way she helps us."

"Shut your mouth, Grel!" growled Osbert. "Maybe you don't mind dying on this godforsaken shore, but I do! You boast that you're Elaar's own chosen swimmer. Why don't you paddle out and secure us that ship? But you're all empty wind. You—"

Aethelstan seized Osbert by the collar of his tattered cloak and shook him like a kitten. "I am still your captain, ashore or at sea!" he roared. "And Grel is still my second-in-command! Will you govern your tongue, Osbert, or will you lose your teeth?"

"I—I—I—" Osbert stammered, trembling. "I ask your pardon, Grel," he finally managed.

Grel shrugged and got up to fetch more driftwood for the fire. He had stacked it well away from the blaze and covered it with a piece of salvaged sail, knowing how the sight of it saddened his friend and captain.

Aethelstan set Osbert on his feet with the parting caution, "Next time, mind your words. Grel built this fire for us in the first place, making wet wood burn when *you* couldn't even get flame from a tinderbox! *And* he dragged your waterlogged brother safely to shore when Elaar would've claimed him, bones and hide. Remember that!"

Osbert hung his head.

Grel stood gazing out at the drifting ship, his arms half full of driftwood. "People on her," he remarked.

Aethelstan peered through the stinging small rain. It was true, there were two or three little shapes moving back and forth aboard the foundering craft like ants on a twig. The ship's mast was snapped away, the rudder most likely gone, and the vessel seemed to float aimlessly. As Aethelstan watched, a humpbacked wave raised itself beneath the keel and sent the ship sliding down to smash against the black breakwater rocks.

Hunks of ship's timbers and the struggling bodies of the survivors filled the sea. Their clothing showed as small bits of brighter color against the gray of the waves. The twelve ragged men waded into the shallows to help the strangers come ashore.

The Braegerd rovers gave no thought to the fact that their own rations were low, that here were more mouths to feed, that the wisest thing to do would be to let the newcomers drown or to help them to do so with a judicious knock on the head. That was not the way of Braegerd men. In a raid or a fair fight they had no qualms about killing any man who challenged them or came between them and their legitimate booty—but this was no raid. Here were only victims of the sea. They would always stand between the sea and her prey, though they died for it.

Ursula's hair streamed down her face, one strand across her lips bitter with the taste of the waves. The storm was dying. The savage rain had gentled into spindrift, stroking her face with cool fingers. Osbert's hand steadied her as she staggered up the shingle and sat down heavily on the dark, wet sand.

The others straggled out of the breakers after her, their clothes heavy on them, the Braegerd men hovering near. Mizriel stumbled and fell, scraping her hands on the sea-cast pebbles. Grel tossed his thick cape over her shoulders.

"Thanks," mumbled Lymri, helping Mizriel to her feet. The sorceress's white hair looked dull as dirty snow. Grel picked her up easily and carried her to the campfire. The rest followed him.

"Women dressed as sailors," Aethelstan muttered into his dripping beard. It stirred faintly, leading him to believe he had picked up a crayfish or two in his swim to land. Osbert had already plucked three small crabs out of his own whiskers and had eaten them. The Braegerd leader studied the castaways as carefully as dim firelight and encroaching mist would allow, and a look of realization slowly filled his face.

"The prize!" he exclaimed, pointing at Alban and Ursula. "The first ship we took! You were aboard her!"

"The Braegerd men," breathed Ursula, "who sold us at Koly-town."

Alban reached for his sword and found nothing. He had surrendered his last blade to King Egdred. Weaponless, he faced old antagonists.

To Alban's surprise, instead of giving orders to make captives of them all, the burly sea rover crushed Alban in a bearhug and roared with hearty laughter.

"By Elaar, it's good to see you alive!"

Alban broke out of Aethelstan's damp embrace, eyes narrowed. "Did you expect to, after selling me to *her?*" He indicated Runegilda, who was wringing out her sopping clothes.

It took Aethelstan some time to connect the bedraggled woman with the elegantly hooded priestess he had last seen in Prince Phalaxsailyn's company. When he did, he said, "Understand one thing, friend: It wasn't my idea to leave you in that gutless princeling's hands, least of all for a human sacrifice. The gold he gave us for you lies under Koly's stream. Huh! You call us barbarians on Braegerd Isle, but there we feed the gods on mead and wine until they're too happy to ask for human hearts."

"Maybe not hearts, but you gave them blood enough to drink when you took the *Elaar's Eye,*" Alban retorted, remembering the fate of her crew. "You're nothing but barbarian pirates!"

"Barbarian pirates," Aethelstan repeated. He spread his hands. "That's what they call us in all the Twelve Kingdoms. Tell me, what kingdom do you call home? That sea-slug prince of Malbenu called you Sombrunian—and a prince, no less! Though if he's any gauge of the breed, princes are an overrated lot. Prince or not, when I first saw you, I *thought* you looked Sombrunian.'' Clearly the matter of Alban's royal blood was secondary to the Braegerd men.

''I am from Sombrunia,'' Alban admitted.

''A fine land. A fat land. When your women have many children, it's cause for rejoicing. When a Sombrunian sires many sons, he doesn't have to weep because there won't be land enough for them to live on when they're grown. If they should fall sick, he doesn't take their deaths as a favor from the gods. If they all die . . .''

Aethelstan's eyes misted with a memory he did not voice. He shook off his private ghosts and continued. ''The Vahrdmen fight as fiercely as we do, take as many slaves, make as many kills, but their kingdom is rich compared to ours. They don't have to fight; they do it for love of war. They have so much. All that we have—all that we love—is the sea.''

Aethelstan spoke with such sincerity that Alban could not find words to reply. As he stood there mute, the sea-thane laid one hand on his shoulder. ''Come, share our fire and your story. We're all in the same boat here. Or out of it.''

Alban hesitated. He still recalled vividly the unfortunate captain of the *Elaar's Eye*, and he was not about to trust Braegerd barbarians too soon. Yet Aethelstan's words had moved him. The Braegerd man looked scarcely older than himself, and perhaps had turned pirate because piracy was the best means of survival open to most men on Braegerd Isle.

''As I see it,'' said Aethelstan when they were all shoulder to shoulder around the fire, ''we won't starve while we stay here. The fishing's good, even when all we've got is sharpened sticks for spears. But we can't drink seawater, so thirst's the enemy here.''

''I wonder where we are?'' said Mizriel. The clouds lightened and blew away on an icy wind, clearing the sky.

''There's our problem, m'lady.'' Athelstan stirred at the fire with a stick. ''We lost our navigator when the storm took us. My men are good fellows, but not much on finding the way. We spotted the Seaman's Star just before the waves caught us, but now I'm not sure where it lies.''

''Are we in the northern or the southern lands?'' asked Osbert. ''We might even be on an island no one knows. Can anyone recognize this beach? From an old traveler's tale, maybe?'' No one did recognize it. It was a common-looking beach shaped in a rough crescent, and the sharp rocks in the breakwater were enough to deter any ship from willingly venturing to land there. A thick wall of trees hemmed the sand in on the inland side, a titan fence with gnarled roots that spread like grasping hands to the very edge of the sea. Sea birds roosted in the topmost branches.

"What trees can drink saltwater and survive?" murmured Mizriel.

A short, solid Braegerd man named Korth spoke up. "If we don't know where we are, Cap'n, we'd better learn. I'll explore a ways into the woodland. Who'll come with me?" Osbert and an amiable youth named Horgist volunteered. The three crashed through a wall of green beyond the beach.

Hours passed; they did not return. Aethelstan dispatched a second party of three to find them. Runegilda whiled away the time by broiling some fish over a small cook-fire. The sun freed itself from the clouds and shone with the faint light of fading day. They ate the fish without ceremony; then Aethelstan wiped his mouth on the back of his hand and sent two more men into the woods.

The sun touched the sea and still no one returned. Brilliant bands of purple and gold lay across the westerly sky. The forest kept its secrets.

Aethelstan strode to the edge of the forest, then back to the edge of the sea. "As if it swallowed them," he muttered. "As if the forest floor split under their feet and covered them up again."

"What will we do now?" Lymri shivered. He did not like the darksome trees. He thought he saw them creeping closer, spreading their distended roots across the sands, slowly intent on devouring the beach.

"We have no choice." Aethelstan was grim. "We must have fresh water. This time we'll all go into the forest together. We'll have to do it sooner or later. Take your spears, catch all the fish you can! We'll cook them here and take them with us tomorrow. No sense entering this unwholesome wood by moonlight."

The fleeing sun, aided by the campfire, had warmed and dried them. Men and women alike took up the makeshift spears and waded into the shallows. Mizriel stood to one side, trying to snare her catch with spells instead of spears. Her cape, spread beside the watermark, soon was well-lined with glittering, squirming, finny bodies.

"Mizriel, is this wise?" Runegilda asked. Her face was calmer than the starry evening above them. "How much true power do you have that you're so generous in spending it to catch fish?"

Mizriel looked at Runegilda with open irritation. The priestess made her feel uncomfortable, and her long silences made her feel edgy. All the time that they had been captives tied hand to hand on Morgeld's ship, Runegilda had said nothing.

"I've got more than word-magic," snapped Mizriel. "Why should I hoard it? If you have the power, there's no end to it."

"Where does the power come from?" Runegilda asked, not looking at Mizriel. "Where does it go once you cast it free? Our very lives are gifts. If our lives must end, must our powers last forever?"

"Oh, pardon *me*," Mizriel replied in mock deference. "How stupid of me to forget that Krisli himself gave you the gift of second sight, my lady. Do you see me at a loss for magic at some future time? Do I cast a spell and have only words left? Share your vision with me! Or is your gift of prophecy something else that must be hoarded?"

"My words are for your own good," said Runegilda. "Do what you will. I see the future written on the ocean sands, changing with every wave that washes over it. Even the rocks wear away at last." She stood tall against the darkening sky, leaning on her spear and looming over Mizriel, who squatted above the tidal waters weaving nets of magic. The young sorceress muttered something under her breath.

"You said?" asked Runegilda.

"Divine it! Why does it matter how I fill my net so long as we have food? You've speared three miserable fish in the time you might have caught three hundred; *if* you had any power worth speaking of! But you have none, so keep your counsels to yourself!"

"Do you think I envy your magic?"

"If you were an honest woman, you'd admit it," returned Mizriel. "But being what you are, you use the mask of wise and prudent counselor to make me hold back my enchantments."

Runegilda stooped to pick up the three fish she had caught and took them to cook over the fire. Dusk rode in on the waves of the sea. The castaways were drawn to the fire, their eyes dancing with the brightness of the flames. No one dared to turn away, not even for a moment, to peer into the blackness of the lowering trees.

They wrapped their cloaks around them and slept. The fire burned down to ashes and embers. Sleeping on the beach in midsummer is pleasant, a night of cool breezes and the drowsy warm scent of salt and seaweed. To sleep on the same beach towards harvest-time is another matter. The silky golden blanket of sand becomes a gritty nuisance, and the morning wind from the sea brings no gentle spells of distant shores, but carries a damp, fever-ridden chill to wrack the body and stun the heart.

One by one the sleepers rose and ate a dull meal of cold fish cooked the night before. After breakfast they looked reluctantly into the trackless wood.

"Well, one step starts our journey," Aethelstan said philosophically, and he drew his sword and loped into the forest with the others behind him. Marching ahead, he slashed at shadows until the blade grew too heavy to bear. He sheathed it and lumbered on.

The forest grew darker all around them; each soul sensed the strangeness of it. They walked by ones and twos, first the Braegerd men, then the women. Alban and Lymri took the rear.

"I mislike this place," said Ursula as they trudged through the brush. "I feel I ought to know its name, but I can't think of it."

"I feel the same," agreed Mizriel. "It's like a place I walked through in an awful dream once."

Runegilda asked, "Why must we know its name? How could that help us? We fear this forest. Isn't our fear enough? Must we give it a name? If a traveler is bitten by a snake, does it help him to know the name of the snake that bit him?"

"Yes," Mizriel countered. "Yes, it helps him. It may even save him! An ignorant man dies soonest. If we could remember the name of this dreary wood, we might also remember the name of any royal highways leading through it."

"Sometimes the wise man and the ignorant man are fated to die in the same hour," said Runegilda. "This is the Naîmlo Wood."

Ursula stopped in her tracks; Mizriel groaned. In all the northern and the southern lands no forest is as vast as the Naîmlo Wood. No man dares cut down a single one of the great oaks that stand in unbroken silence along the forest paths. No maiden delights to wander beneath the pleasant shade of the stout and graceful branches. Evil things are said of the Naîmlo Wood.

Many animals too shun the solemn forest. Those that do dwell there grow fat in the shelter of the trees, unmolested by men. Plump deer and chuckling white squirrels, bright pheasants and well-rounded partridges make their homes there. Wild cattle and sheep join them. Few herd-boys venture after any beast that wanders into that forest. Three kingdoms border it on the east; no common man knows what lies to its west. There are musty charts, made in the days before the gods departed, that claim to contain the secrets of the Naîmlo Wood's innermost depths and western reaches. These venerable scrolls are carefully kept in the libraries of Panomo-Midmists by scholars as wrinkled and yellow as their charges. University students who have studied the old maps under the guidance of their aged keepers have noted that the only point on which the different scrolls agree is that to the farthest west the Naîmlo Wood eventually meets the Lyarian Sea. Students who bring this to the attention of their professors, questioning the scrolls' worth, are given another semester to repeat the course and learn the value of discretion.

"No wonder my men never came back," mused Aethelstan. "There is no way out of this accursed forest."

"Let's not lose heart," suggested Lymri. "Are we really going to believe all that bogey prattle? Why, when I was a student and an amateur bard, I used to invent new legends of the Naîmlo Wood, and I'd seen the place only on a map."

"Lymri is right," said Alban. "Your men are used to the open sea. Why wouldn't they lose their way in a forest? We'll probably find them a few hundred yards ahead of us, angry and hungry. And listen! I think I hear a sound like a running river. All that fish has made me thirsty. Come along!"

What Alban heard turned out to be the feeble trickle of a woodland stream at the foot of an ancient oak. It would take forever to fill their belt-gourds from the pitiful driblet, so they passed it by.

"A better source must be nearby," said Lymri, but by nightfall they regretted having scorned the tiny stream.

"I'm thirsty!" wailed Mizriel.

"And I'm hungry," said Ursula, "so don't complain."

"Do your feet hurt as much as mine?" Lymri asked Grel. Grel nodded.

"There's a little fish left," offered Runegilda.

"You can have my share!" said Aethelstan. "If I eat another morsel of fish, I'll turn into a cod and drown on dry land." He ordered Bern and Octher to gather up deadwood and strike a fire, but the warmth and light did nothing to ease the pangs of hunger and thirst. It was an altogether unfriendly night.

Morning did not restore good spirits. Everyone was still hungry, thirsty, tired, sore, and touchy. They marched on until they encountered another streamlet, and this time they were more appreciative.

"Are we going in the right direction?" asked Ursula.

"What *is* the right direction?" answered Mizriel.

"Where are we?" wondered Aethelstan.

It grew dark again and they stopped to make camp. Here there was not so much dead wood; Aethelstan's men had to hack off living branches with their swords. The green wood burned poorly and made a paltry fire over which they had a meager dinner, the fish almost gone. Runegilda bravely toasted some of the hideous fungi that grew in the woods, and since they did her no harm the company plucked as many of them as they could get and wolfed them raw.

"We can't live on mushrooms," Lymri whispered apart to Alban. "Maybe you can live on love, but I'm going hunting."

"Love," stated Alban, "becomes unimportant when you're starving. Do you know, Lymri, she loves me? She always has. Yet from the time we were shipwrecked she hasn't come near me."

"And do you love her?"

"Once I knew I did. Once I knew I didn't. Now I don't know anything. I have to think."

"If you're going to *think* about it, you'll never know. I wish we still had our instruments. You'd let your fingers wander over the lute strings, playing the old songs of love and beauty, and then you'd know the truth."

Alban's laugh was wistful. "You're still a poet, Lymri. I've grown too old for poetry. There isn't any truth in a rhyme. The world will be saved by a sword, not a song."

"Alban," Lymri spoke gently, "growing hard and growing old are not the same as growing wise. If you only listen to reason, you lose too much. Do you love her?"

"I don't know." He shook himself as if to cast off a persistent dream. "At the moment, I love the thought of a hunt! What weapons do you have?" Lymri produced a small clasp knife. Alban searched himself and found the sailor's dagger Grel had lent him when they entered the wood. He chuckled. "There's good luck for you. No sword, no bow nor arrows; only blades too dull to wound a chipmunk. If we'd landed on civilized shores we'd be dining like kings now."

"Since when do poor sailors dine like kings?" asked Lymri, his voice a comic whine of feigned misery. "What would we steal or sell to pay for our bread?"

For answer Alban tore open the collar of his shirt. Lymri drew a sharp breath of amazement. Green forest light sparkled on a golden collar and dazzled back in rainbows from the heart of the royal diamond set there.

Alban removed the smooth metal neckband and allowed his

trusted friend to see it at close range. The little poet held it gingerly, balancing the exquisite circlet on his fingertips. The body of the necklace was one solid band of gold with a small gap at the back, like the heavy torques many fighters wore, yet the thick metal seemed to bend at a touch, flexible as the most finely linked chain. The diamond was cut in a manner Lymri had never seen before, neither round nor doubly pointed or square. Instead the facets of the stone created an illusion of ever-shifting shape, ever-increasing dazzle, a diamond seen through swiftly running water.

Lymri was almost glad to pass the stone back to Alban.

"Through all our travels," Alban said concealing the collar again, "this has never left me. You shared my life at Panomo-Midmists, but never suspected I wore it. It became a game with me to see how long I could hide it from you." He touched the base of his neck where the diamond nestled. "I'd gladly trade it for a sword now, or a bow."

"It never left you? Never? Not when the Braegerd men took you? Not when Runegilda prepared you to be Krisli's sacrifice?"

"Never," swore Alban. "Or how could it be with me now? I myself am astonished that it eluded the Braegerd men. Whatever else they are, they're thorough plunderers. I wager that when I was in their power and they saw this collar on me they thought it was too gaudy to be real. Paste and gilt done up in poor taste, typical for a wanderer to wear."

"You should be thankful they left it to you."

"Why? What shall I do with it, Lymri? Barter with the squirrels for a bushel of nuts?"

Lymri still stared at the place where he knew the necklace hung. He imagined he could see the jewel winking at him through the fabric of Alban's shirt. "How did you come by that stone in the first place, Alban? Was it a gift from your royal father?"

Alban fingered his shirt collar so that the gem caught a little light, a green beacon in the shadows. "My father, may the gods keep his spirit far from Helagarde, never knew I had this stone. I remember how I came by it well enough. It was on the day they found my elder brother's drowned body washed ashore below the cliffs. Haldin was a strong swimmer. He knew the waters' temper and he knew his own limits. No one ever expected to find him drowned. There was something unnatural about it . . ."

"Men drown," said Lymri. He did not mean it to sound heartless. The waters of river and sea called to his blood, and that call often held some hard truths: Men do drown.

"That is so, Lymri. But knowing what I know now—knowing the name of my enemy—I can't believe my brother's death was entirely mischance. When Father sent me word that my other brothers had died also, I mourned, but now I'll do more than mourn them. I know who took their lives, and I swear that if I ever get out of this forest, I will destroy Mor—"

"Hush!" Lymri waved his hands frantically. "Don't mention his name or he'll come to it!"

The Sombrunian prince did not seem to care. "Let him. I've got business with the Lord of Helagarde, in my brothers' names. Besides, if anyone would know the way out of the Naîmlo Wood, it's Morgeld."

"Well, I'd still feel better if you kept your lips clean of him," said Lymri. "Go on with your tale."

"It was after they brought Haldin's body home," Alban resumed. "I was in my chambers, preparing to depart for Panomo-Midmists. I had only happy thoughts in my head, anticipation of the carefree student's life ahead of me. Then my father came in. He told me what had happened. The news had washed something out of him, bent him, changed him. That was the first time I knew my father was old.

"He wanted me to go down and see Haldin's body. I couldn't, and I said so. He insisted, with some of his old spirit coming back to him; we quarreled. I shoved past him and ran away like a little boy. I was going to hide until Haldin was safely buried. I couldn't stand to see my brother's face and know that he was dead. I'd rather have lived a lie and told myself that he'd swum out into the Opalza Sea and Elaar herself had taken him for a second husband.

"When I was really a little boy, I'd always found the royal storerooms a good place to hide. They lie low in Castle Pibroch, near the treasury, but they're not so strictly guarded. Besides, why should the guards stop a royal prince of Sombrunia?"

"You found the stone in the treasury, then," said Lymri.

Alban shook his head. "Not even the royal princes are allowed to come and go freely in the vaults. My father's stewards and accountants would have seven kinds of conniption fit. The storerooms are another story, full of pretty things, valuble enough in their own way, but not so precious as gold or jewels."

"But *that* is a jewel," Lymri protested, jabbing a finger at the hidden diamond. "It's the all-mother of every diamond in the Twelve Kingdoms!"

"Sshh. Not so loud. There are Braegerd-bred ears nearby."

Lymri clapped a hand to his mouth and looked contrite. His expression made Alban chuckle. In a dramatic whisper the poet asked, "What was such a gem doing out of the royal treasury, in a common storeroom?"

Alban made a gesture of ignorance. "I was just as surprised to find it as you are to hear of it. I came across it . . . rather painfully. A heap of tapestries lay in the room I chose for my hideaway and I threw myself down on them. I got a blow to the stomach that felt like a giant's fist. It took the breath out of me. I found myself asprawl on a huge lump in the tapestry pile. The tousled way the weavings had been thrown down, probably by some lazy servant, cast shadows concealing the lump unless you landed right atop it." He grinned. "I did."

He went on to describe his surprise when he lifted the topmost tapestry and found a small box made of plain pine, unsanded, unpainted. "Curiosity made me pry it open. It was crudely made, a little larger than a lady's pomade jar, and when I cracked it like an egg, *this* was the yolk I found inside." He touched the cloth-covered diamond.

"Why didn't you tell your father?" Lymri asked.

"I intended to . . . but when I tried to speak to him about it, he turned from me and would not speak to me for a fortnight. He was still hurt by my refusal to look at Haldin's body. By the time he was ready to approach me again, I'd grown bitter toward him. I thought he grieved too much for his dead son and didn't care enough for the ones still living. For some time after that I played the fool, just to make him sorry. I marked the time between Haldin's death and my departure for the north by long tavern nights. I kept the gem in my pocket as a kind of talisman of defiance. I thought: If my father only knew! That made me feel wonderful."

"A strange kind of satisfaction. It doesn't sound like you, Alban."

The Sombrunian agreed. "It wasn't me, but grief attacks every man differently; it changes him. One night I showed the gem to my drinking companions. We were talking about the city craftsmen and how the old trademasters stuck to their shops till they died. They kept the younger artisans locked out even though their hands shook, their eyes failed, and they ruined more than half the raw goods their customers entrusted to them. Two of my friends had suffered at the hands of senile tailors, a third went hooded for three months after an ill-omened visit to an elderly barber, and a fourth had a vial of precious sigia-essence turned to stench by a perfumer whose nose had predeceased him.

"I defended the craftsmen. I was drunk and ready to defend anything. The men who'd had their yardgoods mangled dared me to risk something of equal value with a craftsman as old as their cursed tailors. That was when I pulled the diamond from my pocket and asked them if it was a fit subject for the test they had in mind."

"You gave it to an old jeweler to set?" Lymri shuddered at what might befall such a gem in the wrong hands.

"More. I took it to the oldest gemsmith in the city—a man called Eyndor—and I told him I wanted it not only set, but *cut* as well. It was a rough stone I found in that pine box, Lymri. I knew it for a diamond, but untrained eyes might have let it pass all those years in the storeroom as a hunk of rock crystal."

Lymri's eyes did not move from Alban's shirtfront. He ached for another full view of the stone. "At least it's plain that you won your wager. The gem is flawlessly cut and masterfully set. It's a miracle."

"I thought so too. You should have seen how old Eyndor's hands trembled when I walked into his shop and tossed the stone down before him. 'Cut this in a way worthy of the stone,' I said."

"So he did, trembling hands and all," the poet said.

Alban grew sober. "That's the strangest part of this stone's history, Lymri. As soon as Eyndor laid eyes on the stone, the palsy left his hands. I saw it. He placed the gem on a velvet pillow and studied it, then looked up at me. Old Eyndor's a living joke in our city, a man whose mind wanders so far that he claims he walked with the gods when he was young."

"Old men have fancies."

"Yes, but . . . Lymri, when he looked up at me from the gem, his eyes were sharp and clear as an archer's and he said, 'So you are the one to find me first, my lord Prince Alban? I thought it would be otherwise. Well, I am glad now to redeem the promise I made to the gods in better times. What is this stone you bring . . . or does it bring you? Will you make this the love-pledge for your chosen lady?' "

"What lady?" Lymri asked.

"That's what I said. Old Eyndor had a wheezy laugh. 'She will come, she will come.' he said. 'Her coming was not so clearly foretold as my part in it, but she will come. If I can hold Janeela's jewel in my hands again after all these years, if this stone has found you, then so will your lady, my prince. Leave it with me. I will take good care of it and prepare it for its fate. I will make it even lovelier than when it was my daughter's.' ''

Lymri looked completely bewildered. "His *daughter's?* Did the old man mean Janeela? The Silver One died so far back that—'' The poet made a helpless gesture to wave away impossibilities. "His brain must've been half rotted out with age.''

Alban opened his shirt once more to peer at the mysteriously twinkling stone. "All I know is that he called it Janeela's jewel; I don't know why. Perhaps it's cursed; many precious stones are. It must have been guarded by black magic to survive its stay in old Eyndor's shop and come back to me this beautiful.''

"I've heard of other enchanted stones,'' said Lymri. He was re- lieved to speak of legends and tall tales rather than mad old men. "The ruby of King Dramur of Paxnon that never leaves its owner until death, the opal of Heydista that fell to the king's unluckiest son. There's a song that tells of a row of statues in the Desert of Thulain. They're men of garnet, but anyone stupid enough to help himself to a chunk of the stuff might as well cut his own throat . . . *and* the throats of all his kin. Could your stone be touched by evil magic, Alban? Wouldn't Janeela's name cleanse it?''

"All I know is that it sticks to me like a burr and I have never had worse luck than in these past weeks. If we were still on the strand, I'd throw it in the water. Well, a man must live with his luck. Let's tell the others that we're going hunting.''

Mizriel was loudly opposed to the plan. "You'll only get lost, like the others.''

"At least let us go with you,'' said Aethelstan.

"Too many for a hunting party; you'd frighten the game. Don't worry; we'll mark our trail well,'' said Alban.

"Here,'' said Grel. He handed Alban his second dagger, a Brae- gerd blade of perfect weight and balance, meant for throwing. Bern made a similar gift to Lymri.

"Try that direction,'' said Runegilda. "I sense the life-call there.'' Only Ursula said nothing. Alban and Lymri bid their friends a short farewell, promised to return with some game, and struck out northeast.

"Alban,'' piped Lymri before they had quite lost sight of the camp. "Alban, someone is following us.''

Alban looked back over his shoulder. Ursula was coming through the bushes, smashing the branches aside with a sharpened quarter-staff. Lymri discreetly glided out of earshot.

"What are you doing?" demanded Alban.

"Coming with you. I've got a good eye for small game and a good throwing arm."

"We don't need you. You should stay safe in camp with the others."

"No," Ursula said, her voice dangerously low. "I didn't think you needed me." She turned to go, then suddenly whirled and flung her staff at his feet. "Have it your way, Lord Alban!" she exploded. "Who *do* you need? You've never left your princely castle or opened your eyes to the real world, not once, no matter how far you've traveled. You could build a castle out of your pride. You think I scorned you when you were a masquerade minstrel, so now it's your turn to scorn me, is that it? Love is more than just debts and payments, each lover giving only what he gets. It's a game for you, a garden pastime. Sing me a love song, I fall in love with you at once, and we can sail off to the sweet security of your enchanted castle. It doesn't work that way! If you scorn me, I still love you. If you send me to a safe haven, I'll break free and follow you. I've said I love you, but you haven't said a word; you're tired of this game; you're playing another one now. Well, I'm sick of games. Play on without me, Alban. You're a baby playing at being a man."

Ursula took two strides back toward camp, then paused, not looking back. Her words came to him faintly. "When you tire of games, I'll be waiting. Farewell." She plunged into the shadows.

Lymri whistled low when she was gone. "Now what's the answer to love-puzzles?"

"If she had said half those words to me the first night of our escape, I would have died for joy," murmured Alban. "If she would have said as much on board the *Elaar's Eye* . . . But I don't understand love anymore, Lymri; I don't understand it at all." The Sombrunian cut a broad slash on the back of a tree to mark their trail. "I am still Krisli's Fool."

Chapter XV

ALBAN STONESWORD

"This is a strange forest," whispered Lymri as he and Alban walked through the Naîmlo Wood, leaving blazes on the trees.

"A glum place," said Alban.

"Glum and more; I said strange. Beyond the edge of this forest, you know as well as I do that it's autumn, with winter coming on quick. But here I swear we're walking through branches still wearing summer greenery."

"It's your imagination. In the dark, dead leaves can fool your eye into believing they're still green."

"Yes, it's very dark. Let's turn back," said Lymri.

"I suppose we must, before it grows too dark to find our marks on the trees," agreed Alban.

A magnificent deer slipped from behind the weathered bole of a regal oak and paused with her muzzle a handspan from Alban's face. Like autumn smoke she drifted before the hunters' eyes, in no hurry to evade them, seemingly indifferent to their presence.

"Ah!" breathed Lymri, and the doe danced a pace away. "Fresh venison after fish would be welcome." Alban nodded and began to edge after the beckoning deer.

She drew away from them into the leaf-hung darkness and they followed. She was a moving blur through the leaves, a trail of game scent stronger than the smells of moss and mulching leaves rising from the forest floor.

"Lymri," whispered Alban, "I've lost sight of her. Do you still see the deer?"

"Yes, barely. It's getting harder, and—Alban, have you noticed the trees?"

"They still have leaves in autumn, I know."

"No; more than that. I think there's a new perfume coming from them, a blossom scent; a springtime smell, Alban!"

Alban strained his eyes into the dark and saw the doe pass beneath an arch of delicate white flowers. The fragrance in the air was too fresh and new for autumn. He reached up and plucked a spray of snowy flowers. "By Pibroch! There's more than oaks in this forest. I saw no other kind of tree by daylight, but here are apple blossoms in my hand."

"And here," said Lymri, picking other flowers from the trees, "is lilac! And there's linden as well, and cherry trees, and wild crabs and dogwood!" He held the bouquet to his nose for an instant, then let the flowers fall.

"Curious," said Alban. "Look, the doe stops."

"As if she were waiting. I don't like this. No normal deer would act so. She's bewitched. Let's go back."

"Too dark to find our trail now," said Alban. "Here, the deer's not bewitched, just stupid. Let's bring her down. We can still leave a trail in the dark, even if we can't follow one. If we lose the quarry, we'll return empty-handed."

"Onward," said Lymri, without enthusiasm.

The doe allowed them to come closer, then continued her calm stroll, sometimes leaping ahead out of dagger-range, sometimes browsing on tender leaves until they could catch up to her. No matter how dark the night around them grew, the doe was always visible.

"It is the moon," Alban supposed. "Or else her coat's a lighter color than a common deer's. She almost seems to glow."

"Alban!" Lymri called, and the tall Sombrunian saw that his friend had fallen far behind. He waited—and so did the doe. Lymri's legs were too short to keep up with Alban's stride.

"I can't go any further," Lymri panted. "We've marched all day on a mouthful of fish and we've trudged half the night after this beast. Go on alone if you must, but I have to rest." He sank down at the foot of a maple, crushing the dead leaves beneath him.

"Rest, Lymri," said Alban. "I'll come back for you after I've brought her down. Don't worry, I'll blaze my trail well." The doe danced away with him while Lymri fell into a deep sleep.

The little poet woke up alone with the sun high above him. The dead maple leaves of his mattress were a glorious scarlet in the sunshine. The foliage around him blazed with the flames of high autumn.

"Do the seasons themselves wander lost here?" Lymri asked. His voice went echoing piteously among the towering trees. He searched for Alban's trail.

It was not to be found. Lymri ranged a growing circle from the maple tree, examining each trunk for the knife-blaze Alban said he would leave, but he found nothing. "The trail must be here," he said. "Twice, before I fell asleep, I heard his knife scraping bark. And where—*where* are the marks I know the two of us made yesterday?" He made a wider circle, finding nothing but the unscathed trunks of timeless trees.

"I am lost," Lymri told the watching elms and maples. "And Alban is lost too. Our trail's gone, the gods know how. If we ever find each other again, it will be purest luck. And if we ever find the others—" A sweet, sharp, slender face crowned with a fall of whitewater hair rose in his mind's eye.

"Oh, Mizriel!" he cried aloud. Not even an echo came back to comfort him. "Why did I waste my time debating points of love with Alban and never tell you—? Too late . . . too late . . ." Sadly, aimlessly, Lymri wandered in the forest.

The doe suddenly took it into her head to acknowledge that she was being hunted. She broke into a long, lovely, leaping run that left Alban breathless but not spent. His legs were almost as long and swift as hers. Low branches hindered him, sending showers of withered leaves swirling around his head. Then the leaves were gone, and thin black branches clawed at hunter and prey. Dead logs lay in their path, rotting under piles of brown and crumbling leaves.

Alban's legs grew heavy and he thought he couldn't run another pace. Ahead, he saw the deer also slow and stop, her sides heaving. He drew Grel's dagger and flung it at his quarry. It struck the deer hard in the right shoulder and she fell.

She did not move at all when he came near, and he saw that he had killed her. For a moment he was puzzled; the dagger was so small, the deer so big, the blade hardly long enough to reach the heart, yet here the deer lay dead. But then he felt too hungry to question good luck. Day paled the sky as he knelt to dress the dead deer. Its coat was creamy white with a pale trace of almond brown, and very soft. Alban grasped the dagger's hilt and pulled it free. Like

melting snow, the creature faded into the earth, and Alban could
only stare at the wasted winter grass where the deer had lain.

"You lose your quarry just when I find mine. Greetings, Prince.
We have been parted too long."

Alban leaped up and uttered a glad cry to see the wild, black
whiskers and the sage, bespectacled eyes of his father's old counselor, Paragore-Tren. "The deer was of your sending!"

The wizard raised one hand, disclaiming the illusion. "Not mine,
but answering my purpose. The Naîmlo Wood breeds phantoms the
way other woods breed wildflowers."

"Why do you walk in this unhealthy wood?" asked Alban. The
wizard took him by the arm and led him through the trees into a
small clearing. Here a green kettle hissed over a fragrant fire while
a bony, dun-colored mare went about the business of making tea.

"This wood is where I live," said the mage. "Did you think I
flew into the clouds every time I left your father's castle?"

"My father." Alban was suddenly grim. "Lymri told me."

"Lymri wanted to tell you. It seems you are a king now, my boy.
Sit and refresh yourself, Your Majesty, and we'll discuss the ruling
of your kingdom."

"I can't," said Alban. "I can't stay. I left my friends behind.
They'll wonder what's become of me. Send me back to them!"

"Why can't you go back yourself?" The wizard arched one sooty
eyebrow as he poured the tea. A man wearing the bright, loose robes
of the southern lands came to bow humbly before Paragore-Tren
and return two empty plates to the fireside. An insignificant white
dog wagged its tail at the edge of the clearing, then bounded into
the forest. The man followed after.

"I'd swear I've seen that man and his pet before this," said Alban. "How do you happen to have visitors when no one dares to
enter the Naîmlo Wood?"

"Oh, people come here. That fellow, for instance, is an itinerant
player. His name's Mustapha and he comes from the southern lands,
like you: Vair, to be precise. They're very discreet in Vair. He
doesn't want to eavesdrop on our conversation, but I wouldn't put
it past that dog of his . . . Well, never mind them. You've heard
wrongly about this forest. People *do* enter the Naîmlo Wood. They
never talk about it if they escape, that's all; one of the woodland
spells. And the woods are lovely—endless variety, really. Just look
around you."

Alban's eyes circled the clearing. Spring flowers, summer green, autumn glory and winter bleakness formed the walls of the wizard's encampment.

"This is the very center of the forest," explained Paragore-Tren. "The seasons change, but at the same time you'll find all the seasons happening at once, in different parts of the wood. No man can leave a trail on these trees; the wounded bark heals swifter than thought. You could just as well try to blaze a trail on the sea."

The mare trotted up behind the wizard and rested her muzzle on his shoulder. "Shall I set another place for dinner?" she asked. Alban started.

"Don't be afraid." The wizard laughed. "I made her speak so that I could always have some companionship here. You can't depend on visitors. Haven't you sometimes seen me ride her when I came to your father's court?"

Alban stroked the mare's silky muzzle cautiously. "I always wondered why a wizard didn't ride a more impressive horse—or a dragon—begging your pardon, ma'am," he added hastily to placate the mare.

She whickered laughter. "He'll make a diplomat yet, master," she said. She breathed softly in his ear and brushed his neck with her satin lips. Alban scratched her chin and thought that he had never felt anything so soft and fine as a horse's muzzle; hers was mousegray and smelled of fresh grass. She closed her eyes and permitted him to pat her.

They sat down to a modest meal. There was venison stew that came from real deer, not wizards' sendings, and it was serviceably seasoned with wild onions and garlic. Flatbread baked in the campfire ashes sopped up the gravy nicely, with herbal tea to wash it all down. After a diet of cold fish and raw mushrooms, it tasted divine to Alban.

The mare served them, sometimes carrying the teapot in her mouth, sometimes tottering on her hind legs while balancing a tray on her forelegs.

When he had finished eating, the wizard lit a green lacquer pipe of Vairish design and leaned back against the bole of a springtime tree.

Though he was reluctant to disturb Paragore-Tren, thoughts of his friends' plight pressed closer in on Alban the higher the sun hung in the sky. Wherever they were, they were hungry, footsore, and probably worried about him.

"Paragore-Tren." Alban tugged at the mage's sleeve. The wizard's black eyes glittered like volcanic glass behind the gold-rimmed spectacles. He looked displeased.

"What do you want? More food? Here!" he called to the mare. "Get him more!"

"No, please, not food," said Alban gently. "A little help is all. Could you use your arts to guide me back to my friends?"

Paragore-Tren grumbled and knocked the ashes from his pipe. Leaning across his bent knees he favored Alban with a basilisk glare. "My lord Prince Alban," he said slowly, "I have not the faintest intention of helping you. Your father entrusted the news of his death to me, I've seen to it you were informed, and my obligation to you's at an end. Death pays all debts. Why should I waste my spells to help you find your friends? Who are they, anyway? Name them!"

"Lymri—"

"A man without past or parents! A copper-poor poet who's brought you nothing but trouble." The wizard laughed scornfully.

"Ursula—"

"Phaugh, the cause of it all. If you hadn't been besotted with her, you'd be safe on the Sombrunian throne now. You don't still love her, do you? Just as well if you didn't. If you think the Council would ever consent to a queen who turns into a bear willy-nilly—"

"Mizriel," said Alban, his voice growing tense.

"Yes, yes, prides herself on being quite the accomplished sorceress. Gives herself airs, like her sister."

"Runegilda of Malbenu."

"Risking your neck for the woman who almost cut out your heart? Oh, you *are* a sensible man!" The wizard patted Alban's head with the same patronizing smile petty nobles give their jesters.

"And Aethelstan and his men," Alban finished, his face growing hot.

"The best for last, a host of Braegerd pirates. So those are the fine friends I'm supposed to help you find again? Let the forest have them! I'll cast a spell to send you back to Castle Pibroch, and that's all."

"You're not sending me anywhere," snapped Alban, rising quickly. "Keep your spells and keep your help! Death cancels all debts, as you say. You were my father's friend; you're not mine. And so I'll thank you not to criticize the friends I do have."

Alban turned his back on the wizard, wanting nothing more than to rush out of the enchanted clearing and never see him again. Paragore-Tren casually raised one hand and the trees clamped together into a solid wall of wood too impenetrable for a worm to wriggle through.

"I'll be the one to tell you when you can go," he said, still with that easy smile. "Sit down, Alban." Alban folded his arms, silently refusing. Paragore-Tren sighed deeply and hauled himself up. "You are stubborn; a sure sign of childishness. Is that what we've got here? A child who's going to pout because he doesn't get his own way? By all the gods and powers, princeling, you'll listen to my advice, and you'll take it!"

He flung down the green pipe and it exploded at Alban's feet into a roaring wall of flame. The prince shielded his face, but still the awful heat seared at him. The wizard chuckled.

"Have any of your friends *that* kind of power? Can any of them do you all the good I can?" He lowered his voice persuasively. "Your father would have been nothing without my help and advice, and he ruled a peaceful Sombrunia. Times have changed, Alban, but there's no reason your land couldn't enjoy peace throughout anything that might affect the other kingdoms."

Alban regarded the mage suspiciously. "Morgeld is free; you know there won't be peace for anyone now. Why should Sombrunia be spared?"

"Don't concern yourself with it, my lord," purred Paragore-Tren. He flickered his fingers like snakes' tongues and a golden vision of Castle Pibroch hovered in the air between them. "As I said, times change, and wise men learn to change with them. I'll send you back to your friends on one condition."

"Go on," said Alban evenly. His lips were white.

"New times call for new alliances, and the best alliance for your kingdom is clear. Give him the woman he wants. There are more than enough high-born ladies for you to choose from afterward. She'll be taken from you in any case; you might as well acquiesce, and get on Morgeld's good side. The perfect wedding gift: a bride."

Before he entirely realized what he was doing, Alban's fist lashed out and struck the wizard down. Yellow fire glowed behind the clear spectacles. "Do you dare . . ." hissed the wizard. He launched fire from his hands. It crackled blue across the clearing.

Alban dodged and felt a bolt of heat streak past his right ear. He was as good as weaponless, and ordinary weapons were useless against a mage. He braced himself for Paragore-Tren's next attack, and this time when the fires flew he threw himself under them in a desperate leap to stop the wizard bare-handed. He landed with a thud on empty ground and heard Paragore-Tren's laughter.

"What did you intend to do, my lord? Strangle me?" he asked. He loomed tall and forbidding as the trees surrounding him. "Well?"

"He isn't going to have her," Alban began. "Not even for my kingdom. And don't think I'm protecting her out of love, wizard. I'd do the same if you told me it was one of the Braegerd men as the price of my land. I'm not buying a throne with anybody's life."

"Except your own," said Paragore-Tren curtly.

"No," said the prince. "I don't believe I'll even have that much left to offer now. But if I had a sword in my hands—" Alban stopped. The wizard's hand was extended at his heart. He waited for the death-blow.

"You are your father's son," said Paragore-Tren, and his face lightened with amusement. "Well, are you going to lie there all day? Take my hand and get to your feet, Alban. We have important things to discuss."

"What?" asked Alban, bewildered. He let the wizard haul him upright and marveled when the mage laid one brown hand on his shoulder.

"What do you mean, *what*, eh? You're trying to flatter me. I had no idea I was so convincing an actor. It must've rubbed off from my recent guests, though I think the dog's a better player than his master. Either that, or you're still slightly gullible. Well, that doesn't matter. A little gullibility's good in a king, or so his subjects say."

Alban looked wounded. "I don't think I'm gullible."

"Would you prefer it if I called you honest? Honorable? Loyal? You are all of these, Alban of Sombrunia. A man who keeps faith with his friends is hard to find, but one who stands up for his enemies is a rare creature."

"You mean the Braegerd men," said Alban. "They . . . they don't seem so evil as when I first met them."

"A good man can do an awful lot of wickedness. He'll have his reasons, and to him they'll make sense and seem good. Braegerd men are like Malbens, Vahrdmen, even Sombrunians: they're human beings." The wizard winked. "I can't say the same for your friend Lymri."

"Watch what you say about—"

"Peace." Paragore-Tren held up his hand. "It wasn't an insult.

You're to be king of Sombrunia, and Sombrunia does well in the sea trade. I just thought you might care to know that you've got a very special sort of friend who can bring even better luck to your ships.''

Alban wrinkled his nose. *"Lymri?"*

The wizard guffawed. "Now who's insulting the little poet? Yes, Lymri Riverborn. That's a proper name for him, more than he knows. You see, he's not human; he's one of the waterfolk.''

The prince's jaw dropped. "He was a foundling . . .''

Without knowing it, Paragore-Tren echoed Runegilda's words to Mizriel. "The waterfolk have their different races and kingdoms, wars and treacheries, just as we do. Your friend is a refugee from one such war, although he doesn't know it. He was an infant when his kingly clan was destroyed by their enemies, but he was saved from the general slaughter and left on the banks of the Salmlis.'' The wizard smirked. "Our copper-poor poet's as royal as you, in his way.''

"Lymri . . . one of the waterfolk?'' Alban struggled with the new thought. "He *has* always said how much he loves the waters. He claims they call to him.''

"Then you can tell him how right that call has always been when you see him again.''

"And tell him that his family—his blood kin—are all dead? Murdered?'' Alban frowned. "Maybe bring more danger on him than I've already done, if his enemies still live? No, Paragore-Tren; when it's time for him to understand the river's call, he'll do it. Until then, he's happy enough thinking that he's human. Can't we let him be?

The wizard could not hide the serene joy Alban's words brought him. "May the gods favor you, Alban. With love like yours in the world, it can't be long before Sarai All-Mother herself returns to walk with her mortal children. Pay heed now. There is something I have to give you, Alban, and I trust you'll find it more welcome than the so-called advice I gave you a minute ago when I tested you.'' He dipped his hand into his nighted robes and plucked out a smooth blob of clear glass shaped like a teardrop. "The prize, my lord prince,'' he said, handing it over.

"What is this? What are you talking about?'' asked Alban. The glass droplet seemed to weep in his hand.

"I've heard it called many names since the day I first carved it out of a block of northern ice from the lands of magic,'' said the wizard. "Mostly, though, it is called the Kari-Ta: the Mirror of the

Heart, in northern speech. I molded ice into glass clear enough for a man to look into the crystal and read his heart with his mind. For you, my prince, who in spite of all your songs and poetry still believe that the human brain rules alone, it may be your salvation.'' He closed Alban's fingers around it. Alban felt an icy chill followed by a growing warmth that spread up his arm and found the center of his body.

"But I still don't understand," he protested.

"You will," promised the wizard. "And now take the path I'll open for you through the winter trees. This prize I've given you is the first, not the last. It fell to my lot to sound out your heart, but others have different tests in store for you. You are the last of the royal Sombrunian line, the line fated to overthrow Morgeld. It may be that your blood will be his doom, in time, as it was foretold. A prophecy does not always run as straight as we'd like it, and it can be twisted. You are the vessel of prophecy, and so you must be sounded to see whether you are strong enough for what lies ahead. The decision to test you was not mine alone.''

Alban thought of the vision that had come to Malbenu Isle in a sudden storm. "Do you speak of Ayree, the Prince of Warlocks?" he asked, already knowing the answer.

"And others. It's hard for mages to sit back and wait, watching. At least we can do this much for you, help you learn what you are and the limitations bounding you, heart, soul, and mind. It's not much, but it's something; something hard. If you'd rather turn back . . .''

Alban's smile flashed bravely. "What? And lose my reputation for stubbornness?''

Paragore-Tren squeezed Alban's hand. "Go now. You will find your friends at the Inn of the Virgin's Delight.''

Alban paused at the edge of the clearing where a narrow path now showed plainly through the bare silver-gray branches. "Will I see you again?" he asked.

"In Sombrunia," said the wizard, "if ever. Farewell.''

The path took Alban out of sight of the wizard's camp almost immediately. Paragore-Tren sighed and curled his fingers. The trees drew back together behind the Sombrunian prince.

As the wizard bent to retrieve his green pipe, he heard a judicious cough behind him. The Vairish traveler and his dog stood at the edge of the camp.

"How much did you hear?" Paragore-Tren asked casually.

"Master of all power, at a word from you I will become as deaf as a snake and as dumb as—"

"—a dog? Or maybe a mare?" He enjoyed Mustapha's reaction. "My colleague Ayree has told me much about you, Mustapha."

Mustapha started. "Lord of the unseen, your fabulous steed has the gift of human speech, but I have the art of human discretion. If I *had* violated your generous hospitality so blatantly as to overhear your private conversation with that young man, where would be the harm? I would not betray him. We have the same enemies, he and I."

"Enemies whose names you . . . guess?"

The wandering player bowed very low. The small white dog likewise made an enchanting obeisance to the black-haired wizard, wagging his tail wildly as he ground his belly into the dirt.

Paragore-Tren squatted to tickle the dog's back. "Let's not play another scene, Mustapha. I'm still recovering from that little set piece with Alban. I know what brought you into the Naîmlo Wood."

"A mischance," the player said offhandedly. "A bad set of directions on the road. I was bound for Leyaeli—"

"You were bound for Helagarde. Don't try to deceive me, Mustapha. Save your cleverness for another day, when it may save your life. You pursue Tor, Morgeld's servant."

Mustapha and his dog exchanged a somber look that seemed entirely human on both sides. "Tor was once a duke's son," said the performer. "My friends and I entertained at his father's court. There was a lady among us who was so kind and beautiful . . . she was too beautiful."

The dog raised his muzzle and gave a plaintive howl.

"Tor desired her, she refused him, and so he contrived to carry her off by force after the troupe left his father's protection. He and his men overtook them on the road and killed anyone who would defend her." The pain of recounting the tale made Mustapha squeeze his eyes shut, trying to erase the memory of his comrades lying dead on a moonlit road. "But she was too brave for him. She took her own life before she would let him touch her."

Paragore-Tren's voice was tender. "And you survived."

"By fortune only. I was waiting for them farther down the road. We were all going to sail for Malbenu Isle. By the time I came looking for them, it was all over." Mustapha's teeth ground together. "I will kill Tor."

The wizard inclined his head. "It strikes me, Mustapha, that you and I might make an amiable bargain. Do you see this?" He opened one hand. A smooth green stone lay there, cool to the touch, its surface covered with sleek bumps like warts on a toad's back. "This is the waystone of Naîmlo Wood," Paragore-Tren said. "Be guided by it, and it will take you wherever you want to go."

Mustapha folded his hands across his chest and bowed deeply a second time. "This gift, Beneficent One, is too magnificent, too lavish, and I am too unworthy to accept it."

"In other words, you want to know where the hook is, eh?" The wizard stilled Mustapha's incipient protests. "There *is* a hook. If I gave you this stone, I'd have you use it to round up as many of the wanderers in this wood as possible. It's within the waystone's power to find them, never fear. Take them along with you."

"Take them . . . where? Master, I am bound for Helagarde! I go there for my own satisfaction, but I would not compel others to—"

"Take them along," the wizard repeated. "Do this, and you will find you've done more to avenge your friends than you might have done alone."

Mustapha bowed yet again, accepting the terms. The white dog at his feet cocked his head, as if measuring the trustworthiness of this wizard.

Paragore-Tren massaged the beast behind the ears until all doubts vanished in a burst of sensual enjoyment. "Don't worry, little friend," he said as he found all the best places to scratch. "I wouldn't do anything to harm your master. You see, I need his help. Yes! A wizard needs the help of an ordinary man; even a witch-king must rely on mortals now." He looked up to where Alban's path had once cut through the trees.

Alban heard the dun mare whicker once behind him, but he never looked back, as if mistrusting the path that Paragore-Tren had carved for him. Clouds hid the sun and the sky grew milky. A few flakes of wet snow fell and clung to the empty branches.

Alban grew tired. He had marched long, and since the path showed no sign of vanishing, he decided it would be safe to take a short rest. Sitting at the foot of an elm, he pillowed his face against the rough bark and let sleep come.

Through his lowered lids he dreamed that the forest mists were slowly melting into golden light, the whole wood suffused with clear radiance. His soul tugged against the pull of his body and seemed to float free, hovering near to gaze down at the empty shell. From this vantage he watched himself asleep, and suddenly he realized that he was not alone. Very timidly a golden-haired child peeped around the trunk of the elm tree, saw the sleeping prince, and laughed gladly before ducking back out of sight. The baby-face appeared again around the other side of the tree, three other naked babes with him. Gently they touched the empty body and it vanished, but Alban knew he was still there. The children sensed him, too.

They ran to his outstretched arms, seized him by the hand, and dragged him after them while the forest faded around them and the trees flattened to the dull vastness of the Dunenfels Plain, east of Sombrunia. They formed a dancing circle, sparked by the rising silver light of a full moon, and as Alban let himself be whirled around and around in a dance that dizzied his head and lightened his heart, a voice from beyond the moon whispered in his ear, "These are your sons."

The voice turned to a promise, a vision that gave him a choice. He might stay here forever, dancing in the moonlight, playing like a child with his children, none of them ever growing old, none ever losing the others, or . . .

He was an old, old man seated in his father's place on the great throne of Sombrunia. The queen's throne beside him was empty and a messenger had come with news that his son was dead. Tears flowed thick and slow from the old man's eyes for the son he had lost, and also for other deaths he could only vaguely remember.

Brusquely he dropped the small hands that held him. The four naked children clung to each other in the moonlight, then tried to draw him back into the enchanted dancing circle again, but he pulled away. He felt the wrenching in his heart, and yet he turned his face to the far mountains beyond which lay his kingdom, and—he knew this certainly—his lonesome death. Deliberately, he walked away.

The Dunenfels Plain and the moonlight disappeared. He sat at the foot of the elm tree with the children ranged before him, four pairs of his own eyes staring at him sadly. "Father," one said timorously, "Father, why?"

"My beautiful son," cried Alban, holding the child's hands tenderly. "Understand, try to understand. If I were anything else than what I am, I'd gladly give up everything to spend eternity with you. But I can't. You are my boys, and I may lose you painfully someday for this decision, but before that black day comes, I pray to all the gods that you'll understand why I can't abandon my land or my people.'' He gathered all four of them close, their gilt hair shining, soft as flowers. ''I never asked to be a king, but if I must be, I have more children than only you to look after. But never any I'll love more.''

His arms were empty, the children gone. He stumbled to his feet and felt a weight dragging at the back of his neck, then saw the golden mantle, colored like their hair.

The second prize is won, creaked the windblown branches of the elm tree. Sorrowful-eyed, Prince Alban resumed his path through the forest.

The wind blew stronger, and a distant rumble of thunder shook the snow from the trees. The golden mantle whipped like a castle banner in the gust. Without warning a jag of lightning slashed down to split an oak not three paces in front of Alban. Instinctively he raised his arms to shield his face and sprang back.

A naked man brandishing a silver sword leaped shrieking from the smoking cleft and hurled himself at Alban. The prince gaped, and received a buffet from the creature's pale brown leather shield. The white sword descended like a plummeting hawk. Alban rolled aside, hampered by his mantle, and received a slash in the arm. His opponent gave a hoarse cry of triumph and bore down on him. Desperately Alban cast about for something to use as a weapon, and his fingers closed on the thick club of a lightning-felled branch.

Sword against club they fought. Alban had no idea how long the battle lasted. At first all he tried to do was keep his feet and stay alive, using the club to parry the hack and thrust of sword. Inwardly he prayed that the slim blade would hit the thick tree limb at a bad angle and snap, but it was a supple piece of tempered steel, lithe and flexible. It danced through the stormdark air like a captive streak of lightning and pierced Alban's guard. A thread of blood trickled down Alban's thigh.

The second wound seemed to wake him. It enraged him, and suddenly he was no longer merely trying to counter attacking moves, but attacking on his own, using the felled branch as sword and quarterstaff, striking the naked swordsman on ribcage, hip, and leg, breaking through his guard again and again, pressing him backward toward the cloven tree.

Sweat streamed down the naked man's body. His teeth shone silver as his sword, and his lower lip was bloody where he'd bitten himself. Alban kept up a constant hail of blows, and he was stopping fewer and fewer of them with his strangely covered shield. It was Alban's turn to laugh, forcing his enemy to give ground, remembering all the old martial skills he had been taught so long ago in Sombrunia.

His laughter drove his foe to recklessness. He raised the silver sword high, a chopping blow meant to split the prince in two. But it was also the most foolish move a swordsman could make, a maneuver that left his guard down, his body open, and Alban was too quick to be taken with such a clumsy ploy, too smart not to profit by his enemy's stupidity. With one smooth move he dodged the blow, then dealt a sidelong smash of his own that would have caved in a mortal man's ribcage. The silver sword went flying free. It melted into drops of brightness in midair.

Giving a low, squalling cry of despair, the naked man backed into the open wooden heart of the tree, and when Alban brought his club down for a final blow, he felt it reverberate against a sealed and unscorched tree. On the ground among the roots of the oak the brown shield waited. Alban slipped it onto his left arm and went his way.

The third prize is won, hushed the falling grains of snow.

The snow grew deeper as Alban continued, pulling at his feet in drifts, weighing down his steps. He lost his sense of time and wondered whether the gathering darkness was another storm coming on or the first hours of dusk. The trees appeared to ripple and part like the folds of a velvet curtain. The curtain wavered once, then closed against him. He could not find his path through the trees.

As Alban stood there shivering, he became aware of a small light approaching. He thought of other travelers, as lost as he was, and went toward it, but what he took to be the lantern of a snow-weary wanderer soon grew so large and brilliant to his sight that he wondered if there were anything on earth that could shine so brightly.

And the light became a lady, the most beautiful he had ever seen, clothed like a star and with a star bound to her brow. In her hands she held a sword. She held it toward him pommel first, an offering, and she smiled.

"This is the black sword," she said, her voice full of nameless music. "The black sword, one of the Three. Long life to the man who holds it, and the saving of the world. It is yours, Lord Prince

Alban; yours for the taking, as am I. My kingdom lies beneath the forest floor, at the warm heart of the earth. Follow me, take the sword, wield it well, and you shall sit by my side on an ageless throne and rule the riches of the world. Your life will outlast even the sword if you will be my king.''

He drifted toward her, drawn by the sleepy melody of her words. By the lady's silvery aura he saw that the sword she offered was unlike other swords, crafted not of metal, but of black stone. He stretched out his hand to touch it and she clasped it with her own.

''I will come with you,'' he muttered. The lady laughed.

''And what will you bring me as a bride-gift, my lord?'' she demanded. ''A pretty toy?'' His hands went slowly to his throat where the stone old Eyndor had set still hung, but then something, some feeling his mind could not define, made his hands instead thrust themselves into the fold of his tunic where the wizard's crystal nestled. He held it high, and by the lady's light he saw a face shine from the depths of the teardrop: Ursula's face.

A heaviness left him as his fingers closed securely over the Kari-Ta, and he felt its warmth flood up to his heart. Giving the star-bright lady a smile, he knelt before her reverently.

''My lady, another man must share your throne, and your sword as well. I won't break faith with my heart a second time. Forgive me if I offend.''

The lady bade him rise. ''So at last,'' she said. ''At last you have come. The sword is yours; take it. You are chosen to have it. You and your sons are the ones whose lives are the threads of the prophecy, the end of the Evil One. King and hero, father of heroes, bards, and kings: Alban Stonesword. The final prize is won.'' A wind sweet with all the scents of summer whirled the snow up around her in a sparkling cloud, and Alban found himself looking through naked branches at a single luminous star.

Chapter XVI

MASPA OF
WIGGINSDALE

The Inn of the Virgin's Delight was a small, trimly made cottage, white-plastered, well-timbered, fine-thatched. It stood in a bright clearing in the western reaches of the Naîmlo Wood. Four long benches leaned against the outer wall, catching the sun, while a stone well with red roof, shiny bucket, and squeaky pulley stood conveniently close to the front door. Behind the inn was a dovecote, a vegetable patch, and a cream-colored milch cow.

Aethelstan thought he was seeing a mirage when he first laid eyes on the inn. The black-haired, snap-eyed wench drawing water might have been a monster, judging by how he goggled at her. She in turn took one look at him and his party and fled into the house.

"We've done it!" cried Aethelstan, striding forth to conquer the clearing in the name of Braegerd Isle. "We're out of the Naîmlo Wood!"

"No, we're not," said Mizriel. "Not yet. Look." It was true. Beyond the inn the trees continued.

The bear bleated agreement. "We should never have followed that stag. We'll never see Lymri and Alban again. How will they find us here?"

"My lady"—Octher bowed to the bear—"I blazed our trail when we followed the beast, and your friends can follow the trail to us here. But where has that stag gotten to?"

"I wonder that myself," said Aethelstan. When the regal quarry had presented itself to them, they could not resist pursuing it. The lofty span of its snowy antlers tempted them on, and hunger made them lose their heads. And now the stag had vanished.

"We'll be fine here," said Grel. "We've lost the stag. We've lost our comrades. But I won't lose a meal at this tavern. Let's go in."

"But do they serve bears?" wondered Ursula.

"That depends. Do you have fleas?" came a deep, cheery voice from the tavern door.

The innkeeper waddled out to welcome them. He was a large man who looked readier to laugh than cry at anything life might throw him. "I am Maspa of Wigginsdale. We serve all who come this way."

With bits of jokes and snatches of old songs he ushered them inside. A good fire crackled on the hearth. Dry, simple clothing was laid out on benches. The common room was empty except for the snap-eyed wench and a tall, handsome young man who sat glumly over a flagon of ale and took no notice of the newcomers.

"Yonder chap," explained Maspa, "is your fellow lodger. A good man and a brave knight, Sir Errod of Leyaeli."

"How do," Sir Errod said listlessly.

"The wench is my daughter, Brasberia the Silent. Go up and change into fresh clothes, then come have some supper."

Brasberia set ale and a homely stew on the table, preceded by soup and followed by pudding. She was quick and competent, hesitating only a moment when faced with the problem of whether to serve the bear at the table or on the floor.

"Here," said Mizriel, tying a napkin around Ursula's neck and helping her balance her furry bulk on the bench. The bear ate from a bowl as daintily as she could, and drank deeply from a wide-mouthed tankard.

Hunger and thirst satisfied, Octher asked, "Innkeeper, your sweet daugher—was she mute from the cradle?"

"Sweet?" wondered Maspa. "Why, she spoke as well as any, only twenty times as much. A good tavern wench is sociable, but too much chatter drives off business. When I kept the inn at Wigginsdale, her tongue scared away our custom, so we had to move on, then move again. That tongue of hers was a whip to drive us! In Leyaeli, her blither-blather kept even a man dying of thirst from our door. Only Sir Errod came, either in love with Brasberia or eager to go deaf. Well, we couldn't live on his love, and with no business we faced debt and starvation. I became a desperate man, and

I acted it, plunging into the Naîmlo Wood one day in the hopes of opening a small inn within its borders, an inn men would be so glad to find that they would not mind Brasberia.

"But we ourselves grew lost in the accursed forest. We wandered for days, we grew hungry, we thought we were going to die. Happily, we met a wise man of the woods, a wizard who makes his camp hereabouts."

"A wizard!" cried Mizriel. "Can you take us to him?"

"Ah, no, not unless he wished it. And he never shall. He was kind to us when he found us, feeding us, making us comfortable. He called us welcome company. Then Brasberia started to talk." Maspa gave his girl a hard look; she stuck out her tongue in reply. "Bed to breakfast, breakfast to bed, nothing but nitter-natter until she drove away even his wizardly patience. He lifted speech from her tongue then and there."

"Is there no hope?" asked Aethelstan.

"Oh, there may be." Maspa was evasive. "He said he might break the spell one day. He set us up in business here by way of consolation, to give us a place to wait."

"For what?" asked Grel.

"The . . . ah . . . cure." Maspa hesitated. "Truly, I'm in no hurry for it," he added in a lower voice. "We're comfortable here, and—"

"And your daughter is easier to bear without speech?" suggested Ursula.

"Bear, mind your insinuations! You speak of the woman I love!" Sir Errod jumped up from his place and tried to draw his rusty blade. The Braegerd men overpowered him, disarmed him, and returned him to the table. With a melancholy look in his blue eyes, he returned to his ale.

Ursula felt bound to apologize. Touching his hand with her wet snout she said, "I'm sorry. My sister is a sorceress. Can she help Brasberia?"

"I don't know, bear."

"My name is Ursula. I'm enchanted."

"Sir Errod; delighted. The cure is locked in her father's cruel heart. The wizard gave him the cure; he lies if he says differently. But he will not give it to her. So I, who followed her into the Naîmlo Wood, go every day in search of the wizard's camp; each day I return, a failure. My poor steed has died long since, so I explore the woods on foot. It's time I made a sortie now. Excuse me, gentle-folk.''

Sir Errod rose and went to a side cupboard where an ill-kept suit of armor hung. He donned it, clanked to the door, and there tied himself by the waist to a reel of thin rope attached to the jamb, a precaution against getting further lost.

"Poor man," said Mizriel. "Spells to make the dumb speak are so easy! A bit of mallow root, a bulrush heart, a drop of essence of aralda, the whole served in a quart of hot red wine, well spiced, and speech returns in most cases."

Brasberia the Silent overheard and dropped her tray. She ran from the common room in a swirl of petticoats. Maspa watched her with a sad eye, then spoke to Mizriel.

"Ah, lady, why did you have to be so chatty? The recipe you named sounds like the one the wizard gave me, saving the mulled wine."

"It's not needed for the cure, but it makes the other ingredients go down easier," admitted Mizriel.

"And who'll make it easier for me, trapped in this blessed inn all day, forced to hear Brasberia's constant gizzling? Answer me that, madam!"

"Well, Maspa, if Sir Errod marries your daughter, he'll have to listen to her chatter, not you. And if he doesn't, an infusion of convaleria, mesereon, and calaminth taken daily in a pint of the fermented and distilled essence of potatoes will dull your ears pleasantly and make her easier to live with."

"By the gods, I'll reel in Sir Errod at once and *make* him marry her!" shouted Maspa. The smell of mulled wine wafted from the kitchen. The innkeeper waddled to the door to tug at Sir Errod's string and bring him home, then paused on the threshold, never touching the string, and gave a low whistle.

"Ambra give you grace, my lord," he said, kneeling.

Alban—a golden mantle falling from his shoulders, a brown shield on one arm, a black sword in his hand—entered the Inn of the Virgin's Delight. The Braegerd men, the women, the bear—all came forward with glad cries of welcome. But as they drew nearer, something about him made them pause and lower their eyes.

Alban threw off his mantle, dropped his shield. Carefully he laid down his sword and without a word embraced the clumsy, fubsy, furry bear that stared at him in fright. He kissed the hairy snout, hugged the cumbersome paws, and smiled when snout, paws, and form changed.

"Alban," she said softly.

"My love," he answered. "Always my love. I am not Krisli's Fool any longer. I am master of my own heart again, and I share it only with you. As I pray we shall also share the Sombrunian throne, my queen."

"If I share with you the only throne I ever thought worth having," said Ursula, "you can keep your gilded chair." She rested her head gratefully on his shoulder.

He gently stepped away from her to reach inside the collar of his shirt. From his fingers hung a band of gold set with a radiant gemstone. He held it high, and its brilliance seemed to fill the small inn.

"By this token I, Prince Alban of Sombrunia, pledge faith to the lady Ursula of Norm. Let no man challenge me." He slipped the collar around her neck. Aethelstan sent up a wild cheer.

Runegilda stepped forward, her hands before her like a blind woman's, as if she wished to warm them at the fire in the heart of the jewel. Shatterings of rainbow light danced across her cheeks. "I feel the traces of the man who shaped this stone," she murmured.

Alban looked puzzled. "Old Eyndor cut it for me, Runegilda," he said. "He's half daft, but he still has all his skill with gems. It's a good job, but not—"

"You don't know," the priestess whispered, and as her hands glided back and forth before the gem at Ursula's neck, a silvery light played over them. "You call him Eyndor, you call him old and daft, but age is only a mask, jewels are only part of all he shapes and has shaped in his time. Unknown to Morgeld, Eyndor's hands worked the very chains that bound the dark one for so many years. And the work of his body was Janeela."

"Janeela's jewel," Lymri said in a hushed voice.

"His daughter," Alban murmured. "Just as he said."

Twin diamonds gleamed in Runegilda's eyes. "The gods granted a great boon to the mortal gemsmith who served them so well. His years would be long, and no form of death could take him until he had seen the face of one who might avenge his child. Janeela gave her life to bind Morgeld, and the gods departed from the Twelve Kingdoms, knowing he would break free, knowing how he would turn many men to evil. The gods who love us wait on mortal deeds. When the final battles come, when the land is lost or cleansed forever, they will return, to mourn or to rejoice. A stone cut by Eyndor's hands alone will bind the faith of the woman whose child shall be the saving or the losing of the Twelve Kingdoms!"

The spirit of prophecy left Runegilda, and she covered her face with her trembling hands.

The inn exploded with jubilation. Runegilda's weird words were gladly pushed aside by most of the listeners. Prophecy was all a mystery, but the betrothal of two young folk clearly loonbrained for each other—*that* they could understand. The Braegerd men grabbed Mizriel and Runegilda, whirling them around in a wild reel dance of their barbarian island. Sir Errod stumbled across the doorsill to join the merriment and was immediately seized by Brasberia to caper and clank in full armor.

Maspa chuckled, rushing back and forth to lay the plank tables with more food and drink. He plundered the dish rails on the common room walls for plates of red and green and Neimar-blue glaze. He hustled into the kitchen and trundled out barrel after barrel of young ale, tapping the spigots home with a wooden mallet. Once he vanished out the door, and the uproarious whir of wings told everyone that Maspa had besieged the dovecote. He came back inside covered with feathers but empty-handed. Without wasting time on regrets that he wasn't nimbler or the doves slower, Maspa fetched a tub of apples and two crocks of honey from the storeroom.

"Ah, it's been too long since we had a betrothal party!" he gloated. "And such a one, such a one! No expense to be spared; my treat, lords! Ambra bless this day!"

Runegilda pulled away from Grel, her watchful eyes following Mizriel as the white-haired girl tugged at Alban's sleeve and whispered a question. His lips moved in reply, his face solemn, and Mizriel's face went paler than her hair. She glided from the common room like a mourning ghost. Runegilda followed. She found her on a bench outside the inn, sobbing into her slender hands.

"Lymri is lost," said the priestess softly. "You loved him."

Mizriel flashed her a hateful look. "Mind your own business, priestess! Why do you play at reading minds, then tell me to conserve my own magics? I am a sorceress! Only a man of magic is worthy to be my mate! I have no use for a poor little poet."

"When I was young," said Runegilda, "and living in my mother's house, I loved a farmer's son. He tended cattle on the upland meadows. My mother was Casilda, the famed witch of the north. She promised me to Krisli in a dream. All my love she gave to the god before I knew what love was. Still I loved my cowherd. We planned to run away. We would meet on the eve of my dedication to the shrine at Krisli's Point. The night was dark; our plan was discovered. The priestess and the shrine guards came upon us and brought us back. They tied my lover to the altar and made me watch the sacrifice. When it was done, the priestess said to me, 'Why do you grieve, Runegilda? How could you love a common cowherd?' But I did love him; I told him so before he died. It made the final parting easier.''

"But I told Lymri nothing," Mizriel said sadly. She let the priestess stroke the curling white fall of her hair. "I never said a word of love all the time we traveled together. Words are too hard to say, love is hard to know, harder to speak of. I thought a poet could read my heart. But it's too late now. Oh, Runegilda, it's hard to live with regret for company!''

"Let us go inside," said the priestess.

The mood of celebration had hushed. Alban and the others were clustered attentively around Maspa, as close as his portly belly would allow.

"Escape?" echoed the innkeeper. "Yes, I suppose many have escaped the Naîmlo Wood, though you wouldn't find them coming back to tell me about it. Where did you have in mind?''

"The sea!" thundered Aethelstan, slamming his tankard on the table. "Once we make the sea, I ask nothing more of any man. Lead us that far and we'll flag down a passing ship to take us wherever we like!''

"The Braegerd man is right," said Alban. "The old charts say that the Naîmlo Wood ends in the west at the Lyarian Sea. Take us there, if you can.''

"I take you there? No, no, not I,'' disclaimed Maspa. "I'd only get us lost again. But I can certainly arrange for one of my . . . um . . . clients to oblige.''

The company looked about the vacant common room. Apart from themselves there was no evidence that the Inn of the Virgin's Delight ever hosted more than Maspa, Brasberia, Sir Errod, and the occasional mouse. And yet there were many long tables and benches crowded into the room, many tankards and other drinking vessels of varied design hanging from hooks below the plate rails on the cleanly plastered walls. Either Maspa was the prince of optimists or there was indeed more traffic in this inn than at first seemed apparent.

The barrel-bellied innkeeper laughed. "This is no ordinary tavern, friends, just as the Naîmlo Wood is no ordinary forest. It's an evil wood, a fitting place for dark creatures, for sprites and demons, goblins and fiends, imps and wood-nymphs and all the shadowy breed that good men call Morgeld's children. You'd be surprised at the powerful thirst these beings can develop in a single day of wickedness. Accordingly, my inn is their favorite resort of a night, and their nasty spells on my tuns and casks and barrels keep them eternally filled for the creatures' black revels."

"The sun's low," Grel said apprehensively. "Will they come tonight?"

"Every night, sir, every night. But you'll be safe enough. Hide yourselves in the upper chambers. The demons loathe stairs and have no reason to leave the common room. Now listen carefully . . . certain fiends make their homes at the very edges of the Naîmlo Wood, within sight of the haunts of men. Many a mortal guest before you has followed a particular demon out of the woods that way. I know the evil ones and I know which ones to follow."

"Did any man you helped ever get free?" asked Octher.

"Would any man be stupid enough to come back to thank me and risk getting lost a second time?" countered Maspa. "I only hope they escaped."

An orange ray of sunset made Maspa suddenly very businesslike and bustling. "Night's coming on. Get above now, get above! Brasberia, bring supper to the upper rooms. Sir Errod, keep her there and guard her. I'll serve the devils alone tonight. There's a knothole in the floor of the room above; keep watch there. I have only one wooden tankard in all my establishment, and I'll serve it to the fiend who lives farthest to the west, closest to the Lyarian Sea. A wooden one, remember! Now go. The sun is already set."

Sir Errod raced up the ladder, but Brasberia gave a stubborn shake of her head, hid behind the bar, and refused to budge. The others left her there, climbed aloft, and helped Alban draw up the stairs behind them, shutting the trap door. Darkness before moonrise crept like a serpent slowly in at windows of the Inn of the Virgin's Delight.

A damp, sighing, sobbing breeze blew in at the door. Brasberia lit the candles. Maspa laid the fire. It smoked badly and burned with a sulky, sorry light. Thin trails of greasy smoke rose up from the candles as the wind drew closer to chill the struggling flames. There was a scratching at the door.

A small, brown, wizened demon strutted across the threshold. Llew-op-fish the woodland sprite could give himself airs when there were only mortals about, but when the truly terrible demons of the wilderness and the storm came in, he had to take a secondary place. Therefore he made it a point to come early to the Inn of the Virgin's Delight so that for a few moments, at least, he might swagger.

"Wench!" Llew-op-fish roared: a paltry roar. His art was to make lethal toadstools look appetizing. "Wench, bring me wine!" Brasberia brought a cup and pitcher, getting a rude pinch through her skirts for her troubles.

A crew of water-wights tumbled in, merry as the foaming river where they had drowned so many. They clamored for strong drink and raw fish, complained of a bad day and no drowned men to show for all their efforts. Pale blue they were, with frothy white hair and long, clever fingers to pluck unwary passengers from skiffs and boats and dories.

One of them took notice of their fellow guest. He poked his neighbor in the ribs. "Fungus-face is here," he bubbled. All the water-wights tittered and jostled each other until the table was awash with liquor.

"What did you call me?" Llew-op-fish snarled.

"Fungus-face."

"Toadstool-tail."

"Mushroom . . . uh . . . mush," said the least creatively inclined of the group. His brothers emptied their flagons over his head and complained to Brasberia that her father had given them short measure. Stonily, she brought them more drink.

"Maspa gave 'em short measure? Bah! The gods beat 'im to that. Pack of water-shrimps," the little demon spat with contempt.

That was a mistake. The water-wights rushed Llew-op-fish, knocked him from his seat, pinned him to the floor, pried open his jaws, and poured anything liquid and handy down his throat. When the liquor ran out, some of the more enterprising sprites gushed themselves through the demon's innards, not a very enjoyable experience for victim *or* tormentor.

"Don't you *ever* eat green vegetables?" demanded one discomfited transient as he emerged and shook himself off.

The demon broke free and tramped back and forth across the floor, demanding to speak to the manager. Maspa remained prudently preoccupied in the kitchen, ostensibly getting things ready for the midnight rush. When Llew-op-fish complained to Brasberia the Silent, the water-wights set up a competing stream of cavils. Their burblings drowned him out and Llew-op-fish retreated into his winecup, sulking.

Now the tavern began to fill up in earnest. From all walks of the Naîmlo Wood the demons came. A score and more of stocky brown fiends rolled clumsily up to the bar, spirits of boulders that plunge from great heights onto souls beneath. Maspa's strongest cups were bent and dented in their hands.

Next came the forces that cause rotten trees to fall and block the roads; then the genii that coat the rocks across a stream with slippery moss. Last came the more awful demons: ghosts of murders done beneath the trees; nameless terrors of the darkened wood; nightmare shapes that dance beyond the circle of campfire. All came and drank and made strange merriment at the Inn of the Virgin's Delight.

One particularly loathsome being sat apart from the rest, sunk in a humid melancholy. He was a gray and grainy demon with yellow tusks and ochre eyes. Resting his ungainly head on one flabby, pimpled paw, he signaled Maspa to bring him drink, chewing a cattail rush while he waited. To this most miserable of monsters Maspa brought the wooden tankard.

The fiend drank down his measure and ordered more, then more again when that was done, and more and more after that. He did not howl and gibber with his fellow fiends; he did not even speak to them. Drink was his only companion, as if he were too hideous even to associate with another monster. A scattering of lesser imps paid grave respect to him, but he ignored them, bristled snout deep in his flagon.

The night waned. Moon and stars were gone from the sky. The candles guttered lower and the fire abandoned all pretense of burning, fading to hissing embers on the hearth. One by one the children of Morgeld slipped back out into the ebbing blackness.

The monster with the wooden tankard would have gone too, but for the sudden interest his host took in him. He tried to ignore the mortal, but Maspa's friendly overtures came accompanied by a pitcher of the demon's favorite tipple. The inn and the pitcher both were almost empty before the creature deigned to answer Maspa's questions.

"You see I am a person of great status among my own kind." The demon spoke with a voice of breaking nails. "I am honored because of the post I occupy. It's a privilege for any imp to be addressed by me, so I speak to none; they are conceited.''

''What post could be so great, my lord?'' Maspa inquired. ''I know you come from the west, but—''

''To the west? Yes, to the west,'' said the demon, a little fuddled. ''You don't know what lies to the west, eh?''

''Good sir, I prefer the security of my humble inn. But if you would do me the honor of telling me—''

The demon looked around the room, empty except for Brasberia the Silent who was gathering up the pots and flagons in a huge washtub.

''Your generosity''—the demon indicated the now-drained pitcher—''earns you my confidence. Your daughter's well-known affliction makes it safe to speak before her. I am the Demon of the Laidly Marshes.''

A sound of scuffling burst overhead. The demon looked up sharply.

''Mice, my lord,'' Maspa said hastily. ''A common enough complaint in the inkeeping trade. I was hoping you might come up with me now and help me get rid the inn of the vermin once and—''

''Do I look like a cat, fool?'' the demon roared. Dust sifted down from the rafters.

''Ah, no, assuredly not. Pardon me, sir, pardon me. And please, allow me to repay that insult with a second pitcher.''

The demon drank and was calmed. When the second pitcher was empty he spoke, with much slobbering affection for his host, of his duties as guardian of the Laidly Marshes.

''The west is the end of the land.'' The demon's eyes glittered like topazes. ''Beyond the forest lie the marshes and beyond the marshes . . . nothing. Only the sea men call Lyarian. Not many mortals sail it; there are reasons. They fear the Laidly Marshes, and that is wise. The sea birds do not fear them. Do you like a fine, fat gull, eaten raw? A tasty morsel!'' The demon's laugh was gravel in a sieve. He clapped Maspa on the back with a fleshy paw. ''Though not as tasty as other meats I could mention. It grows late. I must go.'' He loped from the inn, leaving a trail of clammy footprints.

At the first rap of Maspa's broom handle to the trapdoor, Alban yanked it up and lowered the steps. Stone sword in hand, he led the others swiftly away on the trail of their unnatural and unknowing guide.

Maspa, Brasberia, and Sir Errod watched them vanish into the pale green mists of the coming dawn. When he could no longer see even the hint of their shadows moving through the trees, Maspa went inside. There he sat and nursed a pipeful of good tobacco by the cold hearthstone. Brasberia retired to the kitchen, Sir Errod in tow. Maspa sighed contentedly at the familiar sounds of Brasberia sloshing soapy water in a basin to do the night's washing.

"Looks like the little white-haired one didn't know much about magicking after all," he sighed happily, enjoying the relative peace.

His reverie shattered with a crash from the kitchen. Brasberia flew to the hearthside and yanked her amazed father to his feet.

"He's asked me to marry him!" she shrieked in a voice Maspa recalled only too well. Brasberia tugged heartily at his sleeve and blathered on about the coming wedding while a sheepish Sir Errod came from the kitchen to stand beside his prospective bride.

Maspa gave his inevitable consent. Privately he would always wonder whether Mizriel's magic or Sir Errod's proposal had been responsible for the return of Brasberia's voice.

Dawn came slowly to the Naîmlo Wood, giving a few more precious hours of night to the things of the darkness. It came without gauzy pinks or golds, but in waves of dank white mist like milk. Through such a dawn they followed the demon of the Laidly Marshes.

It was a slow chase. The demon was drunk and could not go quickly without smashing his rubbery bulk into the trees. They needed secrecy, not speed; the demon frequently stopped short in his tracks to listen, as if he suspected he was not alone.

It was green in that weeping dawn, green as Elaar's realm beneath the sea, thought Mizriel. She smelled the hint of ocean in the air, and before she could draw a second breath of it, they were out of the Naîmlo Wood and standing on the whispering gray sands of the Laidly Marshes.

They were alone. The demon had been swallowed by the sands, sinking to sleep in their gray embrace as a man sinks gratefully into a feather bed. Behind the mortals the trees of the Naîmlo Wood shifted in the mist, edging closer and closer together to form an impenetrable wall of hostile green. There would be no turning back.

Everything was flat and gray before them. Dry rushes fluttered and rustled their feathery heads together in the wind. Pale sands starred with black rocks and yellow pebbles ran down to the unseen sea. Columns of mist rose out of the land to hover for a while above the trembling earth before drifting away out of sight to the west.

"Never have I seen such a marshland," said Runegilda. "I never saw marsh mists form such strange shapes." She shuddered.

"Shapes of mist? Don't fear them," Aethelstan said confidently. "Save your fears for more solid stuff than marsh wraiths. In fact, why fear anything at all?" The well-beloved fragrance of the sea was in his nostrils again, and the barbarian felt like his old, bold self. "Let's go down to the tideline and look for a ship. There's nothing to fear, now that we're out of the forest."

Aethelstan drew his sword and brandished it gladly, then marched for the sea. Grel and Octher fell into step behind their captain and the rest followed. Through the rushes and the rocks, across the rasping sands, and through the whispering grasses—but they never came to the water.

Following Aethelstan, Ursula became aware of something queer about the Laidly Marshes, something that seemed to emanate from the pallid, pilgrim mists. They didn't act like ordinary wisps that arise from the steaming ground to lose themselves in the cooler heights, or miasmal fogs that creep close to the earth. These mists had firmer shapes and ascended with slow, stately grace from the swampland. Just to a certain height they rose, then hovered there unchanging, the color of earth and ashes. They rose from every footfall the travelers left behind.

"There are more of them now," said Ursula. Everyone but Mizriel and Runegilda ignored her. The women looked around them and slowed their pace.

The mists formed pillars in an unseen hall, gently blocking the wanderers' way with hazy forms, leaving only a narrow path clear for them to take. Behind them, all was obscured by a gauzy curtain. The muted sound of distant waves reached them, and the smell of salt, but they could not see the sun.

"What was that?" whispered Ursula, her hand groping for Alban's. Something about the shifting mists made whispering seem necessary.

"I didn't hear—" The sound came again, faint as the rustle of rushes, faint as the boom of the surf, and yet terribly, terribly loud: a baby's cry. It came again, a sound so thin and helpless that even the Braegerd men stared in fright. Every man drew his sword.

"Look," said Mizriel. Her slender arm pointed true down the single clear aisle between the walls of fog. The wall wavered, shifted, and then a single shaft of cloud detached itself, a phantom in the shape of a woman that came slowly nearer, and in its arms it bore a child: not cloud-child, but child of flesh and blood, rosy as a happy morning.

A song drifted on the wind, a sad, longing song, an eerie lullaby as unsubstantial as its singer.

"Ursula . . ." The name was softer than the green spring evening breeze. The living baby cried, a live sound almost drowning out the infinitely soft voice calling, *"Ursula . . ."*

"I am here." She felt on edge, her voice sounding too loud in that place of dreams and shadows. "What do you want? Who are you?"

"No one . . . now. Once I was queen."

"Queen? What queen?" demanded Aethelstan. The phantom floated imperceptibly away from the hard reality of his sword, but otherwise paid him no mind.

"Who sits on the throne of Malbenu?"

Ursula could not answer. She knew the phantom now, and sudden tears choked her. Alban stepped forward instead and replied, "King Egdred has safely returned."

"And Phalaxsailyn?"

"Dead," said Alban flatly. "But you should know that."

"Know?" echoed the shadow in a pathetic voice. *"I do not know. Men know. Men remember. Here there is nothing to recall. I would gladly leave. Yes, I will leave . . ."* The vague womanly shape turned slowly from them, yet they could still see the baby's tiny hands waving through the mist. It cried again. *"Ah!"* the phantom sighed. *"I cannot go. Not yet . . . not yet . . ."*

"Renazca!" Ursula cried. The shadow looked up, its face all at once sharper, plainer to see, recognizable. "Renazca, give him to us. Give us the child; we have come for him."

"The child?" The pale head bent over the baby in its cloudy embrace. Then a shudder shook it, and it seemed to wander back to a sad and desperate hour. *"My son! My prince! Oh, my child, my child, I am dying, I feel it, and he—he wants you dead also. No! No! No strength left . . . for me to go on living. But I will take you*

*with me. I will save you. He shall not have you, my son . . .
my son . . . ''*

"Renazca." Alban's voice was warm, his hand softly touched
her cloudy shoulder. "Your task is over. Your enemies are dead,
your son is safe, and his father waits for him. This is the land of
shadows, and he is a living child. Give him to us; we'll bring him
home. Your son will be a king." He took the baby carefully from
her as he spoke.

It was a while before it noticed that its arms were empty. When
it looked down and saw that the child was gone, another tremor
shook it. Renazca's face grew clearer, recognizable, and recognized the mortals ringing it.

"Ursula!" Sudden urgency was in the voice, making it louder
and stronger. *"Ursula, why are you here—here where the danger
is greatest? Go! You must go! That way, to the sea!"*

"Renazca, wait," pleaded Ursula. "Why are you so afraid for
us? What danger—"

"See where you have stumbled!" The voice rose to a wail. *"See
where no man would go, but many must!"*

A host of other voices spiraled upward, twining their lamenta-
tions with Renazca's, and the mists split at the overwhelming wave
of sound. Burning with a cold and deadly fire, amethyst against the
constant flame of sunset, glittering with fearsome beauty, Helagarde loomed on her perch of ebon rock high over the Lyarian Sea.
Below her the black, oily waters whirled their wolfish tongues about
her proud foundations. Above, the skeletal winds of a dark heaven
howled hungrily through her turrets. At her feet was an open portal
and a narrow bridge of packed earth, a fragile spit of land linking
the castle to the marshland. Across that bridge and through that portal, in misery and sorrow, passed an endless line of smoky shapes.
And none came back.

"Behold what might have been your kingdom, Ursula." The
voice was bitter. *"See, fear, and remember. Now turn back, make
for the sea and do not falter. Lose your way a second time and you
lose your life. Farewell."*

The mists descended again, veiling Helagarde, and Renazca's
phantom faded back among them. Only her child remained, sleeping, smiling at hidden dreams. (The shades had cared well for Prince
Amador . . . but that is another story.)

"This way, she said." Alban led them again. The haze
thinned, the sound of waves and the salty smell grew stronger.

They stood on the clear strand and looked out across the white and leaden waters of a wintry sea. A fleck of brighter white sailed the far horizon, a seagull or a sail. Alban took off his golden cloak to hail it.

"Don't waste your time. No ship will save you." It was the cold and joyless voice of Morgeld.

Chapter XVII

BATTLE

Morgeld was mounted on a horse black as midnight silence, armed with a thin, yellow, smiling blade, sheathed in chain mail supple as a sea snake. Coolly, he gazed down at them, and stroked his left hand with his right. An amethyst ring carved from Helagarde herself glittered in the flat gray light.

"Thanks, my lady Ursula." His voice was falling ashes. "Thanks to your retinue for bringing you back to me so very nicely when so many others have failed." He shot a meaningful look to where Captain Tor stood holding the horse's bridle. The big man cringed inside his scarlet cape.

"But words," Morgeld went on, "are empty thanks. They shall enjoy the hospitality of Helagarde and witness our wedding. But first, let them witness the love-pledge I meant to give you at Dureforte Keep. You were, as I recall, too *shy* in those days to receive it." He held a soft black leather pouch and tilted it into his open palm. A silver collar trickled out, set with an amethyst shining like a violet star. He held it out for her to see. The cold, odd radiance of the stone made the baby in her arms stir and whimper.

Ursula gave the infant prince to Mizriel, who in turn wove magic into a moonlit cradle for him there on the strand. Unseen hands rocked Prince Amador back to sleep, sheltered from Morgeld's icy sorcery by powerful young spells.

"Find another bride," Ursula said calmly. "Save your bridal gift for her. My sister and I both fled to escape you. Our father died trying to save us from you. Many more good men are dead, shielding us from you, but their lives won't be wasted. Look, Morgeld!"

She parted her heavy, honey-gold hair to show Alban's collar glistening warmly on her throat. "I will never wear your token, wearing his. I am Alban's!"

Morgeld shifted uneasily in the saddle; the leather creaked and moaned. "Has it happened? In spite of me, has it?" He leaned forward to stare at the winking gem. "Yes, Eyndor's work, dead Eyndor's doing. I thought I had undone the prophecy when I killed him after he made this trinket for me—the gem the gods foretold, cut by Eyndor's hand alone to bind the mother of heroes . . . or of my sons. When I killed him so easily and no power tried to interfere, I should have suspected . . . but I told myself that lies gather to prophecy like flies to syrup. Truth and myth mingle. The gods' promise that Eyndor would not die—could not be slain—until he had seen the face of his daughter's avenger . . ."

The dark one raised a gloved hand to his eyes. "Janeela's avenger." His voice was rough with many memories, many regrets. "Janeela . . ." He raised his eyes and glared at Alban. "Where did you find *her* gem, princeling?" Without waiting for an answer, he turned again to Ursula.

"So, my lady, you believe this thieving prince will father heroes on you? You wish to be the living fulfillment of empty, ancient prophecies? You would pave the road that will bring back the gods? No," he breathed hoarsely. "They are not born yet, nor shall they be born. They shall not be born!"

Standing high and straight in the stirrups, Morgeld flung open the doors of lightning in the mottled sky. Death-light danced in waves across the palms of his hands, while the amethyst necklace glowed and flamed as if thrust into a furnace. The black horse reared, hooves striking red sparks from the sand, green eyes burning. The earth shifted and complained, as if to give birth to mountains or death to seas.

But they answered Morgeld's summons. They came like frost, covering the ground, budding blackly out of the sand row on row. All on foot, mailed in sable armor, the dark legions of Helagarde came. They seeped up from the sands with swords drawn, dismal and deadly, cloaked in the cold aura of new graves, and they awaited their master's pleasure.

Ursula gasped and took a step back, but Morgeld flung a thread of holding that caught her in midstep, and she fell sprawling.

West of them the sea glittered black and silver, jet touched with foamy pearl. The winter wind hung suspended for a moment in the sky, then swept down raising greedy waves to churn away the shore. Far to the west, the fragile bit of whiteness that might have been a sail came nearer.

In an instant, Alban sprang across Ursula's body, the black sword cutting thick, slow arcs of menace in the air between him and Morgeld. "Call off your minions, Morgeld," he growled. "Call them off and let us pass."

"Step aside? Ah, no. You are a fool, Alban—fools have always reigned at Castle Pibroch. Perhaps that is why I have never really believed a prophecy so senseless as the one promising my death by any child of yours. Let us here put an end to such a useless royal line."

"Morgeld's line will be the line to end!" Runegilda suddenly proclaimed. "The line of Alban Stonesword will be Morgeld's undoing. Let north wed south, the lord's daughter and the king's son, the bear and the sea hawk! The black sword is found; the first is found. When the three are found, the three are one, then a woman's child—"

The silver arrow shone brighter than any sea bird. Runegilda stood entranced, transfigured by prophecy, eyes closed, arms outstretched to welcome the future she saw, her words a hum to blend with the arrow's flight. The arrow made a dull sound as it struck her down. Mizriel caught her as she fell. Tor threw down the crossbow and laughed.

"You see, Mizriel," Runegilda sighed, looking up at her friend. "My words were true. You see it now, how much your friends need your enchantments in the battle that comes. I go at last to be Krisli's sacrifice. He has chosen me on the doorstep of his father's house." The priestess closed her eyes and died.

"Well done, Tor," said Morgeld. "Her nonsense tired me."

"Prophecy!" shouted Mizriel. "Only fools find nonsense in prophecy, and I thank the gods that you are the greatest fool of all, Morgeld!" She was on her feet, glowing white as a burning sword, calling her powers in around her. Tor made a grab to fit a second bolt to his crossbow. The weapon shattered in his hands, glassy shards cutting rills of redness in his flesh.

"Well, little sorceress," Morgeld laughed, "would you challenge me? Another time, perhaps. Tor, clear the sands of them. I must take my chosen bride home."

An icy wind stronger than any blowing across the blasted strand fell like a falcon from the sky. Around and around Morgeld it whirled, whipping out evil tongues of shadow to twine and weave over Ursula and Alban, hiding them from sight. Then it rose, the dark wind, and fled up through the unseen halls between the stars. Morgeld, Ursula, and Alban had disappeared. Morgeld's horse remained, pawing the pallid earth.

Catlike, Tor leaped into the saddle, a hastily drawn sword flickering in his hand. The pitiful remnant of Braegerd men stood with swords ready, ranging themselves around Mizriel until she resembled a blazing star set in a crescent moon of steel.

"You shall all die while Alban dies at my master's hand," said Tor. "But have no fear, gentle lady"—he addressed Mizriel—"you shall be spared for my private pleasures."

"Dead men have no pleasures," replied Mizriel. "These legions you command now are unwilling slaves, made Morgeld's thralls for some small evil they committed in their lifetimes. They have no choice, but you, Tor—you are not like them. You are a living man who gives himself willingly and gladly to serve Morgeld. Beware of that day when the willing servant becomes the slave. You are so full of pride that a touch will burst you, and then you will be his forever, and nothing earthly shall ever set you free."

Tor's dagger flew from his hand, the point striking for her heart, but Aethelstan's arm was swifter. He whipped his heavy mantle around one brawny arm to form a makeshift shield. The dagger struck it and rebounded harmlessly.

"Dog," sneered the barbarian. "No honest man would have you in his ranks. Dog that you are, you go sniffing around the sewers of Morgeld's castle. I stand with the lady Mizriel, devil, and while she counts on my sword, your living days are short."

"And yours will be shorter," snarled Tor. Arm upraised, he turned to command the legions of the dead, but the order froze on his lips. Row on row they waited, the dismal host, swords drawn, covering the ground like fallen leaves; and row on row they vanished. With startled eyes Tor watched them fade and disperse into the unknown regions of the air, row on row melting to nothingness, dark armor dissolving into a pearly mist that drifted languidly away. Mizriel's laugh rang through the salt air above the few rows of phantom warriors left.

"Where is your army now, my captain? The spells of freeing release them at my command. *Mine!* They've returned to the realms of the wandering spirits, free."

"My lady," Aethelstan whispered in her ear. "My lady, why didn't you destroy them all? They still outnumber us."

"Hush," Mizriel hissed back. "Runegilda was right. I freed as many as I could. My powers have limits, and this has almost drained them. Swords must do the rest."

"Then you have no more . . . ?"

"Hush, I said! Tor must not hear—"

"My condolences, lady," Tor drawled. "You have picked a very poor time to lose your arts. It marks you for the neophyte witch after all. A pity. I do not think I will want you for my pleasure in that case." His sword arm flashed down, and he gave the battle cry.

A second war cry answered. Not an echo, but an answering challenge from somewhere beyond the mists where Renazca's spirit wandered—a loud cry, a battle cry repeated—and then the charge. They streamed through the distant banks of fog, cloaks flying, swords gleaming. They fell on Tor's rearguard and hewed them down like trees. Back and back they beat the sullen black troops until Tor's command forced his men to make a stand.

"Fear Morgeld, swine!" He pulled tight the reins of his horse until the great beast reared and wheeled, trumpeting wildly. "Fear Morgeld! Stand! Turn and fight! They are ten to your thirty!"

"My men!" bellowed Aethelstan. "My men, to me! For Braegerd!" A roaring shout of "For Braegerd!" resounded above the din of battle. Mizriel thought she recognized Horgist's gravelly voice.

"Our crew," said Grel, wading into the fray. "The ones we lost in Naîmlo Wood. They're found."

"In a good hour," said Mizriel. A silver bow inlaid with red enamel work appeared in her hands, a silver quiver of red-fletched arrows slung itself on her back. "A good hour for something of my powers to return as well, it seems," she murmured, then plunged ahead with Aethelstan to take Tor's men on both flanks at once.

The black horse rushed into the midst of the churning combat, tossing up huge sprays of sand. The air was loud with screams and mixed battle cries, thick with swords clashing against swords and the sometime hum of Mizriel's arrows. They drove like a wedge into the thick of Morgeld's army, killing the dead.

Mizriel would never forget her first true battle. All around her was a great roaring, as if the sea had risen to crush and wash them all away. When close range made her arrows useless, she pounced on the sword of one of Morgeld's fallen men and wielded it with the blind rage of first combat.

"If I only had a little magic left, just one small spell," she thought longingly. She cast a hurried glance behind her to where Prince Amador slept in his shining cradle, shielded by the invisible armor of her conjuring. Mizriel did not dare remove one hair of that protective spell to gain even a momentary advantage in battle.

The fight advanced up the beach as Tor's men fell back to regroup. The two wings challenging them met, joined, and redoubled their attack against the dark horde. Battle thinned as more men fell, and now Mizriel was able to see clearly the faces of the men who had stormed Morgeld's legions out of the mists.

She saw Braegerd sea rovers, Aethelstan's men who had left the beach campfire to explore the Naîmlo Wood and never returned. A dark-skinned man in robes of the southern lands was at their head, a strange green stone held skyward in his hand. There was a knight in ill-kept armor whom she recognized as the errant Sir Errod, and a young boy who, through some trick of light, seemed to dwindle into a small, white dog.

And there was Lymri. She called his name happily as the last dark-armored deadman fell to the poet's sword.

The battle was over, the dead truly dead at last. Tor alone remained, slashing futilely around him from the vantage of the black warhorse. Aethelstan stooped beneath the blade's arc and seized the horse's bridle, roaring a challenge. His sword stroke caught Tor off balance, smashed against his shield, swept him from the saddle. The horse reared and stampeded across the dunes as Tor fell. His sword tumbled free, tangling itself hopelessly in the thick folds of his scarlet cape. From up and down the silent battlefield they came to watch Aethlstan slay his man.

"Get up, woman-killer," Aethelstan commanded. Tor froze, hunched like a spider, fumbling for his lost sword. Aethelstan laughed humorlessly. "Get up, I said. I'll give you a fair fight. I'm a warrior, not a butcher. Find your sword. I am waiting."

Tor's raven warhorse came slowly back to his master, cat's eyes aglow, whickering curiously as he picked his way among the fallen bodies. Aethelstan stepped back, letting sword and shield rest at his side. It had been the longest battle of his young life and he was tired, but not too tired for one more kill.

"I . . . I . . . can't find it," quavered Tor. "My cape—too thick—I . . . You won't harm me?"

"Find it!" bellowed Aethelstan. "Find it quickly, or . . ." He took a step forward and raised his sword high. It was a feint to frighten Tor to action. No warrior deals a deathblow from that stance, and the shield still hung down, off guard. He only meant to scare Tor enough to get his sword in hand again and fight.

Without warning, Tor leaped to Aethelstan's chest. He clung there like a lizard on a wall, like sea-wet clothes, and the barbarian's great broadsword flailed uselessly above him. Then Tor leaped clear and laughed. There was a black-hilted dagger in Aethelstan's heart. Aethelstan staggered, sword still raised for the killing blow he never gave, then slowly sank to his knees in the sand like a stout ship going down.

Tor snatched up his sword and shield while the others remained too horrified to move. They could not take their eyes from the dagger, from the blood; and in those few moments Tor quickly scanned the beach, saw his men all slain, saw Morgeld not yet returned.

"While he toys with the mortal, I'll be spitted on a Braegerd sword," he muttered. "No, by all the spirits of night; I wasn't meant to die by any man's blade!"

With a desperate lunge he threw himself into the midst of his grief-stricken enemies, and the silver light of Mizriel's hair guided his hand. He seized her by it, pulled her to him by that icy rope, and set the edge of his sword at her neck.

"She dies if you move," he said. He backed away until he could watch them all. "Throw down your swords."

"Let her go!" shouted Lymri. His face was hardened and grimy from battle, his right sleeve torn, a thin line of blood trickling down to weave a web at his wrist. "Fight me, coward, but let the lady go!"

"I mean to," said Tor, ignoring the insult. "Drop your weapons." Lymri read the dark captain's eyes. He did as Tor commanded. The others were less eager to obey. "*Now!*" Tor pressed the sword closer and the girl cried out in pain against the thin bite of steel. Grel snorted, like a bear, and threw down his blade. The rest hesitated until the big Braegerd man shouted, "What choice?" then followed.

"Good," said Tor. "Now hear my terms. I give you your freedom. Yes, you heard rightly. Return to your own lands, and soon! We have the lady Ursula; she is all my master ever desired. The rest of you may go."

Lymri's eyes strayed out to sea. The rag of whiteness above the waves grew larger as he watched, but his hopes were cut down by Tor's harsh, "No! Not by sea. Go back the way you came."

"Through Naîmlo Wood!" The anguished cry might have come from any or all of them. Not one among them—not even the hardiest warrior—cared to turn and see the hated forest again.

"As you say, through Naîmlo Wood. Decide and go! When Morgeld returns from Helagarde, he'll summon up more men against you if you linger here. I promise you, he's one lord that's never short of fighting men." Tor chuckled. "I'm doing you a favor, letting you go. But my patience is not long, so make your choice quickly."

No one moved. Tor made an irritated sound with his teeth. "Then stand there forever, and may Morgeld take you!" he screamed. He whistled suddenly, shrilly, and the black horse answered, racing to his side. He swung to the saddle, dragging Mizriel with him, and they rode off at a gallop toward Helagarde, black hooves gouging out great jets of sand behind them.

"After them!" shouted Lymri, retrieving his sword. "To Helagarde!"

"My lord, my lord," the southern man spoke softly, touching Lymri's arm. "No man here desires to see that human demon die more than I. To Helagarde and the lady's rescue, yes; but what of the child?"

"Friend, the child is well guarded without us," said Lymri. He gestured to where the golden cradle rocked. Clouds of mist from the haunted strand had woven themselves into fierce monster shapes, a cordon of magic around it. The blurred cloud-face of a fair woman looked down at the sleeping child and smiled.

"Ah," said the southerner. At once his mild manner vanished. He drew his blade. Maspa of Wigginsdale had been surprised when Mustapha's wizardry-guided party of wanderers showed up at his door, but he'd had the presence of mind to arm them well before sending them on their way. "Lead me then, my lord. To Helagarde."

"Who else is with me for Helagarde?" The little poet tried to brandish his sword, but it was alien to his harp-trained hands. Still, he kept it high. "We are only a few, but Janeela was only one when she bound Morgeld for all the lost ages. For Janeela!"

Grel's blade danced in his hands, a warrior's hands. "Janeela," he said, "and Braegerd Isle." And the same cry went up from the barbarian rovers, "Janeela and Braegerd Isle!"

* * *

The black horse ran well, but Helagarde lay too near for the beast to reach his full run. Horse and riders tore across the bridge of earth. The wailing shadows parted to let mortals pass.

Tor dismounted in the courtyard and yanked Mizriel down, "So, my lady, I welcome you to Helagarde," he whispered.

Mizriel's eyes glided along the smooth, unbroken violet wall surrounding her. The courtyard was empty, except for their presence. It echoed like a forgotten city. The high citadel walls seemed to rise upward forever, melding into the stormclouded heights.

"Do you find it lonely? Does your heart grow afraid?" Tor's breath was warm at her ear. "That is Helagarde's enchantment. No matter how many enter here, each being remains forever alone, cut off from the others. Come; my master must be done with Alban and your sister by this time. I am eager to present you to him. You will make a sweet-faced subject of his kingdom."

Mizriel closed her eyes. Deep, deep into herself she reached, seeking the source of her powers. Emptiness answered her silent call. No magic welled up, shapeless and strong, to be given form by word and sign. She was a hollow shell tossed up from the depths of the icy sea. Tor grinned.

"Another of Helagarde's attractions, my dear. This is the stronghold of the older magic. Your petty charms fall short within these walls. None but the Masters have any power here, and even they have fallen."

Mizriel knew that his words were true. Helagarde was proof against better wizards than she, or what would have saved this keep from the powers of one like Ayree, born to witchcraft? Or Paragore-Tren, who had labored to master powers that lesser mages never dreamed existed?

If they could not take Helagarde, what could Mizriel hope for? She saw her sister's face and again heard Ursula chiding her for casting hasty spells she did not fully understand and could not lift afterward. Runegilda too was there in her thoughts, counseling Mizriel to have caution above all, knowledge before attempting to wield the great spells. But Mizriel had fancied herself a great sorceress. Oh, what a fine and empty fancy! She gazed up at the glowing purple towers of Morgeld's keep and knew where true power lay.

If it were possible to feel a despair beyond despair, she felt it here. Glassy blackness swam under her feet. Mist crept from the courtyard walls, a dirty gray mist that licked her ankles with snakes' tongues. Faces in the swirling gray gaped up at the white-haired girl, their eyes and mouths empty chasms.

Mizriel felt herself leaning forward without wanting to, craning her neck to make out the features of those ghastly phantoms, a tide of ghosts laving her feet. Were those the features of a soul she knew in life? Was this the face of one of her father's old warriors, fallen in a border skirmish years before?

White hands and bony fingers clasped her gown. How different these lone, hungering creatures were from the ghosts of the Laidly Marshes! All wandered far from rest, but the marsh-spirits would someday find what they sought. Helagarde did not hold them quite so close, nor could Morgeld command them. These—thralls to Helagarde's eternal weird of doom—would break their bonds only when the gods themselves returned to walk with men once more.

"Never." Tor's hiss in her ear made Mizriel start. The eddying mist fled, breaking its hypnotic spell. Morgeld's captain chuckled.

The little sorceress stared at him. Could he read minds through some vile gift of his master's? But his next words banished that thought.

"Never," he repeated. "Never to be free, though they are free of their bodies. That is why they seep from their cells every now and then, when they sense a living being come to Helagarde. They seek to remember their own precious freedoms. You are a ghost's keepsake, my lady. They would drain you of every memory of life if they could."

The shining blackness underfoot turned to prosaic cobblestones, gray and veined with purple, a dark mockery of Cymweh's white, violet-shot paving. These stones rippled and burst apart as flowers arched into the twilit courtyard—bells of deathtoll, the swordlike leaves and waxy blossoms of lichlight, and many another growth familiar to Mizriel. Every good sorceress must know the poisonous plants of the Twelve Kingdoms if she hopes to learn their antidotes.

Tor's boots crushed a patch of hellebore. "I never can abide that flower. Once I meant to treat my elder brother to a cup of wine whose flavor would be . . . enhanced by the addition of that pretty herb." He sighed and shrugged. "If not for the meddling of some busybody traveling players, I might be a duke today."

Mizriel regained a little courage. "The day a worm like you wears a ducal coronet, the sun will shine by night and the moon at noon!"

Morgeld's captain smiled sardonically. "Keep looking down at the paving of this courtyard, my lady, and soon you won't know day from night. Reality shifts underfoot here. Helagarde drinks her powers from the black places of the earth, the realm of the stone-bound night-spirits. Caves are their special love . . . as my lord Morgeld's father learned, too late. It's a fine cave my lord has made himself here; a cave of many illusions.''

A freshening wind blew through the gate behind them. It brought the crash of waves, and a louder clamor of human voices with it. Tor jerked his head toward the sound. There was no trace of despair in those voices, no faint, phantoms' cries. They were the voices of living men, and they shouted for vengeance.

''Let them come,'' said Tor, teeth showing like a fighting dog's. ''Let them enter Helagarde freely, as I did! They'll wander this courtyard alone for as many slips and changes as it takes to confuse them. Helagarde will have her little games. She'll lead them back and forth, up and down, when there is nothing to climb over, under, or around. Illusion! Illusion all! A maze without a maze's twisting inner walls! A castle with a single gate, and no doors to the heart of Helagarde that *they* can see!''

No doors . . . Mizriel's eyes swept the courtyard again, and again she saw nothing but smooth, unbroken amethyst. Once a trailing band of mist seemed to wriggle to the burnished surface, but it sank back into the all-devouring stone. There were no doors to lead from this boxy courtyard. There was just the main gate, and no guards at it to keep Lymri and the others from charging in, slaying Tor, and saving her.

''A hope, my lady?'' Tor's voice was deceptively soft. What she could see of his features told Mizriel that he must have been a hand-some man, once; a courtly one, to judge by his speech and his talk of being a duke's younger son. ''That's a sentiment most out of place in Helagarde. You'll learn, in time. But''—the small look of amusement on his lips vanished—''it seems your friends don't want to give us time. Very well. The spells on these stones underfoot will keep them busy enough until we have found my master. By the time they grow used to the changing horrors surrounding them, we will be back . . . you, and I, and my master's bride . . . and Morgeld.''

''Morgeld will be destroyed!'' The last flame of defiance in Miz-riel's soul blazed up in spite of Helagarde's all-pervasive gloom. ''Your master made his gravest mistake when he swept up Alban and Ursula together in his cursed whirlwind! I tell you, Tor, Morgeld brought his own death home with him. Alban will kill him, and Ursula will—''

He only tapped her cheek with his forefinger, but it was gauntleted with steel. Tears gushed from her eyes and and she tasted blood in her mouth. In pain and anger she spat at Tor's feet. The blood became a crimson snake that slithered across the broken pavement of a ruined city. The illusions of Helagarde were as undying as her spell of hopelessness.

Tor raised his mailed hand. Mizriel cringed, but he never meant to strike her. "Behold," he said. Where there was unmarred amethyst he pulled aside a curtain of air. A line of fire followed the slanting descent of his arm, and became a fiery winged snake, thick as battlespear's shaft. It *skreek*ed harshly, scraping painful echoes from the purple walls, then lashed its tail to its mouth and fastened its jaws onto its own flesh. Wings beating madly, spinning faster and faster, its lithe body growing thinner, spreading outward like a ripple ring, the blazing monster whirled itself into a swiftly opening circle of blackness, a doorway of night. Darkness gaped, and through the worm's gateway Mizriel saw a flight of stone steps that led downward.

Tor gripped her hand and forced her through the cavernous portal. As they descended the broad stairs, Mizriel thought she heard human voices calling her name from the world above. *Lymri!* Her heart ached, wondering what awful apparitions her little poet would have to face in Morgeld's courtyard. She pulled from Tor's grasp and tried to flee back to daylight, but though she ran fast, she had only climbed two steps when she saw the flaming door close like a merchant's drawstring purse. All was black.

Out of the darkness, Tor's voice came. "Silly of you to try escaping. Does my magic surprise you? Forming that doorway is my only trick, alas! A necessary gift from my master for entering his private chambers." A damp sigh brushed Mizriel's cheek. "Sometimes I could almost envy my master's *other* servants. They don't need things like doors to reach Morgeld . . . but not too many of them serve him as gladly as I do. I often wonder whether I could serve him better without the encumbrances of flesh and bone."

"Go back up to the courtyard, coward, and there are more than a dozen good men who'll be happy to help you find out!"

She heard his mail creak and clash against itself. His voice came fainter, and there was the sound of footfalls descending. He was going deeper into the darkness. Her taunt was for nothing.

"Give me your hand," he said. "I am impatient to hear of my master's triumph from his own lips. You'd do best not to try my patience, my lady. I know the way here, but you know nothing; you have nothing in Helagarde but your skin. I can leave you here, all alone in the dark, and come back for you at my leisure. That is, if you are still here to be found. You'd be surprised how much a mortal's skin is worth in Helagarde, and what manner of beings roam these halls, searching for one."

She gave him her hand.

Greenish-lilac light shone like deathglow ahead of them. They entered a low-ceilinged room. A hooded figure awaited, seated with bowed head on a throne of steel. Tor flung Mizriel forward on her knees, then knelt as well.

"Hail, Master. Is it finished?"

"Yes." The seated one's voice was breath. "It is finished . . . for now."

"And where is your bride, my lord Morgeld? Her sister comes to act as bridesmaid." He laughed.

"Elsewhere." Slowly Morgeld lifted his cold eyes to Tor's beaming face. Even for one so long in Morgeld's service, that glance could chill. "She is not quite herself."

"The bear curse." Tor nodded. "Well, we can wait it out. Have you given her the collar, my lord?"

Morgeld unclenched his left hand to let the pallid light sparkle on the silver chain. "A bear's neck is too thick," he murmured.

Tor gave a weird little laugh. "True. She should be grateful to you for ridding her of Alban's collar before the change came over her, or she would have strangled in it."

The lord of Helagarde shook his head. "Alban's collar, as mine, came from Eyndor's hands. Bear or human or sea beast of a thousand spans, Eyndor's work will change with the wearer." Very quietly he added, "All things that Eyndor made were touched with magic."

Tor stood and took a few uneasy steps towards the awful throne. "My lord . . . my lord, are you not content? We should decree a celebration! Let me call your servants and your slaves! Let me call the men who serve you willingly in the secret places! Soon the earth will become your kingdom, from the depths of the silent sea to the realm of the gods!"

"There will be no celebration."

An obsidian blade blacker than a fallen star flickered out of shadow from behind Morgeld's throne. It cut a slab of more wholesome light out of the surrounding darkness, opening the way to vision.

Transfixed, Tor saw Helagarde in miniature float out the the cleanly sliced air. A whirlwind fell on the amethyst castle, a wind made of night and terror. It struck the highest tower with a purple arrow of fire and cracked the walls wide.

The wind seeped away through the same crack it had opened, leaving three figures facing each other in the tower room. Morgeld stood with arms outstretched and a smile of false benediction on his face, as though Alban and Ursula were reluctant lovers and he a kind heart bent on bringing them together. Alban held back but Ursula stepped forward, fascinated by the splendors of the chamber.

Not one of the three was any taller than a man's ring finger. Every detail of the tiny room shone like the work of Cymweh's finest miniaturists. Tor drew off one gauntlet, held up his hand, and saw his master's face reduced to the size of a fingernail yet still able to fill him with fear and desire. Quickly he pulled the mail glove on again. Watching the play of tiny simulacra, Tor felt an eeriness creep into his blood, made sharper when the poppet Morgeld spoke.

"Do you like this chamber?" Gloved hands gestured at priceless silk rugs from Vair, gold-shot tapestries from the Kestrel Mountains, a bed piled deep with silvery furs from the northern wastes and hung with Malben-woven curtains thin as flower petals. A scent of hyacinth clung to their folds. On an ebony perch beside the bed a hooded merlin sat, feathers gleaming like beaten bronze. It might have been cast from bronze, so still it sat there.

Ursula stretched out her fingers to caress the downy feathers of its breast. Her startled cry made Morgeld laugh.

"She is warm with life, isn't she? But she does not breathe. She knows, she feels, she senses everything around her constantly changing, but she is cut off from it. That is what it means to be bound." He struck the merlin from her perch. The bird thudded to the carpet with a sound like a billet of wood falling. Still she did not move.

"She felt that fall," said Morgeld. With mock tenderness he slid her ever-grasping talons back onto their perch and straightened the seed pearls decking the poor creature's samite hood. "Pain is real for her, but she is only a bird. Who knows if she also feels the deeper pains? For you see, one she trusted laid this binding on her, and when will she be free? That rests with me. How different from my own case, for by the grace of what was foretold on the day that I was bound, I was able to break my bonds the day that you were born, my lady.''

Ursula's gasp belled into a bear's bleat. Fur sprouted over her, and the weight of a full-grown bear's body bent her to all fours. Her cry of distress shattered any shock that had been holding Alban back. He might be in the topmost tower of Helagarde, within his foe's mightiest stronghold, but she was his love, and she needed him. He sprang after her, but Morgeld made a dancer's sidestep to bar Alban's way. He made no move to detain Ursula when she ran from the tower room.

(Oh, a tower room smaller than many a lady's jewel box, and a mouse-sized bear, and two small man-dolls at their deadly play! Tor had made his home in Helagarde by choice, but he'd never seen a sight that chilled him as thoroughly as this. No, not from the day he'd staggered across the Laidly Marshes to kneel before Morgeld's castle and offer up a bloodstained sword drawn from beneath his travel-tattered cloak. Ambitious younger son, thwarted fratricide, cool murderer, he'd fled his father's justice to seek a dark dream out of legend and prophecy: Morgeld. And the dream was real; more real than any wished-for coronet. Tor had found the fount of all ambition. He had shaken with sobs of joy as Helagarde's lord opened his arms to welcome the mortal who came to serve him with a willing heart.)

But where was Tor's master now? Only another player on a stage of vision and light. Tor knew what could become of players; he had overseen the murder of an entire company. Looking on as Morgeld's simulacrum performed his part, Tor could not shake off the feeling that other eyes besides his and Mizriel's and the real Morgeld's were watching this scene.

Tor's fears did not affect the fingerling Morgeld in the vision. That one let Ursula go, blocked Alban's pursuit, and then, "What a shame," was all he said. "I wanted to see if she might take this from me now." The heavy silver chain with its Helagarde-hewn amethysts dangled from his left hand. "Well, she can't get too far here. Let her explore. It will be hers soon."

"It will never be hers," Alban answered. The black sword was in his hand.

A gray blade arcing with violet fire slipped into the world. Morgeld made a few experimental slashes with it, playing the expert fencer bored with the present necessity of facing an incompetent opponent. His third pass severed the merlin's hooded head.

"She felt that, too." Then he lunged at Alban.

It was no plain fight of blade against blade. Each cut that Morgeld's sword made opened slits in the powers Helagarde contained. Ghosts trickled from the walls, less solid than the deadmen Tor had led to battle, but Morgeld's unwilling subjects still. Solitude and despair hung in their every tatter. They trailed themselves over Alban, entangling his sword.

The obsidian blade freed itself in a violent series of short, sharp chops. Each cut across the ghost's lingering whiteness filled with clean light. The phantom faces showed astonished joy as the invisible chains holding them to Helagarde were severed. Morgeld gaped, then uttered a curse and called off his remaining slaves. He would not use them now if it meant losing them forever.

Black sword and empurpled gray sword crossed. Still it was not a common battle. Outside the vision, even Tor could feel the assault of Morgeld's thoughts as they pounded into Alban's brain.

I am night and war, foolish mortal. I hold the blood of your most ancient enemies. I am older than the world that spawned you, colder than the death that waits for you, master of all you fear, the sword that will always keep you from your gods! Fight me while it pleases me. In the end you shall die, and that will please me too.

Images of desolation and hopelessness flew through Alban's skull. They met the strength of a man who had loved his unborn children and had already known their loss. The love remained, and it swallowed Morgeld's messengers of despair.

Morgeld leaped back, disengaging his blade from Alban's. The Sombrunian prince knew better than to drop his guard over this minor triumph. He was breathing hard, but his sword remained ready.

An emerald haze hissed from Morgeld's body, a spell that was swollen with all Inota's bloodthirst, all the chaos of the night-spirits' realm. Green heat pulsed in the tower room, turned the silken rugs to sheets of fire underfoot. Alban pulled off his cloak and beat at the flames leaping up around him.

Morgeld laughed. "And you thought to defeat me! This is not even the heart of Helagarde! It was *her* room—Janeela's chamber, and even so far from the castle's core, my strength is beyond measure." He took a step forward, ready to bring the battle to an end.

Alban held up the black sword.

A star shone through the cracked wall of the tower room. A star

balanced on the black sword's point. A star poured its light down
the blade, washing away all Morgeld's nighted powers with a cool
shine. Another hand closed around the black sword's hilt, small but
strong, enfolding Alban's own. A woman made of sweetest brightness stood by Alban's side facing Morgeld.

He knew her, and the knowledge froze him. He knew her too
well.

"Janeela . . ."

Strike, Alban, said the lady. *Strike well, but know it is not your
fate to give the killing blow. Strike, Stonesword.*

She was gone in the moment Alban swung the black blade.

The gate of vision slammed shut, releasing Tor and Mizriel from
its thrall. The Prince of Sombrunia stepped into full view.

"Alban!" Tor's desperate eyes sought Morgeld. In mute answer
Morgeld unclasped his other hand and held it to the light. The
wounds were fresh and deep. That hand would never close comfortably around the hilt of a sword again.

"Go, Tor," Morgeld commanded dully. "The first is finished.
The first is found. Lead them back to the light. But know this, Alban Stonesword"—and an undertone of the ancient hatred came
back into his voice—"know that your war is not yet over. Your
sons—if they live—will still fight it. And their sons as well. I have
time, but you are only a mortal."

"I spared your life in combat," Alban said evenly. "Your sword
lies at the bottom of the Lyarian Sea. What is to stop me from killing
you now?"

"The knowledge that you are not the one. Death will not take
one not meant to die." Morgeld sank back on his dull gray throne
and stared unseeing at his ruined hand.

The room's sickly green glow blazed suddenly violet; then Alban stood with Tor and Mizriel in Helagarde's illusion-filled courtyard. But now there were no illusions left; only ordinary stones,
their ghosts in hiding. From the massive gateway came the sound
of pounding feet and a confusion of war cries. Lymri and his men
spilled into the castle keep.

Tor's mind fought a knot of impossibilities. Why had he been
expelled from Helagarde's heart with these, his master's enemies?
Mizriel and Alban were starting forward to greet their friends, the
white-haired sorceress jubilant. It was wrong! By all that was just,
this conquering rabble should be reduced to mindless quaking
wrecks by now. What trick of time or time's masters had detained

them? Why had they gained the courtyard only now, now when it was free of Morgeld's enchantment, and safe? Had the black sword the power to suspend reality, to play with the threads of time and circumstance as easily as a master weaver played with the strands of warp and weft? A dread certainty struck Tor's heart that he would not live to learn the answer.

Panic rose in Tor's chest. He stared at Mizriel's mane of white hair and saw another face grinning back at him. Did he dare? That arrogant stripling who styled himself Ayree, the Prince of Warlocks—did he dare to send his gloating image into Morgeld's stronghold?

Rage drove panic out of Tor's mind, though it was only in his mind that Ayree's taunting face existed. He would show Morgeld that he was still his faithful servant. He would redeem every pledge and promise he had ever made to the lord of Helagarde. He would drive Ayree from Morgeld's house. And these mortals whom Ayree favored so? He would scoop their triumph hollow with the blade of his sword.

That must be why Morgeld had sent him out of Helagarde with the others. It was a sign that his master wanted Tor to act in his name, to show them how fatally they'd erred in thinking that Morgeld could ever know defeat.

Now Tor was content. He could act calmly. His master loved him. His master would not cast him out. And Tor loved his master. Surely Morgeld must know that Tor loved him beyond ambition or hope of reward. He loved him as a man loves the ideal, and if that ideal were made of night and death and war, there were still many more besides Tor to worship it.

Tor's eyes glittered. Mizriel's back was still to him, a tempting target. Ayree's face had vanished from her hair, but it didn't matter. The sign had been given. Tor could not take his eyes from Mizriel's back, already foreseeing the slash, the blood, the fall. He and she were the only two beings left for him in the courtyard. He drew his sword back for the kill, knowing how much pain, and to how many, this one death would bring.

The heavy brown paw broke his arm. His scream was swallowed by the bear's low growl. The ragged company closed ranks in a ring around them as Tor grabbed his sword up in his left hand. The battle was short and unequal, but for Morgeld's captain it seemed to last a lifetime.

The bear played with him, dodging each jab of the steel, reaching in to rake long claws across any bit of flesh not covered by mail. Tor backed away, his right arm dangling at a crazy angle. There were faces in the ring that he recognized with a strange clarity, even as he fought for his life: the dark face of a southern man he had once glimpsed while he still lived in his father's ducal court and laid fruitless plans for the murder of his elder brother; the sharp face of a small white dog that terror now exaggerated to a wolf's avid gape. Both man and beast shared a great, unspoken satisfaction as they witnessed Tor's death struggle.

Other faces he knew were also watching him from the ring, faces that had no right to be there, faces of the dead. Aethelstan was there, and Krisli's priestess Runegilda, and young Sir Kerris of Malbenu, and more. Tor thought he saw a troupe of ghostly wandering players there, clad in the flimsy finery of their stage costumes. The young actress among them was very beautiful, but her face was iron when she stared at him and slowly brought her hands together in mock applause for Captain Tor's last performance.

He had many deaths on him, and in these final moments they had come again. The walls of Helagarde began to pulse around him like a monstrous purple heart. Now it beat louder, and the roaring of blood filled his ears.

"The walls! The walls!"

He never knew who cried out then. The ring of living faces was gone, and only the misty faces of the dead surrounded him. The bear was there also, still pressing him hard, still with a leering human grin on her face. And the walls of Helagarde began to burn with a green and yellow flame under the rolling clouds until a demon wind descended and extinguished all with a single breath. Tor heard a Braegerd cheer. It still rang in his head at the moment the bear's last blow finished him.

Chapter XVIII

PIBROCH

"Which is worse?" Mizriel asked aloud when the adventurers had returned to the shore of the Lyarian Sea. "To see a battlefield during the worst of the fighting, or to see it afterward?"

There was only the wind. It raced along the beach, scattering a light fall of sand over the dead men. Morgeld's soldiers lay sprawled in their sable armor like so many black beetles. The glitter of it faded, and as Mizriel watched they melted into the wind's breath.

"Truly dead, now." Lymri held her in his arms against the cold, but the chill shaking her did not come from the wind or the sea. "Those twice slain don't rise again. Don't weep, my love. We're safe."

"For dead men, they swung solid swords," said Octher.

Mizriel dried her tears. "And left wounds that are real enough. Help me bind them, Lymri." Their cloaks were sacrificed for bandages. Ursula, still in bear-shape, contented herself with rocking Renazca's child in his star-cradle and crooning him a rumbling, bearish lullaby.

Grel and Octher searched the ranks for their lost shipmates, rejoicing at each Braegerd-born face. "What became of you?" Octher demanded. "You went scouting in Naîmlo Wood and we never thought we'd see you alive again!"

Unfortunately, Grel had already gleaned the tale from some of the survivors. In his mouth, an epic of romance and derring-do devolved into a market list. "They got lost. A man named Mustapha found them. A wizard sent him. They found other lost ones. They found an inn. They got swords. They marched west. They came through the mists. They saw our peril. They attacked Morgeld's men. We won."

"When you cut a long story short, Grel," Octher said, "you do it with an ax."

They carved shallow graves for the dead with their swords and raised low cairns of shells and stones over them. Mizriel performed the rites of final sleeping. Aethelstan's men stood apart, whispering and ill at ease.

"What's amiss?" asked Sir Errod. He had joined Lymri's band of wanderers when they passed the inn.

"It's hard explaining to one not of our Braegerd blood," said Osbert. "We've our own funeral rites and we lack the means to perform them here. Aethelstan was our chief, son of a Braegerd chieftain. He merits full honors. We can't slight his spirit, but how can we do otherwise?"

"What honor does he lack? We buried him with sword and shield," said Lymri. "We can build his cairn up higher than the others, for all the good it does him now, poor fellow. What more?"

"He was a seagoing man," said Grel. "In death we send our men back to the waves. The sea takes them, if she's of a mind to. Aethelstan loved her. To leave him buried here, where he can hear the waves and never touch them—to bury him just out of reach of his one love—that seems cruel. He should sail to the far lands of sleeping in a fine, stout ship, but we've no means of making one. O Aethelstan, I'd offer you my own poor hide if they could make you a ship from it, my friend!" He knelt at Aethelstan's cairn and broke his sword in two across his knee, tossing the pieces onto the stones. Then the Braegerd barbarian wept.

"Grel . . . Grel . . ." His name came out of the booming of the surf. "Grel . . . Grel . . ." Grel looked out to sea.

A tall man, pale as the foam, his Braegerd garb all white, stood with one foot in the shallows and the other on the gangplank of a misty ship. White as a pearl, ivory-white her sails; white and shining as a star the lady who stood in her prow. The tall man boarded the ship and smiled at Grel as he sailed away.

"We have no need of honors"—the voice rushed in among them like the tide—"who hold the tribute of your hearts."

Grel wiped his eyes roughly on his hand. He wondered if he was the only one who had seen. The southerner's little dog stood by, wagging his tail. He looked up at Grel. Absently he patted the beast and got to his feet.

"The ship!" shouted Octher. "Look to the ship!"

"Did you see, too—" But it was impossible; the white ship was gone.

Octher waved his arms wildly, dancing up and down on the sand. The others joined in his weird cavorting. Grel shook his head as the ship—the earthly ship—came closer to shore, the bright saffron banner of Vair flying from its masthead.

With a glad shout, Grel stripped off his armor and plunged into the sea, swimming out to greet the lucky vessel.

The cabin was small but pleasingly furnished. A brazier made it cozy, large cushions in the southern manner made it comfortable, and a decanter of Vair's ruby wine made it cheerful. Through the cabin door came the enticing smells of roasting fowls, and meats baking in delicate sauces. Silver cups of broth were on hand to see the passengers through until suppertime.

The captain was a fat, infinitely hospitable young man. When he learned that his unexpected passengers were people of rank, he tried to make Prince Alban an outright gift of his sapphire earrings and gold neck chains.

"I live to serve you, puissant lord!" Alban and the ladies fought down laughter at the sight of his complicated ceremonial contortions. "I am your slave, Phoenix of the Western Reaches! May you live a thousand years and may your lady give you fifty sons and a single daughter like a water lotus blossom. Ask anything of me and it is yours."

"Captain, please," Alban said, smiling. "Passage to Sombrunia for us and passage home for our friends is all."

The captain literally shook all over with delight. "My lord, I shall even convey the barbarians back to Braegerd if they will guarantee not to steal the ship once we get there."

"We won't." Grel drained a goblet of wine. "You have Grel Aaregson's word. Put all my men ashore there but me. I'd like to sail on with you, Captain. I want to learn the merchant's trade."

"A Braegerd man turned merchant?" The captain's rosy jowls trembled with astonishment.

"Why not?" said Grel. "One way of pirating's as good as another."

One bonny day the heights of Sombrunia appeared off the starboard bow. Alban pointed out the dim shape of Castle Pibroch to

Ursula. They docked to the welcoming music of drums and trumpets. Alban wondered aloud how his Council could have learned of his return.

"A simple matter, Your Majesty." Paragore-Tren waved a greeting from the shore, but his voice flew where he sent it.

Ursula and Mizriel spoke apart in the moments before the gangplank was lowered.

"You're not coming with me?"

Mizriel shook her head. "My place is in the northern lands. I have much to do there, and much to learn. Our father's lands must be protected. Or regained, if Lord Thaumas has taken advantage of our absence."

"You won't stay even for a little while?"

"Who knows when the next ship sails for Cymweh? I don't dare be stranded here all winter. Besides, we must return the infant prince to Malbenu as well."

"I see," said Ursula. "Someone else sails north on this ship. You don't love northern ice and snow so much, or fear Lord Thaumas so greatly. It is the little poet."

Mizriel's face colored, and the glow of it even seemed to touch her frosty hair with its warmth. "He and I have been through many things together. I think it was meant to be. He's no hero, but he makes pretty rhymes and sweet music. Now he's working on an epic in Alban's honor: 'Lo, Helagarde Has Fallen!' It has a nice ring."

"My love goes with you both. Come back to see me in the spring. You'll have a warm welcome and a captive audience for all of Lymri's rhymes." The sisters embraced.

There was much music and a few speeches when Ursula and Alban came down the gangplank to meet the waiting nobles. Mizriel, Lymri, and the Braegerd men watched from the quarterdeck. There were fireworks that night, and at the peak of the display the ship glided discreetly out to sea.

The city populace was crowded almost to a man into the castle's public gardens. Feasting and entertainments had been arranged to celebrate Lord Alban's return. Two lone figures were left unnoticed on the dock to see off the Vairish ship, and one of these was merely a little dog.

"By the Treasure of the Hidden Caverns," said the man in southern robes. "This has been a wondrous strange adventure. Did you hear, Elcoloq? That stern young man is king! Ah, by all the pearls in Elaar's palace, I—"

"I'm hungry. Save your musings for another audience and find us some dinner."

Mustapha stared at the dog for a moment, then picked up their meager belongings, and together they turned their steps toward the stony heights of Castle Pibroch.

The CHRONICLES OF THE TWELVE KINGDOMS
include

The Books of Prophecy
   In which the Scroll of Oran is found, and a great evil is unloosed
   Mustapha and His Wise Dog
   Spells of Mortal Weaving
   The Witchwood Cradle

The Books of Initiation
   In which the White Sword and the Green Sword are discovered, and dynasties founded

The Books of Inheritance
   In which the Companions are bonded, and sinister Beasts are conjured

and

The Books of Fulfillment
   In which the secrets of the Scroll of Oran are revealed

Esther M. Friesner was born in Brooklyn, but left to attend Vassar and later Yale, where she earned a Ph.D in Spanish. After teaching at Yale for some years, she quit to write fantasy and science fiction full-time. Her short stories have appeared in *Isaac Asimov's Science Fiction Magazine*, *Amazing*, and *Fantasy Book*, as well as several paperback anthologies.

Presently Ms. Friesner lives in Madison, CT with her husband and two children. She writes, "I'm a member of the local Society for Creative Anachronism group, where my pseudo-medieval plays enjoy frequent nonprofessional production. I am also a camp follower of the Fifth Connecticut Regiment, a colonial re-creation military group for which my husband is company drummer. The drummer used to have to bury the dead. So far we've been lucky."